If there was o...
Daniel Cash u...
perfectly, it wa... ...attle.

"I'm helping you on with your damn coat," he said between his teeth.

Daniel was slowly buttoning up every button on her stupid coat. Winning the battle. His knuckles brushed her breasts as he reached the middle button, and he heard the slightest intake of her breath. His finger froze.

It was probably a little twisted, getting turned on while you were wrestling with a woman for the dubious privilege of helping her on with her coat, but Grace McKenna had been giving him the strangest ideas since the day he met her.

He watched his own fingers slowly unfasten the buttons on her coat, then he slid his hands inside.

"Daniel?"

"Don't say it's a mistake," he whispered thickly. "Please don't say it's a mistake."

She pulled his head up to hers. "I won't...."

Dear Reader,

The 20th anniversary excitement continues as we bring you a 2-in-1 collection containing brand-new novellas by two of your favorite authors: Maggie Shayne and Marilyn Pappano. *Who Do You Love?* It's an interesting question—made more complicated for these heroes and heroines because they're not quite what they seem, making the path to happily-ever-after an especially twisty one. Enjoy!

A YEAR OF LOVING DANGEROUSLY continues with *Her Secret Weapon* by bestselling writer Beverly Barton. This is a great secret-baby story—with a forgotten night of passion thrown in to make things even more exciting. Our in-line 36 HOURS spin-off continues with *A Thanksgiving To Remember,* by Margaret Watson. Suspenseful and sensual, this story shows off her talents to their fullest. Applaud the return of Justine Davis with *The Return of Luke McGuire.* There's something irresistible about a bad boy turned hero, and Justine's compelling and emotional handling of the theme will win your heart. In *The Lawman Meets His Bride,* Meagan McKinney brings her MATCHED IN MONTANA miniseries over from Desire with an exciting romance featuring a to-die-for hero. Finally, pick up *The Virgin Beauty* by Claire King and discover why this relative newcomer already has people talking about her talent.

Share the excitement—and come back next month for more!

Leslie J. Wainger
Executive Senior Editor

Please address questions and book requests to:
Silhouette Reader Service
U.S.: 3010 Walden Ave., P.O. Box 1325, Buffalo, NY 14269
Canadian: P.O. Box 609, Fort Erie, Ont. L2A 5X3

THE VIRGIN BEAUTY

CLAIRE KING

Silhouette®

INTIMATE™ MOMENTS®

Published by Silhouette Books

America's Publisher of Contemporary Romance

To Suzie
The bravest, best woman I know.

A special thanks to Sue Vos
For her generous advice and the invaluable
loan of her Merck Manual.

 SILHOUETTE BOOKS

ISBN 0-373-27108-5

THE VIRGIN BEAUTY

Copyright © 2000 by Claire King

CLAIRE KING

lives with her husband, her son, a dozen goats and too many cows on her family's cattle ranch in Idaho. An award-winning agricultural columnist and seasoned cowpuncher, Claire lives for the spare minutes she can dedicate to reading and writing about people who fall helplessly in love, because, she says, "The romantic lives of my cattle just aren't as interesting as people might think."

IT'S OUR 20ᵗʰ ANNIVERSARY!
We'll be celebrating all year,
Continuing with these fabulous titles,
On sale in October 2000.

Desire

#1321 The Dakota Man
Joan Hohl

#1322 Rancher's Proposition
Anne Marie Winston

#1323 First Comes Love
Elizabeth Bevarly

#1324 Fortune's Secret Child
Shawna Delacorte

#1325 Marooned With a Marine
Maureen Child

#1326 Baby: MacAllister-Made
Joan Elliott Pickart

Romance

#1474 The Acquired Bride
Teresa Southwick

#1475 Jessie's Expecting
Kasey Michaels

#1476 Snowbound Sweetheart
Judy Christenberry

#1477 The Nanny Proposal
Donna Clayton

#1478 Raising Baby Jane
Lilian Darcy

#1479 One Fiancée To Go, Please
Jackie Braun

Special Edition

#1351 Bachelor's Baby Promise
Barbara McMahon

#1352 Marrying a Delacourt
Sherryl Woods

#1353 Millionaire Takes a Bride
Pamela Toth

#1354 A Bundle of Miracles
Amy Frazier

#1355 Hidden in a Heartbeat
Patricia McLinn

#1356 Stranger in a Small Town
Ann Roth

Intimate Moments

#1033 Who Do You Love?
Maggie Shayne/
Marilyn Pappano

#1034 Her Secret Weapon
Beverly Barton

#1035 A Thanksgiving to Remember
Margaret Watson

#1036 The Return of Luke McGuire
Justine Davis

#1037 The Lawman Meets His Bride
Meagan McKinney

#1038 The Virgin Beauty
Claire King

Chapter 1

Grace McKenna did not want to get out of her truck. Hadn't wanted to for five minutes, and still didn't want to. Didn't suppose she'd ever want to, in fact. So she sat in the cab, considering her options.

She could drive back to her hometown in Washington State. People knew her there, were accustomed to the sight of her. She was hardly ever whispered about, hardly ever asked a single, stupid question about basketball or the weather "up there."

Or she could go back to the practice she'd left in eastern Washington, where she stayed in the clinic most of the time, working with the animals, who didn't care in the least what she looked like.

Or she could get out of this cramped pickup and start her new life and let the people talk. She knew from experience they'd find something else to talk about after a time. A year, maybe. Or twenty.

She sighed, looked around a little.

A new town.

It made her nervous. It always did. No matter where she went, she couldn't escape who she was—didn't really even want to. But she always dreaded the first day. Until people got used to the look of her, she felt something like a weed suddenly sprouted green and tall in the middle of an even field of wheat. The eye couldn't help but be drawn to it, opinions formed, discussions begun. It was something to which she was certainly accustomed—having been a conspicuous weed kind of person since she was twelve years old—but she never got over the apprehension of it.

A new town, a new job. A thousand new faces and facts and places.

She looked around at the dusty little Western outpost. Well, maybe not a thousand.

She was on the main street; homey-looking and not too long, with grand winter skeletons of ash trees that in summer would shade it from the ruthless Idaho sun. On the one street was one grocery store, one supply store, one clothing store with fading Wrangler Jeans on sale in the front window. And a Dairy Queen, of course. She'd lived in the west all her life and had yet to see a town of any size without a Dairy Queen. Thank goodness, she thought as she smiled over at the jumble of old pickups and used sports cars in the parking lot. Every teenager west of the Mississippi would starve to death otherwise.

And that was about the size of Nobel, Idaho. She smiled again, a little more confidently. In a little town like this, people would quickly get used to the look of her. With any luck, she'd only spend the first year or so shaking off the whispers that had followed her since puberty.

Time to be brave, Gracie, she told herself. Time to meet your new town. Time to start your new life.

She unfolded herself from the front of her pickup, a rather long chore considering the length of her legs and her reluctance. She snagged two boxes of supplies from the bed of the truck, balanced them in one hand as she unlocked the glass front door of the small cinder-block-and-tin-roof building in front of her, and welcomed herself—there was no one else to do it—into her new home.

Nobel County Veterinary Clinic, here I am.

Daniel Cash leaned against the icy bumper of his pickup and watched her with narrowed eyes. Nice to know he was such a miserable jerk that he could hate a woman on sight, he thought to himself. His mother would swat him a good one if she knew just how much he wanted to stalk across the street to tell that amazingly long drink of water that she didn't belong in his town, didn't belong in his county, and she sure as hell did not belong in his building.

Yep. Hated her on sight. Too damn bad for him she was the most interesting-looking female he'd seen since…ever. Too bad she looked a mile long from where he was sitting, and most of that leg. Too bad her butt sat up as high as a fence post and her hips moved kind of slinky-like. That wasn't going to make a bit of difference. She was in his building, doing his job, living his life. And he wasn't happy about it.

He'd been waiting for her, brooding about her. When he'd drunk as much coffee as he could hold in the café across the street from the old vet clinic—the *new* vet clinic, he supposed people would call it now—he'd come back to the truck to brood in the cold spring wind, hoping it'd take the edge off. It hadn't.

He levered himself off the bumper and crossed the street without looking for cars. There hardly ever were any. Nobel, Idaho, was not bustling. Half the storefronts that in his childhood had glowed with prosperity and the promise of worldly goods now stood dark; the half that were still hanging on by their fingernails were mostly just wasting electricity. The huge warehouse stores and supply companies and chain groceries in nearby Twin Falls were too much temptation for Nobel's formerly loyal consumers.

Not that he was thinking about his town's faltering economy just now. She'd come back out of the building and was headed for her truck, which was parked on the street. She didn't notice him there—which gave him a good indication of just how preoccupied she was, settling into what was supposed to have been his life. He was a hard man to miss. She leaned in and grabbed another couple of bulky boxes from the back. Without a word, he took what looked to be the heaviest right out of her hands.

Lord. The woman was tall, was all Daniel could think as she straightened. Rose, and rose still. She'd looked tall from across the street, but this was…tall.

He was a good bit over six foot four inches, and was accustomed to being just about the tallest man around. And to looking at the tops of every woman's head; at uptilted eyes with flirty lashes, at the downslopes of noses, at those darling little whorls of hair every woman had at the top of her head she didn't know about, as distinguishing as fingerprints. But this girl—

Woman, he corrected himself. Nothing girlish about this Amazon. She met him almost inch for inch. If she was under six-two he'd eat his cap. His eyes widened at the sheer damned length of her. And the blood rushed into his face almost as fast as it rushed south to his groin. He couldn't for the life of him explain either reaction.

Grace felt the package go and gave a little dismayed whimper. Her extra meds were in that box; darn expensive to get and half in glass bottles. She dipped her knees to try to catch it as it fell, but it didn't fall at all. It swooped into the air instead and landed against the broadest, nicest chest she'd had the pleasure of coming across in years. She straightened slowly, wishing she didn't have to.

"Thanks," Grace said, holding her arm out to receive the box he'd nabbed, "but I can get it."

He didn't answer her so she frowned at him. She was

used to those wide-eyed stares, and was, she told herself sternly, resigned to being a freak of nature. But the man was young and handsome in that Western, aw-shucks kind of way, and she was a little embarrassed he'd dropped his jaw the way he had. Embarrassed and exasperated. Surely even this big, dumb cowboy knew it was rude to stare. Apparently not…

Daniel ignored the frown, knowing enough about women to understand when he was being reprimanded. And why. But he just couldn't get over it. Over her.

He knew she wasn't wearing high heels; he would have noticed that from across the street. He had a definite thing for high heels. He looked down at her feet, anyway. Nope. Boots, low-heeled and clunky.

Well, something had to explain why this woman looked him straight in the eye. Why she was the first woman he'd come across in all his wide and varied experience whose shoulders wouldn't graze his belly, whose head couldn't snuggle up under his chin, whose eyes he'd never see head-on unless she was scooted all the way up onto the pillows of his bed.

Grace glared at him. Wonderful. Now he was staring at her feet. They were, naturally, not dainty. She would have tipped over every time she walked if they had been, but she was still a little self-conscious about them. If he was so flabbergasted by their size, she thought, drawing her brows together, maybe she should just kick him with one and show him how useful they could be.

"Excuse me," she said sharply. He looked up, blinking, his gaze sidetracked briefly in the general vicinity of her chest, as though he somehow expected her face to be there and was surprised when it wasn't. At least he wasn't gawking at her feet any longer.

She meant to raise her eyebrows at him when he finally

got all the way up to looking at her. Give him a disdainful stare, she told herself. The one she practiced in the mirror for occasions just such as these, when people—when men— made her feel like some kind of circus curiosity for something genetic and completely beyond her control.

But she didn't raise her eyebrows. When she met his eyes, she felt the oddest jolt. They were mossy-green, the color of the lichen on the trees in her native state. And intense. And looking at her not as an oddity of nature, but as someone who might be backed up against the pickup behind her and pressed against. Taken. Right in front of the Nobel County Veterinary Clinic.

"Uh…" She couldn't get out another single syllable.

Daniel just stared at her. He was trying to remember why he wasn't supposed to like this woman. He'd sulked for days about her coming here, and waited in the cold so he could give her a little trouble. That was reason enough why he shouldn't squeeze up against that long body to see if it fit his as well as he imagined it might. Wasn't it?

For several seconds he couldn't answer his own question. Until she shook her head, breaking their strange and electrifying eye contact, and made a grab for the box he was holding.

Daniel recovered, barely, and sidestepped her effort to get her box back. He wanted inside the building, inside the boxes, and this was his chance. Besides, even though he disliked her on principle, that whole long length of her was making him twitch like a teenager, and he was man enough to admit he'd like the feeling to continue awhile.

"I got it," he said. He stepped in front of her and through the open door as if he owned the place. He put the box down—it clinked and he knew there was medicine in there; his fingers itched to get at it—and looked around.

"You just get into town?" he asked as she came in behind him, though he knew perfectly well she had.

"About five minutes ago," she said, annoyed and surprised at herself. She was unsettled, and nerves she hadn't known she had were zinging around inside her like marbles in a centrifuge. This big man had grabbed her box of expensive medicine without warning, gaped at her like a rube, and then short-circuited something important, she was sure, inside her normally very good brain.

Thankfully, she had enough sense left to know now wasn't a good time to make a blathering fool of herself in front of this, her first townsperson. The people of Nobel, including this giant, were going to be her lifeblood. Or their animals were, anyway. She stuck out a hand. "Grace McKenna. I'm the new vet."

"I know who you are," he said shortly. It made his blood simmer just thinking about who she was, what she was doing in his town. He took her hand anyway. "Daniel Cash."

"Oh, my landlord." She pumped his hand a couple times, was pleased beyond reckoning to find it was bigger than hers, and tried to pull hers back. He held on. "Uh, excuse me."

He let her hand go when she tugged the second time. He couldn't decide whether he'd kept it in some kind of perverse power play, or because it felt perfectly right in his; not butterfly small and crushable like so many women's hands had, but strong and long-fingered, like his own.

"So...the place is going to be great, I think," Grace said awkwardly. "Smells like you just had it painted. Thanks."

He nodded, still taking her in with a pair of depthless, moss-green eyes.

"Dr. Niebaur said you would. Paint it for me. I bought the practice sight unseen." And she was dying to see it, if this bruiser with the pretty eyes would get out of her way. "But he assured me you took good care of the building."

He nodded again.

"So—" She moved to open her boxes, wanting something to do. She'd always been a little shy around men, owing mostly to their drop-jawed expressions when they got a good look at her, and this one, with his sudden appearance and intense expression, intimidated her more than most. She felt an old, despised clumsiness as she bobbled the box on the counter and watched him automatically dip his knees to catch it before it crashed to the floor.

"Thanks. So," she began again after a deep breath, "are you the Nobel welcoming committee, or do you hang around town waiting to help carry boxes around?"

"I was passing by."

"Well, thanks for the help." She started lifting items, two-handed, from the boxes.

He'd seen Niebaur's old vet box bolted into the back of her pickup, knew she'd bought it with the practice she was taking over from the retired vet. This was extra medication, animal supplements, promotional items from feed companies, other fascinating stuff. He could barely keep from brushing her hands away.

"I don't want to keep you," she said after an extended, uncomfortable silence between them.

Daniel ignored her polite but pointed comment. She wanted him to leave. Too bad. He shifted so he could get a better look at what she was unpacking, and brushed up against her in the process, making them both jump.

"'Scuse me," he mumbled.

"Uh-huh," she said, giving him room. He seemed to need it. He was huge, at least an inch taller than she was. Maybe two, she thought, and a good fifty pounds heavier. His shirt stretched tight at his shoulders, and his forearms, bare despite the weather, looked like tree trunks. She didn't want to go lower, because she already felt crowded, but she got the impression of narrow hips and long, long legs.

He was less interested in her legs than she was in his, Grace noticed in something resembling relief. He was studying the felt-wrapped bundle she'd laid on the reception counter.

"My surgical tools," she said.

He grunted and chewed his lower lip. "Mind?"

"Um…" She looked at him warily. He had hardly said two words together. "I don't think so."

His dark brows snapped together. Not too difficult to figure out what she was thinking. "I'm not going to attack you with them," he scolded.

Her brown eyes widened fractionally. "So you say."

He shot her a look that told her not to be an idiot, and reverently unwrapped the instruments. He picked up a scalpel and examined it.

"You didn't get these from Niebaur."

Funny he'd know such a thing, Grace mused nervously. "No. I bought his vet box, but I got these as a gift from my folks when I graduated from vet school."

Another little grunt. "They look pretty new."

Nastily said, she thought. That cleared her head, got her back up a little. "They've been used. I've been out of school for almost two years."

"Two years, huh?" He put down the set of hide clamps he'd been absently weighing in his hand and looked at her, surprised all over again at how her eyes met level with his. She was slim, but not skinny the way so many tall women tended to be. Nice, wide hips, a nipped-in waist, high, heavy breasts on a gorgeous chest. He glared at her in a rush of lust and annoyance. "This your first practice then?"

"My first on my own," she conceded.

"It's a big job for a new vet."

"I'm not new," she repeated slowly. "As I said, I've been practicing veterinary medicine for two years, mostly large animal work, which is what the bulk of Dr. Niebaur's practice consists of. I'm good."

"I'm not saying you're not. I'm saying you're young. What are you, twenty-five? I'm saying this is a big area for one vet, much less one just out of W.A.S.U."

Oh, so he knew where she'd studied, did he? Niebaur

must have told him. He'd used the slang term for Washington State University, pronounced "wazoo," where she'd received her veterinary medicine degree. It made her mad, but because she was accustomed to men making her mad, she just smiled.

"I think I can handle it. And my age is really of no relevance." He'd underbid her age by a couple years, pleasing her in spite of herself.

He made a sound with his teeth and cheek, and nodded dubiously.

Oh, he was hostile, all right. She didn't know why, but she could guess. Some men, especially these rangy, manly types, automatically went into full browbeat mode the minute they got a look at her. They were used to walking tall in their little towns, and women such as her unmanned them. Well, tough.

Grace straightened her spine and lifted her chin to give herself every inch and advantage. She watched his Adam's apple move in his throat as she did. Probably in irritation.

"You want to see my diploma?" she challenged.

Daniel almost drooled. Her neck was long, like a swan's, like Audrey Hepburn's, for crying out loud. And when she got huffy her shoulders seemed to widen until he wanted to take them between his hands and measure their width, dig his fingers in a little, test their resilience. Lord, she was one long, cool drink of water. He was suddenly parched.

"No. Niebaur would have been careful with his practice." He'd wanted to say yes, just to needle her a little.

"Oh," she said. "Well, good." Naturally good-natured and easily mollified, she tried a closemouthed smile on him, a dismissal and peace offering in one. She didn't like his attitude, but she also wasn't in any position to alienate a potential client. She couldn't remember seeing his name on Niebaur's client list, but he might have a cat he needed spayed someday.

She looked at his sharp face, his vast size, and decided

no. No cats for this one. And certainly not anything spayed. This man would have a dog, a wolfhound or something, blissfully un-neutered so as not to offend his manly sensibilities.

"I should probably get busy in here, Mr. Cash. If you would excuse me."

"It's Daniel. Where are you living?"

She stared at him. "I beg your pardon?"

"Where are you living?" he repeated, ignoring her ruffled feathers. He knew he was being rude. He knew why, of course. She was in his building, with the practice that should have been his, would have been his if not for fate and a horrible lie he'd never been able to disprove. What he didn't know was why he was so reluctant to slink out and leave her to her unpacking. He hoped it was because he was small and petty and bitter, all manageable, if not particularly honorable, emotions. And not because she was just so damn tall and because he could vividly picture where she'd fit if he shoved her up against that newly painted wall she seemed to like and wedged his knee between her thighs. That was not manageable. Not manageable at all.

"Where am I living?" she echoed. She thought of a million reasons he shouldn't know, all big-city, woman-alone reasons. But what difference did it make, really? She was this town's vet now, the only one in a hundred square miles. She'd have to post her home phone and address for her patient's owners anyway, sooner or later. "I've rented a house."

"Here in town?"

"What—what—" Now she was stuttering. Wonderful. She wondered if punching Daniel Cash, landlord and probably Noble County scion, her first day in town would lose her many customers. "Why do you want to know, Mr. Cash?"

"Daniel." He corrected her again. "I have some other properties here in town. Just curious."

She doubted that. "On Fourth."

"Mrs. Hensen's old house? Did she get those front steps fixed?"

"I don't know. Also sight unseen."

"You have plans for dinner tonight?"

She almost laughed. "No."

"Want some?"

Her eyes went wide. "With you? I don't think so."

"Why not?"

She cocked her head, looked him up and down. She'd been right about the length of his legs, but she ignored the tiny buzz of interest in them. She put her hands on her hips and gave him her most confident glare. "Because you seem a little unbalanced, frankly. What's the matter with you?"

He frowned at her. "'Unbalanced'?"

"Yes," she said. "Unbalanced. You nab my box of meds without introducing yourself, play with those surgical instruments like some kind of serial killer, grill me on my credentials and my qualifications and then ask me where I live? Not to mention I met you all of three minutes ago. And I'm supposed to go out to dinner with you?"

"Oh, I thought you meant unbalanced because I was asking you to dinner." He flashed a quick grin at her, making that sharp face go gorgeous. "Like maybe you don't get many dinner invitations."

She flushed, because she didn't, because she knew he was baiting her. "I get thousands. I need to hire a secretary just to handle them all."

He gave her the long look this time, his head tilted to match hers. "I'll bet. So what about it?"

"No, thanks."

He narrowed his eyes on her. She was spoiling his plans. He wanted to know what kind of vet Niebaur had sold his damn practice to, and interrogating her over some fried chicken at the café was as good a way of finding out as any. The fact that he was very nearly aroused to the point of discomfort just standing next to her had nothing to do with it.

"Just a Welcome-to-Nobel dinner. I can give you my folks' phone number. They'll vouch for me."

"Parents never know. Besides, I have a million things to do. I haven't even been to my house yet."

"Okay." He could count on one hand the number of times a woman had turned down a dinner invitation from him. But he supposed a girl such as this, with those legs and that wit and a face like a Klimt painting, was turning them away by the truckload. He shrugged, took one last lingering look at both the legs and the veterinary supplies he wanted to get his hands on. "Welcome to Nobel, anyway, Dr. Mc-Kenna. I'll see you around."

"Yes. All right. And thank you for the help. My office will be open for business Monday, if you have animals that need tending."

He considered for a moment. "I have a couple. I'll be in touch."

He pushed out the front door and strode across the street without giving so much as a glance around for potential traffic. Grace watched him go with a dead even mix of relief and disappointment.

He'd pronounced it "noble," the name of his town. She'd been calling it "no-bell," like the prize. She'd remember that. It was always important, when you were doomed to make a bad first impression, to remember what you could to make a decent second one.

Chapter 2

He walked into his mother's kitchen late in the afternoon, not surprised to find it empty. Ever since he and his brother had taken over the running of the family cattle ranch at the base of the hills that shadowed Nobel, his mother and father had run amok.

He poked his head into the refrigerator, looking for a little fuel to keep him until dinner, an hour away and nothing much to look forward to anyhow, since he'd be having it alone.

"Mom?" he shouted, just to give general warning he was here and in her refrigerator. "Dad?"

They were probably out playing an afternoon rubber of bridge or something equally goofy and unproductive. They seemed to have taken to the goofy and unproductive since they retired, and he couldn't have been happier for them. They'd worked like dogs every minute he'd known them, with the cattle and the hay and the occasional field of potatoes or sweet corn or wheat when the futures looked good. Had worked even harder to help him through college and then vet school. They deserved a break. He was more than happy to give it to them.

He pulled out a beer, twisted off the top, pinched the cap between his thumb and middle finger and flicked it across the kitchen, where it rebounded off the wall and landed in the trash.

Of course, he'd planned it all differently. They'd have still had their retirement, but Frank would have had the ranch on his own now, with Lisa helping full-time, and he'd have been in that cinder-block building instead of Grace Mc-Kenna, living in town with his wife and the life they'd planned together.

His wife. The phrase left a bitter taste in his mouth and he took a slow pull off his beer to wash it away. Julie had left him to face his disgrace and his failure alone. They'd only been married seven months when his life had started to come apart, so he supposed it was unfair of him to have expected her to ride out the trouble. But he had expected it. And he'd found, during the three years since she'd left, that it was as hard to forgive her betrayal as it was to face his own failure.

Today, standing in the office he'd always thought would someday be his, had brought it all back to him. Not that he ever forgot it, really. It was always there, haunting his days, tainting his nights. But he could back-burner it most of the time. Not today. Not watching Grace McKenna drive through town with *his* vet box bolted in the back of her truck, opening *his* office as the official new vet of Nobel County, Idaho.

He didn't blame the woman for having his life. That would be deranged and foolish. He didn't blame her.

He leaned back against the kitchen counter, his mossy eyes going dark and flat. Oh, hell, he blamed her a little.

Grace McKenna. Damn her. He took a long swallow of beer, his head tipped back. He wondered if when her mama named her she knew she'd grow into the kind of woman

who needed a bigger name. Grace was a name for a petite
blond woman with tiny feet and dainty hands. A blue-eyes
belle, who never did anything nastier with those hands than
pour afternoon tea for her garden club.

He could think of a dozen better names for Grace Mc-
Kenna. Strong, mythic names, such as Hera, Diana, Minerva.
He smirked into his beer. Okay, not Minerva. But a name
for a woman with power and height, and that cap of dark
curly hair that looked so soft, as though it belonged on a
baby.

He knew what Grace McKenna did with her hands. For
nearly twenty years he'd trained to do the same thing. She
pushed her hands into the back ends of sick or pregnant
cattle. She made stud colts into geldings. He'd bet she did
not belong to a garden club or pour tea for anyone.

Quite suddenly and against his will, he started to wonder
what else Grace McKenna might be capable of doing with
those hands. More than a few ideas popped up in full color
right in front of his glassy eyes.

He dug his thumb and forefinger into his eye sockets. Oh,
jeez, where had that stuff come from? The last thing he
needed was to start his feeble mind down that particular road
with this particular woman.

"Danny!"

He jumped and almost bobbled his beer, feeling as if his
mother had caught him looking at dirty pictures up in his
room. Again.

"Mom!" He gave her a kiss as she went past, her hands
full of grocery bags. "Any more outside?"

"Your dad's getting them, sugar. What are you doing
here?"

What was he doing here? He'd been pissed off and feeling
sorry for himself all day, ever since he'd awakened and realized this was the day the new vet came to town. He'd tried
to fight it out with the person in question, then tried to sweat
it out all day working the herd. Neither tack had taken. Now

he wanted a little comfort. And this was the place he'd always come for that.

"Nothing. Just checking in on you guys. Wanted to make sure you hadn't taken up golf yet or anything."

His mother laughed. "Not yet. Put them on the counter, Howard."

Daniel's father came in, loaded down. "I know where to put groceries, Liz. I've been bringing in your groceries for a hundred years. Hi, Danny."

"Hey, Dad."

"What are you doing here?"

"You know, I could name fifty people right now who would kill to get a visit from their son."

"Not a son who drinks the good beer." He pulled one out for himself. "I keep the cheap stuff in the can for you and Frank."

Daniel grinned. "I'll keep that in mind."

"Do that. You see the new vet?"

Daniel's green eyes went flat again. "Yeah, I saw her."

"Figured you had. Just saw Pat down to the grocery store and he said you'd been staring out the window of the Early Bird for pert near an hour this morning before she showed up."

Daniel moved his ax-handle shoulders. "I just wanted to make sure she got settled in."

Howard tossed his wife a glance. "Right. Did she?"

"She was getting there. She already had Doc Niebaur's vet box bolted into the back of her truck, but she hadn't even been to her new house, so I guess she's got her priorities set." He took another slug of beer, to wash the acid taste of animosity down his throat.

"Where's she living?"

"The little house of Fourth. The one I tried to buy from Mrs. Hensen last year."

"I hope she fixed that front stoop, the old skinflint."

"She did. I went by to check on it."

Howard and his wife exchanged another apprehensive look. Daniel watched his father take in a deep breath, knew from experience a lecture was coming. "Now, son—" he began.

Daniel warded him off with a raised hand. "It's okay, Dad. I was just being neighborly." They were both looking at him, his father's arm slung across his mother's plump shoulders, united in their love and concern for him. He smiled. "Really. She seems like a nice person. I just wanted to make sure she wasn't going to go through her front porch on her first day, is all."

His mother eyed him. "Sugar, I think you need to just let the whole thing go."

"I know, Mom. I'm getting there."

"Well, I hear she's a big gal," Howard said his booming voice emphasizing the "big." "Pat said she was six foot if she was an inch."

Daniel smiled. "More like six-two or three. Tall, but not skinny. She looks pretty good, actually." He took another drink, dropped the bomb. "I asked her out to dinner."

His parents goggled at him.

"Now, honey—" his mother began.

"Hell, boy—" his father said at the same time.

Daniel put both hands up this time, the long fingers of one stretched around the neck of his beer bottle. "She said no anyhow, but I didn't ask her out because I'm interested in her. She could have been a troll for all I care, or a man. I was just going to grill her about her plans for my practice."

"Oh, Danny," his mother said. She shook her head at him. "It would have been better if you had asked her out because she's good-looking."

He grinned at her, to make that worry line between her brows disappear. Dammit, he hadn't meant to say "my" practice. It had just slipped out. "I make it a policy to not date women who can take me in an arm wrestle."

"Bad policy," his father said under his breath, making Daniel laugh.

"I won't have you harassing the girl," his mother warned.

"I wasn't harassing her. Exactly. Anyway, she caught me at it and made some nasty comment about my mental health." Which, somehow, had both stung a little and made him want to laugh. He couldn't figure it. "And she told me she wouldn't have dinner with me, so I came to ask you guys if you want to go out. My treat. We can call Frank if you want to. Lisa, too, if she's not doing anything."

"I don't think I can take an evening with Frank tonight," Liz said, sighing. She put the last of the groceries away. "Besides, we have a canasta game."

"Which we can cancel," Howard countered. "You know I hate to play with the O'Sullivans, anyway. Harry cheats at cards like a lying dog."

"Ha," Liz said. "When it comes to cards, I wouldn't talk about lying dogs if I were you."

"I don't cheat at cards!"

"Ha again! I've played poker with you, buddy boy. I know a cheater when I see a cheater."

"Just at strip poker, Liz." He leered at her stupidly, making her laugh.

Daniel smiled, threw his arms around them both. "I'll get you back in time for your canasta game." He headed them out the kitchen door. "I'd hate for you to miss anything as goofy as that."

Grace's day had turned out plenty goofy. First of all, there had been people everywhere. Not under her feet exactly, but close enough. They'd started coming by the minute Daniel Cash and his splendid body and Neanderthal brain had loped, flat-footed, back to whatever cave he'd come from.

She noticed the kid first, riding back and forth on his bike. He was all of eleven, she thought, and he'd passed the office a dozen times before getting up the nerve to come in to gawk sideways at her while pretending a remarkably intense interest in bovine nose pliers. She let him gawk. Better to get it over with.

Then a couple old men, bored with checkers and coffee or whatever occupied the long days of retired farmers, had sauntered over from the café across the street, made a complimentary comment or two about Doc Niebaur, wished her the best. They'd gawked at her, too. One of them taking to calling her "Stretch" in the middle of their short conversation.

One by one, two by two, people had come by, most too shy to poke their heads inside to say hello to the new vet, but hardly a soul in Nobel willing to miss out on the chance to get a load of the lady veterinarian who looked "pert near tall enough to be in the circus or something."

She'd gone about her work vaguely accustomed to it all. She'd been the junior vet in three other offices since graduation and she'd always encountered these kinds of reactions. She supposed it would have been the same if she'd chosen secretarial work as her profession, or grocery clerking. Anything but women's basketball or modeling. She'd never had the interest in one, the looks or the intellectual indifference required for the other.

She'd unpacked her boxes, snooped through the cabinets in the examining/operating room, though from the inventory list Niebaur had sent her when she'd bought his practice, she'd known almost to the syringe what was in there. She'd checked the kennel cages and taken a quick run through the files, trying not to look for "Cash, Daniel" on the folder labels. She'd found it, anyway, and dug it out.

A thousand head of cattle! No, she'd thought, that couldn't be right. But there it was. Daniel and Frank Cash—a father, or a brother, maybe—owned Cash Cattle, Incorporated, and a thousand head of mother cows. A huge operation.

He'd said he had a couple animals. What a smart aleck. She shook her head in memory of his smug grin.

She'd riffled through the file again, found the brucellosis vaccination records for the past ten years, the trich tests results on fifty Angus bulls, lapsed for three years now. He'd gone to artificial insemination then, she'd noted, and felt a little thrill when she'd realized she'd get to do it this year. A lucrative thing. The A.I. business. If he continued to go to a vet for it rather than hire one of the freelance A.I. technicians. Which he might do, considering his inexplicable animosity toward her earlier in the day.

She hoped he wouldn't, though. She needed the income. Her parents had borrowed against everything they owned to help her pay for this practice, and she was determined to make it work. It was a huge risk, but she liked the idea of a small-town, large animal practice, and although this part of Idaho didn't have an abundance of humans, it had enough dairy cows and beef cattle and hobby farms with spoiled horses to get her by. She hoped.

She'd squeezed the folder back into the file cabinet, promising she'd get the Cash Cattle file on computer, along with everyone else's just as soon as she found an assistant. Niebaur's office manager had promised to come in a couple of days a week for a while, but she was retiring, too. Couldn't see herself working for another woman, she'd said. No offense.

Grace hadn't taken offense, of course. She hadn't wanted to work for anyone else, either.

Picking up the phone book, she glanced at the wall clock. 9:10 p.m. She riffled through the book for the number to the county newspaper and recorded her ad onto the machine that picked up.

She stretched out her long legs, hooking her heels on the edge of the reception desk. She looked out into dark main street of Nobel, Idaho, and congratulated herself. She had every single thing she wanted, now.

Minutes later she dozed off with a satisfied smile on her face.

* * *

He hadn't meant to come by. He'd dropped his folks off at their house, intending to go home to his own small ranch house, just a half mile down the road from the house where he'd grown up. Instead his pickup truck—of its own accord, he'd swear—found its way the eleven miles back into town and past the building he owned, bought when his future looked exactly as he'd wanted it to look. The lights were on. He glanced at his watch. It was past ten, and he'd bet a hundred bucks she hadn't been home all day.

He wheeled the truck into a casually illegal U-turn and brought it to rest behind hers by the curb. He scooped up the nameless old barn cat he'd brought with him as an excuse for coming by and tucked it under his arm, trying not to moon over the vet box in Grace's truck as he made for the office door. He almost managed it, walking past with just a quick yearning glance.

Grace had her feet up on the desk in the reception area and her chin on her chest. Sound asleep. He watched her for a minute, the cat purring happily under his arm, then rapped on the glass of the door with the back of his hand.

She jerked awake and he saw in her brown eyes the instant cognizance of a doctor awakened from a sound sleep. She could perform surgery right now, he knew; intubate a calf, cesarean a breech foal. She had that look as she stared out at him. That completely-awake-and-aware look.

She stood and came toward him. He felt a sudden zip up his spine, a heated pooling of blood between his legs.

Man, oh, man. He'd wasted half the day away wondering if she'd really been the goddess he'd seen that morning, or if he'd imagined that her legs went up to her neck and her hips were narrow and smooth-jointed when she walked and her mouth was wide and lush. He didn't much like this woman who was stealing his dreams, but he sure as hell wanted her.

For crying out loud, he reprimanded himself pitilessly.

Grow up, Cash. He'd gone hard just watching her walk. Heaven only knew what would happen when she got the door open. He smoothed his free hand along the flank of his cat, hoping the thick fur would absorb the sudden dampness there. Didn't want the goddess to know she'd made him sweat.

She stopped on the other side of the door. She didn't smile, couldn't. If she thought he'd been intense this morning, he looked positively dangerous now. It was only common sense and the bone-deep knowledge that she could never, in a million years, with her utter lack of experience and confidence, handle a man with that kind of lust in his eyes, that kept her from throwing the lock on the door and letting him take her.

"Mr. Cash," she said through the glass.

He cleared his throat. "Doctor McKenna."

She glanced at the contented bit of fur tucked into his elbow. "Nice cat."

"Thank you."

"He looks pretty healthy. Any reason you're bringing him to my office at—" she checked her watch "—ten-eighteen p.m.?"

"He's been in a fight."

Grace frowned. "Really?"

"Would I lie about something like that?" he asked solemnly. Of course he would, but she didn't need to know that.

"I don't know. Would you?"

"No. Open the door, McKenna."

She considered him for a full minute, but her active sense of self-preservation just couldn't hold up against an injured animal she knew she could help. She reached up and turned the dead bolt.

"Take him back to the examining room." She relocked the door and followed behind him as he unerringly found

the examining room. She did her best not to study his rear
end as he walked.

She washed her hands at the little sink and felt a familiar
little zing of adrenaline. Her first client in her own practice.
Could there be a more productive sensation than that? She
turned to find the cat lounging on her stainless-steel examining table, the Neanderthal leaning against it with his hands
widespread, watching her.

"Your cat is purring," she pointed out.

"He's in shock."

"Hmm." She took the cat in her hands. It rolled onto its
back to have its belly scratched. Grace obliged automatically
while looking for evidence of the fight. "What's his name?"

"Uh, Tiger," Daniel said, though the cat had been called
"Cat" since the day it was born.

Grace looked up at him. "Tiger, huh?"

Daniel shrugged. "My brother named it."

"Well, Tiger here has certainly been in a fight."

"Yeah," Daniel said, his mouth pursed in studied concern. "I thought I'd better bring him in."

"And two weeks ago, I might have thought so, too. Mr.
Cash." She lifted the cat and dropped it into Daniel's arms.
He cradled it against his chest automatically, his fingers fold-
ing over its small head to scratch between its ears. Grace
noted how unaware he was that he was doing it, how utterly
at ease the cat was under his fingers. He'd probably spent
hours sitting in some dusty old barn somewhere, that cat on
his lap. She forced herself not to imagine it. "But probably
not even then. The scratches were pretty minor even at the
time they were inflicted. They are almost completely healed
now."

Daniel nodded, pretending ignorance. "So, you think he
just needs a little antibiotic cream or something?"

"No, I don't think he needs a little antibiotic cream or
something." She washed her hands. "I think he needs to go
home. I think you need to go home. I think I need to go

home." She stalked out of the exam room, muttering something about wasted time.

Daniel ignored her. "Well, that's a relief," he said, following her through the office. "I'm glad I dropped by."

"You didn't drop by, Mr. Cash." She unlocked the door and opened it wide. "Your home is eleven miles south of town."

"How did you know that?"

"I looked through your file. I figured since you knew where I lived, I should know where you lived. In case I ever had to call the police on you or something."

"Good thinking." He paused in the doorway. "So, what are you doing here?"

"I work here."

"So late."

"I was just getting ready to go home."

"Have you even been there yet?"

"I drove by it earlier."

"Not good enough. I'll see you home if you're ready."

She cocked her head. "I don't think so."

"Come on." He jerked his head in the direction of her truck and his, then held up his cat as proof of his honor. "I own a cat. How bad a person could I be?"

"I believe the number-one choice of pets for crazy people is a cat."

Man, she was cute. And quick. "Come on. Trust me," Daniel said.

She did, for some idiotic reason. He didn't look particularly trustworthy, despite the blissed-out cat in his arms. Something to do with that lingering gleam of reluctant lust in his green eyes, she thought. And he certainly didn't feel trustworthy. She wasn't experienced enough to know what it was she felt from him, but she knew she shouldn't trust it.

Yet somehow... Grace went back for her bag and coat, flicked off the lights, and followed him onto the sidewalk, locking the door behind her. A cold wind sneaked under her sweatshirt and she shivered, ducking her head as much in reflex to the cold as to keep from meeting his eyes. She fumbled with her coat. It was snatched out of her hands at the same instant a cat began winding itself around her legs. She couldn't decide which was more startling.

"Here," Daniel said. He tucked her into her jacket, took the zipper between his fingers and pulled it up. If his knuckles brushed against the inside of her breast so slightly, if his hands lingered at the collar for one second too long, that didn't make him a creep, right? He wasn't harassing her. He was just being gentlemanly, and accidents happen. He bent and picked up Cat from where he'd dumped him unceremoniously on the sidewalk. Before touching her became less accidental.

"Get in your truck before you freeze solid."

"Is it always so cold in March?" she asked pertly, to keep her mind off how gentle his hands had been, and how personal.

"Yes. March is a bitch. But January and February are worse, so by March you hardly notice how miserable you are."

He'd walked her to her truck, stood while she dug in her purse for her keys. "I don't need an escort home," she said. "I know where I live."

"Barely." He took the keys and unlocked her door, then stepped back before the urge to put his hands on her again got to be too much to resist. He kept reminding himself how much he resented her, how much he couldn't get involved with another woman who would betray him the minute she heard about his past.

"Why didn't you tell me this morning you had a thousand head of beef cattle?" she asked, a little accusingly.

He shrugged. "I figured Niebaur would have told you."

"He didn't. I thought you were a real estate agent or something."

He laughed despite his uncertain mood. "A real estate agent. Is that what I look like?"

She brought her shoulders to her ears, shy again. She didn't want to say out loud what he looked like to her. It would have sounded silly, telling him he looked big and strong, man enough to make her feel small and feminine. For once. "I don't know. You own this building, and you said you had others in town."

"Oh." He scratched his nose, knitted his brows in annoyance and embarrassment. "That was kind of a stretch of the truth. I own this building and a little house on Temple. Well, I own part and the bank owns part. I bought them both three years ago when I thought I'd— When I thought about moving to town."

"Good thing you changed your mind about moving. I imagine it'd be hard on the neighbors to have a thousand head of cattle in town. It's a big herd. Are you looking for a new vet?"

"I thought you were the new vet."

"You know what I mean. Are you going to someone else now that Niebaur's retired?"

He looked at her for a minute. Glared at her, she might have said if she could think of a single reason he might do so.

"We'll try it out," he finally said. "I've got some heifers need checking week after next."

"Okay." While she didn't appreciate his antagonistic attitude, her practical heart wanted to sigh in relief. "Okay. Good. I could use the business."

They stood on the sidewalk, staring at each other, unsure of what to say or do. They were having a moment, it occurred to both of them; what that meant, they hadn't the slightest idea.

"So," Daniel began slowly, "Niebaur still have all his files on paper?"

Grace smiled, relieved. She'd been scrambling for something to say, anything to break the peculiar, tingly tension between them. "Yes. I have to find an assistant right away so I can get started on getting them on computer. I don't know how he ever managed to keep his billing straight."

"I don't know, either, but he must have. Frank and I have paid out enough to him over the years to prove it."

"Is Frank your dad?"

"My brother and business partner. Are you cold?"

Grace wondered at the way his face closed at the mention of his brother. "A little. I'd better get home. I still have my suitcases in the back of the truck."

"Come on, then," He slapped the side of her truck, shuffled off grim thoughts of his brother. "I'll follow you."

"I'll be fine."

"Do you argue this much with everyone?" he asked testily. He wanted to feel testy; he wanted the low-level anger and bitterness he'd lived with for three years to shoot back into his system. Because if it didn't he was very much afraid he was going to grab the woman and kiss her. Damn the male sexual response, anyway. He needed to think with his brain right now, but his other, more aggressive organs were pushing for equal time, it seemed.

He closed the door, jogged back to his own truck, tossed in Cat and hoisted himself inside.

Grace didn't get lost, that would have taken a 14-carat idiot in a town the size of Nobel, but she drove five miles an hour down her street until she spotted the little house. It was as dark as a tomb.

They got out of their respective vehicles and stood looking at it.

"You should have gone in when it was still light out," he whispered in deference to the late hour, the quiet neighborhood, the breath he could barely catch, just standing next to her, with her shoulder against his.

"I should have," she conceded in the same quiet tone.

His breath had moved her hair aside, brushed against her temple. She blinked. "It looks pretty dark in there."

He glanced at her out of the corner of his eye. He gritted his teeth, rolled his eyes, sighed. It didn't help. He still wanted to take that anxious look out of her eyes. But that would be it, he told himself. She was no little girl, no damsel in distress. She was the personification of every single thing that had pissed him off for three long years. He'd look around her dark little house and then he and Cat would head home for a long, comforting brood.

"I'll come in with you," he offered reluctantly.

Oh, she should say no. She should tell him she could handle herself just fine, thanks. But she wanted him to come in with her, chase out all the spooks and spiders. It was a rare thing, a man offering to do such a thing. Not since her father, not since her brothers, had a man looked beyond the size of her to the tender, sometimes fragile woman beneath.

"What about Tiger?"

"Who?"

She looked at him. "Your cat?"

"He's okay in the truck. He's sleeping in my rain slicker."

"Oh." She chewed on her lower lip a moment. "Okay. Thanks. Sorry."

He walked in front of her. "For what?"

"For asking you to do this."

"You didn't ask me," he rumbled crossly.

"Oh. Well, just thanks, then."

He nodded shortly.

He walked up the steps, unlocked the door with her key, and flicked on the lights. The place was furnished sufficiently, if a shade shabbily, and was well-lighted and thickly draped. She'd be safe enough in here. He walked through the rooms, leaving her in the living room, snapping on the lights as we went. It didn't take long. The house was tiny.

"Everything looks okay."

"Good. Thanks again."

"No problem."

They stood across the room from each other. He pretended to look at the structure of the room, scanning the ceiling for signs of a leaky roof, bouncing lightly on his toes to listen for a creaky floor. She studied the furniture, the worn carpet, to keep from looking at him. Finally she took in a deep breath, then let it out.

He heeded the signal. "Well, I better be going."

"Yes. It's late. Thanks again."

"You said that already," he noted brusquely. "A couple times."

"Oh. Well."

He walked toward the door, toward her. She wanted to move out of his way, desperately, but found herself rooted to the spot. It was as if her mind was certain she should do one thing, the safe and sensible thing, but her body, her unruly, nothing-but-trouble body, was making the decisions.

He came to her slowly, brushed against her shoulder as he reached for the doorknob. And stood so still she could hear him swallow. Just stood there, his right shoulder against hers, for the space of ten heartbeats. He stared at the door, his throat working. She stared unseeing into the room, her heart pounding.

Then he turned his head slightly, and nuzzled her neck. Her breath caught and held while her face went a dozen shades of scalding red. She was paralyzed with arousal and shock. No one had ever nuzzled her neck. Not ever! Never anything so simple, so erotic. He took his time, let her flush redder, kissing his way up her neck to her ear, taking her earlobe between his teeth.

She'd heard people say, countless times, that their knees went weak, but she'd never believed it actually happened. No empirical scientific evidence to support such a claim. She had some now. She reached out a hand to steady herself, found nothing there, and let the hand hang in midair.

He made his way to her jaw, nipped it gently when she didn't turn her head, drop it back. She hadn't known she was meant to until then, and when she did, he kissed her.

The most amazing kiss. Wet and deep and slow. Her head turned fully to his, his turned to hers, both necks arched back in greed and surrender, the kiss made sweeter, more erotic because they touched in not a single other spot. When his tongue flicked forward, licked at her mouth, she managed to choke back only half the moan that slid up from her chest.

That little sound shot all the way down to his toes and he had to dig his short nails into his palms to keep from grabbing those wide shoulders of hers, turning her to face him. He wanted to, possibly more than he'd ever wanted anything. More even than he'd wanted her job, he wanted her. And that scared the hell out of him. He reared back suddenly, his mouth wet, his brain scrambled, his blood roaring. He met her wide-open eyes for the briefest moment, then fumbled for the doorknob. Without so much as a second glance in her direction, Daniel walked out into the cold night.

Grace's knees did buckle then, and as she slumped to the floor, she laughed. A gasping, dumbfounded, girlish little giggle of complete surprise and joy.

Chapter 3

Grace's office had been a zoo all week, populated by a large assortment of domesticated animals, some of which, like Daniel's cat, did not have a thing wrong with them. Which was more than Grace could have honestly said about some of their owners.

The kid with the bike was back today, with a perfectly healthy white rat who rode happily in a plastic milk crate he'd strapped to the handlebars with a bungee cord. She'd looked over the rat while the kid looked over her. The rat was quiet and polite, the boy was not, giving her a little headache with questions about how tall she was, and had she ever played basketball for the Utah Jazz, and could she change a lightbulb without getting on a chair?

Why Mrs. Handleman had sent the child and a perfectly healthy animal back into the examining room was a question Grace posed the first chance she got.

"Because his mother has an account with this clinic," Mrs. Handleman explained, gravely affronted at having her authority questioned, Grace gathered from her tone. "And I didn't want that filthy vermin in the front office. You're the vet. You deal with the filthy vermin.''

Grace *was* the vet, and everyone in town seemed to know it. The company she'd had moving in was nothing compared to the rush during her first official week. Several times she sent up a quick prayer to thank Dr. Niebaur for lending her Mrs. Handleman until she found an assistant. A prayer that was almost always followed by a curse. Under her breath, of course.

She'd had just one applicant for Mrs. Handleman's job. A woman who'd shown up at the clinic before Grace's ad had even appeared in the newspaper. Lisa Cash, a relative of the hunk, she presumed. Grace secretly decided ''Lisa'' was a rather plain name for a rather flashy young woman. She'd come into the office in tight jeans and a pearl-buttoned cowboy shirt pressed to within an inch of its life. Her hair was bleached until it was more dead straw than live follicle, with what looked like intentionally dark roots. She wore a good quarter pound of eye makeup, as well, which only added to the barmaid aspect of her. Grace was thrilled with her, and envious. As much as it would have galled her to look in the mirror and have a yellow head and Bride of Frankenstein eyes staring back at her, she'd always secretly wished she could work up the courage to look like a hooker every once in a while. For novelty. As a change from looking like someone an eleven-year-old rat owner might mistake for a member of the starting lineup of the Utah Jazz.

Lisa didn't have any experience in a vet's office, but she was good on a computer, she said, and could file and take appointments. Grace hired her on the spot. Anyone who looked like Lisa Cash would be unlikely to sniff at something so inconsequential as a rat, and besides, Grace couldn't *wait* to get rid of Mrs. Handleman.

The woman was bossy, tyrannical and territorial. And if she mentioned how Dr. Niebaur did things one more time, Grace was going to put her fingers in her ears and start screaming. But she knew everyone who came through the door, whatever their species, and filed them back to the examining room in a reasonably orderly manner, so Grace fought off the urge to fire her before Lisa was trained.

"You have the dairy call at two," Mrs. Handleman reminded Grace again, at a quarter to the hour. "It's a good ten miles out of town. Dr. Niebaur would have left by now."

"Uh-huh. Right. Thanks."

Grace was tempted to make a face at the old woman's wide, retreating back. She only just managed to pull in her imaginary tongue when the woman looked back, suspicious.

"Anything else?" Grace asked innocently, peeling off her lab coat and reaching for the hook behind her door for her coveralls.

Mrs. Handleman gave her a cross, distrustful look, then stomped officiously down the hall. Grace almost giggled.

Even Mrs. Handleman couldn't puncture Grace's good mood, apparently. Her first dairy call, and she could hardly contain her excitement. Nobel County had several large dairies, mostly transplants from California, where dairymen had been all but zoned out of the crowded suburban landscape. Grace was happy they had been. She loved working with the big, gentle dairy cattle, but wanted, too, the kind of rural lifestyle only a sparsely populated place such as Idaho could offer. The best of both worlds, she thought, smiling.

"You look pretty when you do that."

Him. She stopped short, halfway wiggled into her insulated coveralls. Oh, the gorgeous, giant Daniel Cash. The man who had kissed her until she was a wide, giggling ooze of pudding on her living-room floor, then hadn't called her for a week. Weren't men who kissed you that way supposed to call you right after? Or at least the next day? Or the day after that? She didn't know, but she thought so. She turned down the corners of her mouth. Wouldn't do to have him think the smile was for him.

"Mr. Cash."

"Dr. McKenna." He gestured to the coveralls. "Don't let me keep you."

She finished worming her way into the coveralls with as much dignity as ten pounds of stiff canvas and padding would allow.

Daniel watched her worming, and fought back the little thrill it gave him. She toed off her sneakers and stepped into her boots. He hid an unexpected smile at the picture she made. The bulky coveralls, with the right sleeve cut off as befits a large animal vet, fit her fine in the torso, but the legs were a good five inches short, and her heeled boots gave her another inch, making her look a little like a stork wearing a winter coat. He doubted she'd have appreciated the analogy.

Grace knew exactly how she looked, and she would have given a lot at that moment to have been dressed in anything else. She furrowed her brows, shook off the wave of self-consciousness. She was a vet, she had a call to make. The last thing she needed was to be worrying about the fashion opinion of some man.

"How's Tiger?"

"Who?"

"Tiger," she offered blandly. "Your cat?"

"Oh." He looked a little sheepish. "Tiger's good. Where are you headed?"

"I have a dairy call. Spandell's."

"Dairy call?" Daniel's brain kicked automatically into a familiar, low-level hum of excitement. It had been the same for him since he was a kid, when he'd splinted the broken leg of a pup his dad had run over. Doc Niebaur had told he'd make a hell of a vet someday. Had used the word "hell" even, which at ten was forbidden to Daniel, and had made him feel like a man. He'd hoped, after all this time, the buzz would fade. No damn luck, evidently. "What've you got?"

"Mild fever, probably."

He nearly rubbed his hands together. Milk fever. He could

have cured that in his sleep. Then again, so, probably, could have most dairymen. "Spandell call you in?"

She nodded. "About twenty minutes ago. He sounded pretty worried about it. He seems to have a very close attachment to his cows. Plus, I think he wants a look at me."

Daniel narrowed his eyes fractionally. "I bet."

Grace didn't know whether to be flattered or annoyed by the glower that had come over his face. "I've got to go. I'm going to be late as it is."

"I'll ride along with you."

"I don't think so."

"Why not?"

"Because it's my first call on this place. I want to make a good impression."

"Then you should have gotten some longer coveralls."

Grace's face dropped, then flamed.

Daniel watched the transformation of her face and felt an uncomfortable little bite of regret gnaw through him. He'd been teasing, of course, didn't realize she'd be so sensitive. She seemed so confident. A woman the likes of Grace McKenna, embarrassed by a silly thing like her coveralls?

"I was just kidding you," he said roughly. He couldn't remember the last time he'd felt like such a heel.

She smiled gamely. "I know. They are funny, aren't they?"

"Look, Doc—"

"I got them as long as I could, but the only ones they had in my length were so big in the torso I couldn't swing my arms when I walked. I looked like Frankenstein."

"I'm sorry I said anything."

"It's okay. Seriously. I'm used to teasing." But not from him. Since he'd kissed her, she'd been working up to wondering if maybe this man saw her as someone desirable, feminine maybe, and possibly even, when she was sitting down and her big feet were tucked under, a little bit delicate.

She'd always wanted one man, someday, to consider her a little bit delicate. "I really do have to go."

He'd hurt her feelings, Daniel knew. Being…well, a man, he wasn't quite sure why, but he felt like a jackass.

"Let me ride along. I went to high school with Larry Spandell. He won't mind."

She considered him a minute, looked down at his boots. "Well, since you already have manure on your boots, I guess you can come. But don't get in my way."

Get in her way? She was in *his* way, and had been ever since she'd stepped down from her truck with *his* vet box in the back. Get in her way. He jammed his cowboy hat onto his head, vexed with both of them. "I won't."

Larry Spandell had a small operation, milked just seventy-eight Holsteins on a place his mother had inherited from her mother. Every cow was his baby, and the one with milk fever was his favorite. When Grace and Daniel walked into his milk barn, Larry was worrying over the sick cow like a nanny over a fevered child.

"Mr. Spandell? I'm Grace McKenna."

He shook her hand, didn't give her more than a glance. Daniel saw how she'd braced herself for the introduction, how relieved she was when Larry didn't gape up at her from his five feet, eight inches. Daniel filed that observation away. He'd kick it around later, when the nearness of the woman and the excitement of the job wasn't clouding his judgment.

"Doc. This is her."

Grace could see that. She could tell it was milk fever from the position of the cow; lying on her sternum with her head displaced to the right, turned into the flank.

She sterilized her hands and knelt to the cow, already reaching for her bag. Daniel placed it in her hands.

"Parturient paresis," he murmured absently, using the diagnostic name for the affliction. Grace glanced at him in surprise. He was taking the cow's pulse at the carotid artery.

"Muzzle's dry, extremities cool, temperature below normal."

Grace decided she'd be curious about Daniel Cash later. She turned to the dairyman. "When'd she calve?"

"Yesterday."

"Pulse is seventy-five, pupils dilated," Daniel mumbled, talking to himself.

"Thank you," Grace said tightly. She took a brown bottle from her vet bag. "When'd she go down?"

"'Bout an hour ago. I called your office as soon as I saw."

"Good." She filled a syringe, injected it smoothly into the thick vein on the cow's neck. "She's an old cow, Mr. Spandell. I'm giving her some calcium borogluconate. She should be up soon, but next calf I want you to give her a single dose of ten million units of crystalline Vitamin D eight days before calving. That should prevent this happening again."

Daniel rose. "Your older cows should be on high-phosphorus, low-calcium feed, Larry. I told you that last time you had a cow go down with milk fever."

"I know, Dan, but I'm on a budget here, you know."

"Be harder on your budget to lose a cow."

Grace shot Daniel a glare, then turned to the dairyman. "Call my office in a couple hours. If she's not up by then, I'll come back on my way home and treat her again."

"You may have to inflate the udder," Daniel said.

Grace whipped around, said in a low voice, "I know my job, thanks."

Daniel nodded, sucked in his cheeks. Geez, he'd made her mad, and no wonder. But he didn't care. It had felt so right, so incredibly good, kneeling beside this old cow in this milk-smelling barn. He'd wanted it to go on all day, treat every one of Larry Spandell's seventy-eight Holsteins for problems they didn't even have.

"Okay, Mr. Spandell?" she was worried he hadn't heard

her, mooning over his downed cow the way he was. "You'll call me?" She pressed one of her new business cards against his shoulder. He reached up and absently pushed it into his shirt pocket. "That card has my home number and my pager number on it."

"I will. Thanks a million, Doc. Doc Niebaur said you was a good vet."

"Thanks. I think she'll be fine. You take care now."

Daniel, had anyone asked, would have had to say Dr. Grace McKenna practically stomped out of that milking barn. And a woman like her made a powerful physical statement, stomping around in a full-on snit, he decided.

"Doc!"

But she had already tossed her bag back into her vet box and was gunning the truck. He loped over and scooted inside just as she roared off.

"Listen, McKenna—"

"You better not talk to me right now, *Cash*."

"I can explain."

"You don't have to explain. I know exactly what was going on back there."

"You do." Well, of course, she would. Nobel was a small town, and she'd been here a week. Surely she'd heard from a dozen people already how he'd been drummed out of vet school just months shy of graduation, for cheating. For cheating! Something that never would have occurred to him.

"I do," she said through gritted teeth.

He put a booted foot on the dash and glared out the window. "Well, I'm interested to hear what you have to say about it." The old, helpless sense of anger nearly overwhelmed him. The injustice of it had almost killed him at the time, and now this woman was going to tell him all about how *she'd* managed to get through vet school without stealing any test results.

"I think you don't trust me and you came with me today

to make sure I didn't kill any of your high school buddy's precious cows!''

His foot hit the floorboard with a thump. "What?"

She yanked the wheel of the truck, screamed onto the shoulder, spitting gravel twenty feet behind her, and came to a sliding halt. She shoved the stick into neutral and turned on him. "I've seen you driving by, don't think I haven't."

"You're on Main Street, McKenna. I can't come to town without passing your office."

"And Mrs. Handleman told me you'd gone out into the clinic's corral Monday to look at that mule Katie Reed brought in while I was on a call."

Handleman! What a snitch. She'd been ratting him out since he was ten. "Katie asked me to," Daniel argued stubbornly. And he'd been flattered, thrilled.

"I think you've been checking up on me since the very minute I got into this town because you don't think I can do this job. Well, you're wrong! I can, and I will. And for your information, pal—" She reached out a long finger and poked him in the chest as he turned to stare, dumbfounded, at her. "The day I need anyone's help diagnosing parturient paresis is the day I sell my vet box and start a bakery!"

He couldn't help it. He was angry and she was angry, and now wasn't the time, but a bakery? He could just picture her wearing an apron. He laughed.

She was going to punch him. He may have had the most beautiful eyes and a glorious body and he may have been tall enough to kiss her without craning her neck toward the heavens, but she was going to punch him anyway. It was a matter of principle. She balled up her fist.

"Wait, wait," he said. "Wait a minute. I'm not laughing at you."

She glared at him.

"Okay, I am, but just at the thought of you in a bakery. Do you even know how to bake?"

"You think just because I look like this I can't bake,"

she shouted at him. Hideous tears burned at the back of her throat. Silly, girlish tears. She could have screamed in frustration. "I am still a woman."

"What's that got to do with it?" he yelled back at her. "My mother can't bake worth a damn. And look like what?" He knew what she meant, couldn't let it pass no matter how much he wanted to. No matter how angry he was, or how desperately he did not want to be attracted to this woman, he couldn't let her think he meant she wasn't desirable as hell. "Tall and willowy as a wheat stalk? Beautiful? Sexy? Mouthwatering? No, I think because you're a young vet with a busy new practice you might not have had the time to learn to bake cookies."

"Well, I haven't!" she yelled.

"That's all I was saying," he bellowed.

"Look, I don't need you or anyone else looking over my shoulder, Cash. I'm a hell of a vet. Born to it, I've had people say."

People had said the same thing to him. "Fine. Fabulous. You're the best vet around, McKenna."

"Stop yelling at me!"

"You're yelling at me."

"Because you laughed about the baking thing." She turned back in her seat, folded her arms across her chest and stared out the front window. "If you're not checking up on me, Cash, then why hang around in some stinking barn with a sick cow?"

He pulled at his jaw, stalling. When he couldn't think of anything better to tell her than the truth, he said, "Because it's what I was trained to do."

She turned her head. "I beg your pardon?"

Daniel dropped his head back, and when that gave him no comfort, scrubbed his face with his hands. "Never mind."

"What do you mean, it's what you were trained to do?"

"It's none of your business."

"You're a vet?"

"No, dammit, I'm not a vet."

"You're shouting again."

"You bring it out in me."

She barked out a laugh. "I doubt it's my fault. You've acted like a jackass since the instant I met you, and except for one rather bizarre moment last week which we won't mention despite the fact that you didn't even call me afterward, when that would have been the polite thing to do, and I should give you hell for that—" she took a deep breath, struggling to keep on the matter at hand "—you've been a jackass ever since. This just tops it."

He scowled at her. She was right about the jackass part, damn her, and that just made her all the more insufferable. But call her? After that mind-slaughtering kiss? Did she think he was a masochist, too?

Okay. Good enough. He reached for the door handle and jerked open the truck door. He was over it now. Over whatever weird, obsessive sexual witchcraft she wielded that had made him kiss her in the first place, that had drawn him back to her office to see her this afternoon despite the fact that it was the last place he wanted to be. He was cleansed, free. Her witchy power was helpless against his stronger will. Ha!

"I'll walk back to town."

"Great!"

"I don't need this kind of aggravation from a woman I hardly know," he muttered.

"I imagine most women would have to get in their aggravation where they could with you," she muttered back. "They wouldn't want to have to wait until you did get to know them before they started aggravating you!"

"What?"

"You know what I mean." She always got flustered when she was nervous. And this huge man breathing fire was making her very nervous. "You're very hard to be around!"

"Fine."

"Fine!"

"See you around."

"What did you mean you were trained to hang around barns treating sick animals?"

He'd reared back in preparation for giving Grace McKenna's passenger door a slam she'd not soon forget, but he froze halfway into it. He scowled at her, a bluff as much as anything. He didn't particularly want this gorgeous woman with her snotty attitude and *his* vet practice to know what a failure he'd been.

"I'm not going to stand here on the side of the road and discuss this with you."

"Are you really going to walk back to town?"

"You betcha."

She'd been ready to soften, but he'd snapped at her. Again. She wasn't such a wimp that she'd let Daniel Cash bully her around.

She raised her patrician eyebrows. "Have a nice walk, then."

"I will."

"Do," she retorted primly.

"Thank you," he yelled back incensed.

"You're welcome!"

He did slam the door then, and was gratified when she sat there awhile longer, truck idling, as he started off down the long road to town.

When she finally roared past him, her truck tires sprayed a fine coating of sand and gravel over him, head to toe.

He glared at the retreating vehicle and shook dust out of his hair. He sucked a clod of dirt off his bottom lip.

Witch.

He was glad he was no longer under her spell.

He walked for almost an hour before he saw the truck coming toward him. Five miles, he figured he'd walked in his cowboy boots on this damn country road. If he ever saw

Grace McKenna again, and he fervently hoped he wouldn't, he was going to give her a pretty big, pretty loud, piece of his mind. And then he was going to tell her he could check his own damn heifers, and the law be damned. And then he might just tell her the reason he didn't call her after he kissed her was because he kissed a lot of women. *A lot.* And that one kiss in her living room didn't mean anything to him.

That's what he'd tell her. And at least most of it was true.

The truck slowed as the driver caught sight of him. Daniel sighed as he recognized both the rig and its driver. Hell, he would rather have just kept on walking.

"Hey, Danny," his brother called as the truck stopped.

Daniel walked across the road, leaned in the open window.

"Frank."

Frank looked around idly. "You're a ways from home."

"Very observant," he snapped. "I need a lift back to town."

"Hop in."

Daniel rounded the hood and got in on the passenger side. Frank flipped a U-turn on the empty road and headed back the way he'd come.

"Your rig broke down?"

"No," was the terse reply.

There was a long silence. "Just out for some exercise?"

"Shut up."

Frank scratched idly at his jaw. "I saw the new lady vet come tearing into her parking space 'bout forty-five minutes ago while I was having lunch at the café. She looked mad. And sorta scary. I'd hate for her to be mad at me."

Daniel stared out his window.

"That have anything to do with you walking this road in the middle of the afternoon?"

"Frank, I'm warning you—"

"Okay, okay. I wanted to talk to you, anyway, Danny. That's why I came into town."

Daniel sighed again, knowing what was coming. "What do you want, Frank?"

"You know what I want. I want out."

"I know."

"But you're not going to do it."

"No."

Another silence.

"I've been thinking about it," Frank said.

"If you spent half as much time thinking about getting on with your life as you do thinking about how to sell this ranch, you'd be better off."

"Thanks for the advice, Danny. You can shove it."

Daniel eyed his little brother. "Nice talk."

"Better yet, take a little of that advice yourself. I was with you when it all came down up at W.A.S.U., Danny, and I was right there when you put Julie on that plane back to her parents. You haven't been the same since. Maybe you should get on with your own life."

Daniel pulled his bottom lip through his teeth, a habit when he was mad. "What do you want, Frank?" he asked, though he already knew.

"Borrow on your shares of Cash Cattle. Buy me out."

"We've gone over this a million times. I owe more on the property in town than I own. I'm stretched. The bank will never loan me enough to buy your shares in the corporation. I don't want them, anyway."

"You'd be majority shareholder."

"So what? I could boss Mom and Dad around then?"

"What about Lisa?"

"What about her?"

"She could buy my shares."

Daniel stared at his brother. "She doesn't have that kind of money."

Frank thrust out his chin. "I think she does."

Daniel's cousin Lisa worked for them, putting up hay in the summer, helping with calving in the spring, feeding the cattle during the long winter. Daniel knew exactly what she made.

Daniel shook his head. "It doesn't matter if she has it or not. You're not selling." He looked at his brother. "What about all we've talked about? What about keeping the ranch between the two of us, for our children? It was what Grandad wanted, what Mom and Dad want. How many ways do you want to parcel it out? You want the rest of the cousins in? How about the neighbors?"

"Children?" Frank's handsome, weathered face drained of color. He'd taken hold of that single word like a man on a lifeline. "Our children?"

"Oh, hell, Frank. I'm sorry."

"We're not going to have children, Danny. I'm sure as hell not going to, and you're not moving in that direction as far as I can tell, either. You've had—what?— a dozen dates since Julie left you. Two dozen? How many of those women you considered having kids with? What children are we going to give this place to?"

Daniel turned his head, watched the farmland and dairies go by. Frank was right. He wouldn't have children, would never marry again, would never fall in love. The first go-around had taught him more about loss and betrayal than he'd ever wanted to know. A second such lesson would probably kill him.

And Frank was less likely to have children than even he was. Frank's wife, the silly, laughing Sara he'd married two weeks after they'd graduated from high school, had died three years ago on an icy highway between Nobel and Boise. Daniel thought Frank could have gotten over that, eventually. Could have outgrown his grief, go on to be the man he was meant to be.

But the accident had taken a baby, as well. Frank and Sara's firstborn. Frank was only twenty-five years old. And already three years gone to his grave.

"Do you really love the place so much?" Frank asked finally. "Is it really that important to you?"

"It's important to me." Daniel moved his shoulders restlessly. He hated putting emotions into words. It was a sorry, unmanly habit to get into. "As much as anything, though, it's the folks. They poured their lives into Cash Cattle so they could give it over to us."

Frank eyed him. "You liar," he said flatly, and snorted when Daniel's fists clenched. "That isn't why you won't sell out, Danny. You think because of the thing at W.A.S.U., you have to hold on to the ranch with both hands. You don't want to fail again, and you don't care who gets in the way in the meantime. This isn't about the folks and their 'dream' for us. And even if it were, I don't want that dream. And until you got booted out of vet school, you didn't want it, either."

"You know I was always going to keep a hand in."

"While I was stuck running the place on my own."

"You wanted it, Frank. Remember? And you had Lisa there. She loves the ranch as much as we do. Did." Daniel shook his head. "Why the hell are we discussing this now? It didn't work out that way, it worked out this way. We both have to live with it."

"That's what I'm saying. We don't. We could sell the outfit, lock, stock and barrel. Get a fresh start somewhere else."

"And how would Mom and Dad live? We don't have enough equity in the land to give them a big chunk of money all at once, and the capital gains taxes would take what we did make off it. Would we just leave here and let them fend for themselves after everything they've sacrificed for us?"

Frank slumped over the wheel of the truck, studying the road ahead of him. "We could work around that."

"No, we couldn't." After a long silence Daniel said, "I need you there, Frank. I need you, and I'm not about to pay you to leave." He ran his hands down his face, pulled re-

flexively at his bottom lip. "Look, I know you're frustrated.
I know you're overworked. Maybe we can see our way clear
to hire on a summer rider. That'd leave me free to help you
and Lisa with the farming."

"She's getting a job in town."

"Lisa? Where?"

"With the new vet. Heard about it down at the Rowdy
Cowboy, I guess. She doesn't know much about vetting, but
she took those secretary courses in high school, and those
computer classes a couple years back."

"Huh. I didn't know she wanted a job in town."

"Guess she does."

"We're about to start farming."

Frank shrugged. "We'll have to hire someone else."

"Is she moving to town?"

"No. She said she'll stay out in her house. Cost her too
much to rent in town."

"Huh," he said again, though the longer he considered,
the more sense it made. Lisa had been complaining, albeit
gently, subtly, for months about Frank's erratic behavior. It
was no wonder she wanted out. "I guess I'll have to hire a
rider, after all. You'll need help with the farming until we
find someone."

"Whatever."

"Frank—"

Frank turned pleading eyes to his brother. "I can't take
much more, Danny. I swear to God."

"You'll be okay, Frank. You're just feeling blue right
now."

"I'm not just feeling blue. It's more than that."

"I can see that it is." He could, quite clearly. "Have you
thought about seeing someone about it?"

"You were an animal doctor, Danny, not a human doctor."

"I wasn't either. But it's been three years, Frankie. You need some help."

"Yep." His brother pulled up to the curb, behind Daniel's pickup. "And I keep hoping you'll give me some."

Chapter 4

Daniel watched his brother drive away until he could no longer see the truck. He was opening the door to his own pickup when Dr. Grace McKenna herself stepped out onto the sidewalk.

Instantly his eyes narrowed and he ruthlessly pushed his brother from his mind. He had a bone to pick with this lady vet, and now was as good a time as any.

"Hey, McKenna!"

Her head jerked around at the sound of his voice. Oh, she should have known. She'd just been about to go back out after him, and here he was. Probably used those hunky long legs of his to run all the way back to town, she thought resentfully. She'd wasted an entire hour feeling guilty about leaving him stranded.

She walked slowly over to where he stood, hip-cocked and fuming.

"You made good time."

He wasn't about tell her he got a ride. Let her suffer. "I'm fast."

"That wasn't a very good display of common sense, walking back."

"You never miss a chance at a shot, do you, McKenna?"

"I'm just saying—"

"I know what you're saying." She'd cleaned up since she got back, was in her office clothes. Damn if those prim pleated pants and the sensible blouse didn't distract him. In her coveralls, he could think of her as just another vet, and his nemesis. In this getup she looked like a woman. She smelled like a woman. She certainly made every instinct and cell and nerve ending in his body sit up and take notice of her as a woman. Now, what had he been planning to say? Oh, to hell with it. "Have dinner with me tonight."

She blinked those big brown eyes at him. "Are you kidding me?"

"No, I'm not kidding you," he said, exasperated. "Why the hell is it every time I ask you to dinner you act as if I've just asked you to saw off my arm or something?"

"That wasn't asking me to dinner. That was telling me to have dinner with you. Besides, you don't even like me." It came out a little less snippy, a little less confident than she wanted it to.

Daniel caught the edge of hurt in her voice. Wondered at it.

He frowned. "I still have to eat. And so do you."

"Not together."

His lips thinned. "Okay, Doc. I'm not going to beg you." He turned on his boot heel and went back to his truck. And just as quickly turned back. He went toe-to-toe, face-to-face. "Listen, why do you have to make this so hard? You look nice in that outfit. I thought maybe we could talk. I don't dislike talking to you, except when you get all huffy. And dinner at the café with me is not going to kill you."

"'Huffy,'" she said, cocking her head to peer up at him. "'Huffy.'" She stood her ground, though he was close enough that their breaths mingled. When she couldn't quite manage to hold his green gaze a moment longer, she looked up at the hazy spring sky. "And he asks me why I'm making it so hard."

Grace shook her head, conscious of the fact they were standing on the sidewalk, and every client she could hope to have could come by at any minute and see the county vet in a knock-down, drag-out with one of the biggest cattlemen in the state. She lowered her voice, leaned in. "Let's do a rundown, shall we?"

He couldn't help it. He loved how her voice went from little-girl vulnerable to snotty in less than a moment. Yeah, she was huffy, and it made her darn near irresistible. He inched closer. Her breath tasted like coffee. And he could smell her hair.

"Run it down, Doc."

"You come into my office the first day I'm in town and practically write down your grievances. I'm too young. I'm inexperienced. I'm a woman."

"I never said anything about you being a woman."

She ignored his interruption. "Then, in the middle of the night you bring me a cat that is clearly not in need of my attention, wasting my time. You don't even know the cat's name. It may not even be your cat!"

"It was not the middle of the night. And his name is…Boots!"

"Tiger. Then you take me home and act very gentlemanly and kiss me brainless."

"Brainless?" He had more than enough healthy male ego for that to make him grin.

Grace ignored the grin, too. "Then I don't see or hear from you for a week."

That reminded him. "Look, Doc, I kiss a *lot*—"

She interrupted him this time. "Then you show up today and I think, Okay, he doesn't seem that weird. He's totally humorless, but maybe I imagined all that surliness and bad temper. Maybe he's just a nice man and he can come on my first dairy call with me because he seems to want to and we can talk and maybe he'll kiss me again.''

His green eyes flashed at that, and too late Grace realized she'd said more—much more—than she should have. Typical. Her temper was usually very even, but when she lost it, she lost it big.

''Then this thing at the dairy,'' she rushed on, ''and you jump out of the truck and walk ten miles back to town? What is wrong with you?''

''You want me to kiss you again?''

''No!'' she shouted at him, forgetting the sidewalk and her potential clients.

He smiled. ''All you have to do is ask,'' he said mildly.

''Oh, forget it,'' she said, swinging away.

She would have sworn later that he barely touched her. But suddenly she was backed up against the side of his dusty pickup and caged between his tree-trunk arms.

''Everything you say is true, Doc,'' he murmured. He brushed against her, took another whiff of that baby-soft hair. ''I'm a bastard.''

''You are.'' Her nerve endings were zinging, and her breath was coming short. He needed to stop nuzzling her hair if she was going to be able to think coherently. ''Get off me. We're on the street.''

''In a minute,'' he said, indulging himself. She was right; he didn't much like her—a fact he had to remind himself of on a near-daily basis—but he could overlook that in the face of this raging attraction. ''How do you work with animals all day and still smell this good?''

''That's not— What does that—? Daniel, *stop!*''

Vulnerable again, Daniel thought, and just stopped himself from biting her earlobe. Anyway, his hands were slippery on the hood of his truck, and if he didn't stop now, he'd end up making a town spectacle of them both.

''You want to know what I meant today?''

She was trembling. ''About what?'' she asked, dazed.

"About being trained to stand in stinking barns with sick cattle?"

She barely knew what he was talking about. "Um. Okay."

"Then meet me at the Early Bird and we'll have dinner."

"I don't think that's—"

"God, you're a mule. You can pay for your own meal if it'll make you feel better."

She took a deep, calming breath. It didn't help. She could smell him, and he smelled amazing. Like a big, tough man. "It probably would."

"Fine. When you get done in there—" he nodded toward the clinic; the clinic he was slowly, reluctantly beginning to think of as *hers* "—come on over."

"All right," she agreed, suspicious and hesitant.

"And, Doc?" he whispered, leaning back in.

"Yes?"

He kissed her. Right in front of God and everyone who happened by on Main Street, Nobel, Idaho. Kissed her hard and slow and thoroughly. His mouth made a small sucking sound when he pulled away. She could only stare at him.

"I may be humorless, but I can follow orders pretty well." He grinned in her stunned, wide-eyed face and pushed away. "You just have to make your needs clear."

"It's not— My needs are— That was a despicable—"

"You stutter when you're turned on, Doc," he said, low, into her ear. "Against my better judgment, I have to wonder what else you do."

"What else— What else—" She clamped her mouth shut before she proved him right. She fisted her hands before they grabbed the lapels of his sheepskin cowboy coat and yanked him back against her.

"See ya, Doc."

He walked away—swaggered away, Grace thought dazedly—and left her backed up against his truck unable to string two thoughts together.

* * *

He met her outside the Early Bird, had the distinct plea-sure of watching her cross the street on those gams.

"Hey."

"Hey." She felt bashful, and wasn't surprised. It wasn't that she was unaccustomed to being with men; in her busi-ness she spent most of her time with men. Dairies and ranches were primarily run or owned by men, and her fellow vets were mostly men. And she had brothers; three irritating, smelly, pompous and pushy brothers she adored.

But this man was different from any of those. Certainly.

"Have you been waiting over here all afternoon?"

"No, I had some other business in town." He'd walked around for a couple hours, ostensibly doing business, but actually trying to walk off a little of the heat that had ex-ploded into his system when he'd kissed her. He'd meant it as a sort of lesson, a salve to his ego after the fight—that she'd won—out at the dairy, but he'd ended up learning more than he wanted to. Less than an hour ago he'd stood right at this spot, tempted to go to her office and drag her out. He'd decided against it. Urges as strong as the ones Grace McKenna gave him were probably best resisted, for the time being.

They sat in a back booth. Daniel was grateful the place was Monday-night empty. Everyone in Nobel was well ac-quainted with his miserable tale of woe. It had been dis-cussed and dissected and gossiped about until, like most sto-ries started in small towns, the truth was almost completely obscured by rumor and innuendo. But he'd been back for years; other more scandalous legends had boiled up and over and his disgrace had cooled. He would have hated to stir the pot again.

The waitress came and Grace ordered a salad and an iced tea. She wasn't exactly sure what a person was supposed to order on an occasion such as this, but she was sure it wasn't what one normally ate. Daniel smiled into his menu, then ordered two long-neck beers and enough food to feed three people.

"You hired my cousin, I hear," Daniel said in the way of small talk after the waitress left. He was in no hurry to spill his guts.

Grace nodded. "I assumed from her last name she was related to you. Her résumé said she worked for your outfit."

"Lisa had a résumé?"

Grace smiled. "It was short. Yours was the only name on it. She's worked for you since high school."

"Yeah. She's a pretty hard worker. Once a month, though, you have to give her a couple of days off if you don't want your head ripped off for the slightest little thing."

"Chauvinist."

"Wait and see."

Grace smiled in spite of herself. "Okay, I'll keep it in mind. Why does she want to work in town all of a sudden? You cut her pay?"

"No. I don't know why exactly," he hedged. "I haven't talked to her. She wasn't supposed to start farming until the middle of next month, and I haven't seen much of her. I think she'll work out well for you, though."

"Will you have to hire someone else?"

"Yeah. Maybe a couple more people, if I can afford it. My brother—" He trailed off.

"Your brother?" Grace prompted. He had that look again, that furrowed-brow look that made her think his relationship with his brother was not a smooth one.

"Nothing. It's nothing," he said again, making Grace sure it was something. "Here comes our food."

He watched the waitress slap the plates onto the table, then, without a word, he slid half of what he'd ordered onto one plate and shoved it over to her, along with one of the beers.

"You'll starve to death on that rabbit food."

"I like salad." But her mouth watered at the smell of the

fried chicken he'd just pushed her way. She took a pull off the beer, straight from the bottle. When she put the bottle down and saw Daniel grinning at her, she frowned. Should have poured it into the glass, she thought belatedly.

"I like to see a woman eat something when I take her out."

"You're not taking me out. It's Dutch treat, remember?"

"Fine. Then you can pay for that beer."

"Fine." She forked up a dainty bite of salad, though her stomach growled over the chicken. "You said you were going to explain to me why you were interfering with my diagnosis out at Spandell's."

"I wouldn't call it interfering," he muttered. He took a drink from his own beer; from the bottle, which made Grace feel slightly better. "I was in vet school for a while."

She nodded. "I figured that out after I calmed down. You certainly seemed to know what you were doing out there."

His heart expanded a little at the compliment. He had known, had always known. It was an instinct.

"I worked for Niebaur before I went to college, then during the summers. I learned a lot, even before I went to W.A.S.U."

"Why did you drop out? You'd have made a good vet."

"I didn't drop out. I was expelled."

She put her fork down, stared at him. So many vet students dropped out of school. It was extremely difficult, exhausting, and mentally and physically taxing as any medical school; only you didn't have to learn just the ailments that could attack a single species, as M.D.s did, but a whole range of species, from fish to horses to goats, and everything in between. But she only knew of a couple people who had been expelled. And that was for—

"Cheating," she breathed, hardly able to believe it.

His teeth clamped down at her automatic assumption. He wouldn't defend himself. He'd tired of that back at school.

He'd just tell her the facts and let the chips fall where they would.

"I was accused of cheating on the infectious diseases exam, final year. I was expelled."

She blinked. "How horrible."

"It was pretty bad," he agreed. He could remember exactly where he'd been when he found he was being suspended. Standing in the dean's office, sick, dumbfounded and furious, his hands in fists and his heart in his throat.

"Did you have a hearing?"

Daniel grimaced. "Yeah. The dean gave me the choice. Go quietly and he'd hush it up for me, promising doctor and all-around nice guy that I was, or I could demand a hearing and have it aired in front of the whole faculty. I chose to have a hearing, of course. I thought certainly the truth would come out."

"And did it?"

He met her beautiful brown eyes, irrationally annoyed that she didn't believe, instantly, that he hadn't done it.

He shrugged, though it cost him to do so. "They found the exam answers in my apartment, they found notes I had allegedly taken from the professor's files, a whole stack of evidence against me. It took the hearing board about two minutes to boot my butt out of there."

"Why didn't you enroll somewhere else? You only had a few months to go."

"I applied at U.C. Davis, University of Kansas, a couple other places, but, Doc, think. How easy is it for anyone to get into vet school, much less someone who's been tossed out of a place like Washington State University for cheating on an infectious diseases exam?" Infectious diseases. It still galled him. He knew that stuff by heart, backward and forward. Most of it he'd learned before he ever left high school, right at Dr. Niebaur's side.

Grace nodded, sympathetic. She'd begun applying to vet schools her sophomore year in college, as soon as she'd declared her major in veterinary pre-med. There were just a couple vet schools in the west, and they were packed, with interminable waiting lists. Because of the overcrowding, only the best students, with the most spotless academic reputations, got in.

"How did you live with it?"

"I didn't, very well, for a while." He smiled, a half-hearted thing that mostly just twisted his lips. "I got divorced, just about first thing. Then started getting drunk pretty regular, drove my family crazy. Classic textbook reaction. Eventually I got tired of that and started back working at the ranch. It got easier to deal with. My brother was in trouble here, and it wasn't fair to leave him alone, with all the responsibilities. I decided maybe it was for the best, that the ranch and my family needed me there as much as this county needed another vet."

She was suddenly having a tough time with a wedge of lettuce that refused to move past her esophagus. "Divorced?"

"I was married. My wife left me a couple days after I was expelled."

"Why?"

He made a sound in the back of his throat. "I don't imagine she wanted to be married to someone who cheated on an infectious diseases exam," he said nonchalantly, and had to take another pull off his beer to wash down the bitter taste in his mouth. "We were only married seven months. After I left school, she decided since I wasn't going to be a veterinarian, and there was no way in hell she was going to live on the ranch, it would be better if we cut our losses."

He sounded very matter-of-fact, Grace thought. But she wondered at the vein that had started to throb at the base of his neck.

"Why was your being a vet so important to her?"

"Because she was a vet. She'd graduated the year before, was already working in a practice in Pullman. We were go-

ing to come back here eventually, take over Niebaur's practice. She'd cover the small animal aspect of the practice, I'd
cover the large animal. When I got kicked out, those plans
had to be scrapped. The marriage was scrapped along with
them.'' He took a bit of chicken. It tasted like chalk in his
mouth. ''Julie was a good vet. She said she didn't want her
reputation to be tainted by mine.'' He shrugged, and Grace
could see how it cost him. ''Can't blame her.''

But you do, Grace thought. And somehow, that censure
extends to me.

''Why didn't you work as an assistant to Dr. Niebaur?
You obviously still love working with the animals.''

''I don't know. Pride, as much as anything, I guess.'' He
smiled again, easier this time, and cut another slice of his
fried chicken. He'd rather have picked it up and gnawed it
off the bone, but he was on his best behavior. ''I'd been his
pup-dog, following him around, for eleven years. I couldn't
go back to it.''

''I can understand that.''

He chewed slowly, watching her pull the plate of food
he'd passed her onto her paper place mat. She picked up a
piece of chicken with her fingers and bit into it. She licked
the juice from her lips, hummed pleasure without knowing
it. Daniel wanted to hum a little himself, just watching her

''So.'' She had to know, but she asked casually, around
the chicken, just as though the answer wouldn't matter to
her. ''Did you do it?''

He gave her a long, steady look, ashamed of her for asking, ashamed of himself for wanting so badly for her to
believe in him.

''What do you think?''

She chewed for a long time, wanting to get the chicken
into tiny pieces so she wouldn't choke on it. ''I think no.
don't know how much I like you, Daniel Cash,'' Grace said
finally, quietly. ''But I doubt you'd cheat on anything.''

Daniel's jaw worked back and forth for a minute and he

ran his tongue over his teeth. He considered her awhile, making her pulse jump curiously. "I think you like me," he said in that same low, persuasive voice he'd used on her when he'd had her backed up, achy and needy, against his pickup. "I think you like me in exactly the same way I like you. Someday we may have to do something about that."

Grace stared across the table at him. She opened her mouth, but nothing came out. Satisfied, Daniel went back to his meal.

Grace cleared her throat, cleared it again. She had to say something or she was going to dissolve with mortification, and just maybe desire.

"I feel the same way about this practice," she said after a minute. "What you said about Niebaur," she added quickly when he raised his brows at her. "It's pride as much as anything. I've worked in some good, solid practices since I finished vet school, where the other vets were well respected and had an extensive client base."

"But there's something about having your own place."

She smiled. "True. I saw Dr. Niebaur's ad for the practice in the back of a vet magazine. The large animal side of it, the small town, walking into a well-established practice, I couldn't resist it. I want to be my own boss. I don't want to be anyone's junior partner anymore."

The waitress came over to check on them.

"Do you want dessert?" Daniel asked Grace.

She looked down at her plate. Just bones left. Aah! How had that happened?

"No, thank you."

He smiled at the waitress, then turned his attention back to Grace. "You should come out to the ranch," he said casually. "I'd like you to see it."

"I'm scheduled to check your heifers next week."

"I meant now." Inviting her had been an impulse, but the more he thought about it, the better the idea sounded. He wanted her to see the success he'd made of himself after the mess he'd made of vet school. He wanted her respect, if nothing else. Having another female vet looking down her nose at him for his failures was something he didn't think he could stand. "Tonight."

"Tonight?"

"It's early yet. won't be full dark for at least an hour, then we've got a full moon."

"I can't. I'm on call."

"It's not that far out, Doc. Your pager will work. Come on." He stood and tossed some bills onto the table. He held out his hand. "Finished?"

She glanced again, dismayed, at her plate. It seemed she was. She looked up at him, at his outstretched hand and the invitation she understood it implied. And thought, What the heck? I've just eaten half his dinner. How much more embarrassing could the evening get?

They drove in separate pickups at her insistence. She wasn't being coy—she would have sworn she didn't know how to be—but sensible. She was on call, she'd told him again, nervous in spite of herself. And he was miles out, no need for him to go all the way back into town. Too, she needed her vet box. And she should get to know the roads, anyway, in case she needed to come this way again. And it was late.

She'd had a couple other arguments ready, but he'd finally given in and gotten into his truck, shaking his head.

He drove out to the ranch, past the folks' house, saw their lights blazing and the flicker of the television set from behind the drapes. It would have been the polite thing to do to drop by and introduce the new vet, but he didn't feel particularly polite tonight. Maybe confessions brought it out in him, but he felt restless, hungry. For what, he had a pretty good idea. He turned into his driveway. He left the engine running while he jumped out and strode back to her truck.

"Come on," he said, pulling her door open. She barely

had time to turn the key before he took her hand and practically yanked her from her seat, but plenty of time to realize what a stupid move it had been to come out here, in the dark, with this bruiser of a man and his pushy manner.

"You know what—?" she began, pulling back like a reluctant filly.

"Yeah, I do. You want to go home." He turned to her, looked into her moonlit eyes. They shone up at him, strong, determined, and a little afraid, and he had a fleeting, amazing sensation that he could see into them, into her. "Don't be a wuss, McKenna. I want to show you my ranch and I can't do that if you're driving in a different vehicle. Just come with me." He tugged and stepped backward when she would have fallen into him. He lifted his chin, daring her. "Come on, Grace."

She couldn't resist him when he called her Grace, and wouldn't have backed away from the challenge in his eyes in any case. She followed him to his idling pickup, holding his hand, which really did feel just perfect cupped protectively over hers. He opened her door, then jogged around and hopped in. He was practically giddy now, she thought. Comparatively, anyway. Now that she was his captive.

Oh, Grace, settle down. You are a wuss, she told herself. The whole way out to his ranch she'd vacillated between a nauseating sort of excitement about being with him, alone, in the hush and coming darkness of an Idaho spring evening, and a head-banging regret. What was she thinking, become involved with any man at this point in her life? She had a practice to establish, priorities to set.

But more than that, she had her heart to consider. It had been safely, steadily beating in her chest for twenty-seven years now, while she went about the business of making her dreams come true. Now wasn't the time to test its vulnerability, to hare off into the night with a man to try to prove, for the first time, that she could do what other women seemed to do so easily. Attract a man, capture his heart.

Frankly, the thought of doing that scared the hell out of her. The thought of not being able to do that scared her even more.

She pulled her bottom lip between her teeth and clamped down. Wuss? That was hardly the word. She'd made excuses for years about why she couldn't—wouldn't—be with a man. It had been easy to do—had even been, in the view of many people in her life, the responsible, if vaguely dissatisfying, path to take. After all, she was a vet now, a good one, with the kind of practice she'd always wanted. See how her focus had paid off?

She wondered when she'd come to see it all for the lie it was.

Daniel turned to her, smiling slightly as he described his wheat and hay rotation, and she knew the answer to that question. Just about the minute she'd met Daniel Cash.

She hadn't been responsible, she'd been afraid. If she never fell in love…if she never allowed herself to feel the heart-pounding, eye-popping, finger-tingling excitement she felt being with Daniel, then she could never get hurt. Then no one would ever say to her, "How can I love you? Just look at you."

It was what she feared most in the world. Just look at me, she thought. The circus freak, with a man like Daniel Cash. She may be a diversion for him, she thought morosely, but if she wasn't careful, he could become vital for her. She'd felt it that first afternoon in her office. Vital.

And then one day he'd look her up and down and realize that nothing in the world could make her into the small, delicate female a man could love forever. His diversion would be over, and her safe, steady heart would be broken.

They drove all over the ranch, across fields that looked ready for a hot summer and a chance to produce. They stopped in big pastures, and Grace got a shadowy impression of fat heifers and lazy cows and spooky, jumpy little spring calves. Daniel told her about his grazing schedule on the federal lands that surrounded his ranch, surrounded the town of Nobel. She listened to him, listened more to the timber and tone of his deep voice, and reminded herself to be careful.

When they came to a gate, she hopped out of the truck and opened it. He tried to beat her to it the first couple gates, but gave in when she glared at him.

"I know the rules, Cash," she said. "Shotgun always opens the gates." She cocked her head, trying to lighten her somber mood. "Is that the real reason we took your pickup out here?"

"You bet." He wasn't sorry they had, actually. After the initial, intense discomfort of sitting in the truck while she worked a gate wore off, he had to admit it was a sight worth seeing. Her butt in those long, slim trousers in his headlights. A man could die happy from a sight like that.

The ranch was huge; it took them hours to get across it and back. By the time they returned to his house it was dark out, with a milk-white moon coming across the desert that stretched east to Twin Falls.

They talked until they were hoarse. About clinical protozoology and grass tetany, about college and the professors they'd shared, about the diagnosis of equine influenza and how the moon shone off the reservoir that watered his fields. Daniel felt an ease with her he hadn't felt with a woman since Julie, and chalked it up to their common body of knowledge. He'd not spoken of his love of veterinary medicine in three long years. It was a relief, palpable and chest-loosening, to do so with her.

He remembered how he and Julie would stay up late, poring over their Merck manuals, testing each other. He'd loved doing that, had never experienced quite the same pleasure doing anything else, before or since. He'd fallen in love with her during those late-night sessions, amazed at her brain, connected to her through a mutual passion.

He brought himself up short. There was a treacherous

memory. Grace and Julie shared the same profession, but nothing more than that. He wouldn't fall in love with Grace McKenna. Even if he didn't take exception to the role she was playing in his life, in his hometown, he wouldn't fall in love with her. He wouldn't fall in love with anyone, not ever again. Love was a sort of madness he couldn't afford anymore. It had left him open to all manner of failure.

He set his jaw, annoyed with himself, and looked over at Grace.

"You look tired."

"I am." She smothered a yawn. "I've enjoyed the tour, though. It's a beautiful place." She smiled sleepily. "What I could see of it. You should be proud."

"I am. My grandfather and my parents put their lives into Cash Cattle. I'm glad Frank and I have been able to keep it going for them."

"It's a tough business. Not many make it."

"We will."

That confidence again, and that flash of intensity, of almost-desperate resolve. She knew instinctively where it had come from, and wondered if he'd ever get over what had happened to him up at W.A.S.U. She doubted it. She never would have. She sighed, fingered the handle on her door. All the more reason to stay away from this man.

"I should get going."

He got out to open her door, but she was already standing beside the truck by the time he made it around the hood. "You'll be out next week, then," he said.

"Yes." She resisted twisting her hands together. How did women ever do this? This hadn't even been a date—more like a business meeting—and still the ending was uncomfortably awkward.

"We could go into Twin Falls after. Get something to eat."

She stared at him. "I don't think so."

He ran his hand over his hair. "God, you drive me nuts."

"I know I do. You have essentially the same effect on me."

"You know, you can go superior and snotty faster than any woman I've ever known."

She raised her chin, straightened her spine. Years of being called far worse names than "snotty and superior" had given her a phalanx of defense mechanisms. "It's a gift," she said coolly.

He regarded her in the dim moonlight. "And yet, when I kiss you, you go all soft and breathy. Wonder why that is?"

"Hormonal aberration."

He had to laugh. "You kill me."

She didn't much like being laughed at. It was a leftover from always being the object of laughter while she was growing up, and up. Her fists balled at her sides. "I'm leaving."

He cocked a single dark brow. It made him look like a pirate, Grace thought.

"Who's stopping you?"

"Not you," she said. "No one can stop me when I want to go."

"I'm sure they can't. You're a big girl. Go ahead."

Big girl? She glared at him. "You're holding on to my arm," she said stiffly.

He was, and hadn't even known it. His thumb was stroking against the sleeve of her coat even now. He wanted, badly, to know what the skin felt like beneath. He dropped his hand.

"Good night, Doc."

Big girl. She couldn't believe he'd called her a big girl. She could have smacked him for that. She grabbed the collar of his coat with one hand instead.

"Good night," she snapped, and yanked him forward. She'd show him "big girl."

He met her, mouth open, his arms clamping around her in an instant.

Yes! Was all Daniel could think. He'd been wanting to get his hands on her since the first night he'd kissed her in that tiny, dark living room. The kiss on the sidewalk had only made him hungrier, more obsessed. It had taken all the discipline he'd been born with and every ounce he'd gained since then to keep from doing something unforgivably rash on that public sidewalk. But now he was loosed from those particular hobbles. He held her closer.

Every promise the woman made with that amazing long body, she kept in one fiery kiss. He sealed his mouth to hers and plundered. His tongue swept through and he dragged out the moan she tried to bite back. He unclenched his arms, streaked under her coat, tugged her blouse from her waistband. Skin. He needed to touch skin. He'd kissed her twice now and had never touched her skin.

He swore against her mouth, a dark and dangerous oath, and felt her shiver at the sound of it. Her skin was as smooth and cool as her walk. He rested his thumbs in her navel, torturing himself. She wasn't what he wanted in his life, but he was certain he had to have her.

"Grace, come inside and lie down with me."

That thick voice…that heavy, quick, desperate command cut through the haze of lust. Some of her lifelong good sense surfaced, dammit. "I can't."

"You can." His thumbs came up from their little nest in her belly button, brushed the undersides of her breasts, making his point for him.

She couldn't have stopped the gasp that escaped her if she'd had her mouth sewn shut. "I hardly know you."

"You know me."

"I don't even like you."

He grinned wickedly. "Yeah, you do."

"You don't like me."

"Yeah," he admitted slowly. "I do." His smile softened. Her nipples were like eraser tips. He ran his thumbs across them again. "A little."

He was doing something shocking now, something she definitely shouldn't allow. She'd kissed men before and had never let them— Oh, that was lovely. He really had better not stop doing that. She'd have to kill him if he stopped doing that.

He kissed her again, more urgently. His tongue came in again, invited hers to meet his. Their mouths opened wide together and he slid one hand around to the soft skin at the small of her back. He urged her closer, loving how their long bodies met, center to center.

"Let's go inside," he whispered when he could breathe again. He pulled away slightly and looked into her face. Her eyes were closed, and she was frowning.

"No." She was impatient with him, pulled his hair until he came back to kiss her.

Fine, she wouldn't go inside. He could work around that. He was a resourceful kind of guy. He simply fused her mouth to his and picked her up in his arms.

She squealed against his mouth, jerked her head back.

"What are you doing?" she huffed at him, mortified.

"Getting more comfortable," he said. He carried her around the pickup as if she weighed nothing and came down on his knees with her on to the spring-greening lawn in front of his house. She wiggled out of his arms, but before she could escape he landed on her, pinning her with his legs. If he happened to bump a very delicate, very aroused part of his anatomy against her hip on the way down, that was purely accidental. If he happened to leave it there, pressed against her, even grinding a little bit, well, he couldn't be held accountable for that. He was so turned on he was surprised the top of his head didn't blow off.

"You picked me up," she said, sounding amazed. He ignored her, focused instead on how he could get her to unzip her parka, unbutton her blouse. Hell, he'd just do it himself.

She batted at his hands. "Daniel."

"Hmm?" He had the parka unzipped, one button undone. Maybe the rest would just pop off if he pulled hard enough. He gave an experimental yank.

"I've never been picked up before."

He tried to pay attention, knew that was the correct and considerate thing to do, especially since he could dimly hear the wonder in her voice over the roaring in his ears, but he frankly didn't want to. He wanted inside. Inside her shirt, inside her pants, inside her skin.

"Shut up, Doc, and let me touch you." He had to or he was going to die. He was reasonably sure of that.

He shifted onto his back and pulled her on top of him. He could feel the damp grass beneath him, could see the white moon behind her head. Could feel the weight of her pressed into every cell of his body. She kept her hands on either side of his face, rasped at his beard stubble with her thumbs as they kissed. He stroked her back, petted her bottom, kneaded it, pressing her into him so there'd be no mistaking his response to her.

She had no doubt. She could feel him, practically pulsing beneath her. She moved instinctively against him, back and forth, up and down.

It drove him mad. He laid flat palms at the small of her back, pushed them into the waistband of her slacks. "Take your pants off, Grace."

"Out here?"

He managed to laugh at her incredulous tone. "Or inside, if I can make it inside. No, wait, out here. Now. Quickly, Grace."

An hour before, a lifetime before, she would have placed the odds of her obeying such an order at about a million to one. She rolled over and wriggled out of her pants in three seconds flat.

Oh, Daniel thought, light-headed. Those legs. The woman had legs up to her armpits. She came back down on top of him and while they kissed he ran his hands the length of

her long thighs, again and again, from the backs of her knees
up to the perfect curve of her bottom. He could feel firm
muscle and soft skin and thought he might explode in his
jeans for the first time since Darla Lee Gilbert let him touch
her breasts in the ninth grade.

She was wriggling again. She knew it was probably un-
ladylike and not what one was supposed to do in these sit-
uations. She'd ordered the salad at dinner but now she was
ruining the whole image of relaxed, casual femininity by
writhing on top of him like a maniac.

But she was magnificently aroused and her body would
not be still. His hands, oh, what were they doing back there?
Oh, yes, a little higher now, Daniel, she thought frantically,
opening her legs. A little—oh! He smoothed back down her
thighs again. If he didn't touch her soon, she was going to—
Ah, there. There, Daniel, there.

She was wet. He could feel it through the cotton of her
prim white panties. He slipped his fingers beneath the elastic, brushed against damp curls, and lost his mind. So wet.
His fingers were slippery with her and he used that moisture
to open her, slide in, feel everything.

He'd meant to take this a little slower. Kiss her for an
hour or two, open her blouse, play with her, pull a nipple
into his mouth and roll it gently between his teeth until she
clutched at him. Oh, yeah, he would have loved to do that.
But this was as good; better, astonishing. He'd do the other
stuff later.

She stopped writhing, lay perfectly still against him. They
stopped kissing, stopped moving, stopped breathing. He
used the fingers of both hands, stroked inside her, played
with the little button she had hidden there until it was as
hard and swollen as he was.

"Grace," he said, his eyes closed in concentration.

She quivered against his hand. It hit her hard, knocked

the breath out of her in a loud, long moan. Daniel wondered absently as he felt the contractions around his fingers if his parents could hear her over the sound of their television set.

He couldn't have cared less.

Chapter 5

They lay perfectly still for a minute as he played with her, bringing her to a smaller peak, a smaller one still, until her body calmed and her nerve endings were soothed.

She buried her face against his neck.

"Grace?" He tried to lift her head, but she shook it, dropped it into the hollow of his neck again. He felt her kiss him there, lick up the sweat she'd left on him.

"Come on, Doc," he said hoarsely. "Look at me."

"No."

He smiled. She sounded very young, very shy. "Why not?"

"It's—" She shook her head again.

"It's what?"

"It's embarrassing."

"Yeah." He chuckled low in his throat. "I'm really embarrassed. You can probably feel how embarrassed I am. As a matter of fact—" he nipped her shoulder "—I insist. I want you to feel how embarrassed I am."

Her face still hidden against him, she reached tentatively

down between their bodies, shifting a little so she could
reach him. She measured him, felt a sensible jolt of apprehension at his size, then cupped him in her hand. He strained
upward, torturing himself against her hand, cursing the
denim that separated them.

"I want to make love to you, Grace."

"I think you just did," she said, her voice muffled.

"Grace. Be brave. Look at me now."

She did, and he smiled to see how flushed she was, how
satisfied and muddled and aroused she looked still.

"Are we going to?"

She kept her hand on him, stroking. But her face lost that
confused look, went serious. "I don't think so."

He made a little sound at the back of his throat. Frustration. He wanted to howl with it; would have, but he knew
his parents *would* hear that, no matter how loudly they had
the television turned up. "Why the hell not?"

"Because it's not a good idea."

"Right now, right this minute, Grace, that doesn't seem
like much of an answer."

"I know." She could hardly give him the real one. What
kind of neurotic mess told a man she wouldn't make love
with him because she was still a virgin at twenty-seven?
That she was so afraid of the shock, or laughter, once any
man got a good look at her, that she'd denied herself any
kind of normal experimentation? That she was afraid of this
man in particular, because she had a feeling his shock, or
laughter, could destroy her. "It's too soon."

"Not from where I stand. Or lie. Do better."

She worried her lower lip. "We don't have any protection."

"I'm twenty steps from my nightstand, Grace."

She had to smile. He looked a little crazed.

"I don't know your sexual history."

"I'm disease free and I had a shower this afternoon." She
was quiet a moment. "That's all you've got?"

"That's all I've got."

"Well, sweetheart, you either need to come up with something better, like you have a prosthetic leg and if I jostle it too hard I'll pull it off, or stop stroking me."

She was still stroking. "Really?" She looked down into his face. "Stop?"

He swallowed hard. "No. Don't stop."

They lay together, panting like teenagers, for a minute. Grace felt goose bumps go up the back of her legs as her body temperature cooled. His hands were still there, petting her, while his body, underneath her, involuntarily pulsed and strained upward.

Oh, she was curious. Curious and aroused, and somehow certain she'd never again get a chance such as this. He certainly wasn't going to want to do this with her again. It was the moon, and the confession in the diner, and a thousand other stimulants that had nothing at all to do with her personally. Once he came to his senses, he'd go back to being impossible for her and she'd go back to being clearly *not* what any man wanted.

She was a doctor of veterinary medicine, a grown woman with a family full of earthy and talkative men and an excellent idea of how the male human body responded to stimulus. Not so differently from the male of any other species, as a matter of fact. But as for hands-on experience, so to speak, she had bupkiss. And suddenly she knew this would be her last chance to get some. She took a deep breath and scooted out from under those amazing hands of his.

She unzipped him carefully. He almost levitated from the shock of it.

"What are you doing? I thought we weren't—" His eyes rolled back in his head. "Oh, man."

"I just want a quick peek." She knelt between his legs and held him in her hands. His skin was like satin and unbelievably hot. She felt awkward and inquisitive; stunningly, affectionately so. She leaned over, gave him a delicate kiss that made him moan. She didn't want to hurt him or disgrace herself with her inexperience, but after that guttural moan, she wouldn't have stopped touching him for the world. "I've never done this before," she murmured.

He didn't understand the meaning behind that, didn't, at the moment, comprehend the innocence of it. His body was already bowed, heels and shoulder blades dug into the grass, anticipating her. "Please, Grace. Anything you do will be—"

He never finished his sentence. Couldn't speak at all, in fact, for several long, glorious minutes.

When it was finished he did what hasty reparations he could, feeling a little foolish. He hoped she wouldn't see the flush he felt high on his cheekbones, the goofy grin coming to his lips. It had been a long time, a very long time, since a woman had touched his body that way. He didn't want to take the chance of looking into her eyes, having her touch his heart, as well.

"Getting cold?" he asked roughly.

"A little."

He got up, and before she could voice a single protest, picked her right off the damp ground and carried her to his truck. He tossed her in, resisting the urge to pat her cotton-clad bottom, and went back for her slacks. He handed them to her, turned on the truck, switched up the heater full-blast. He felt a little better, a little less like a randy teenage idiot doing that, taking care of her. Until he met her eyes and caught her staring. He felt the flush creep up again.

"What?"

She shook her head, looked away. "Nothing."

He frowned. "Look, sorry about that. I couldn't help myself."

"I don't even know how you do it," she blurted.

His felt his face go even warmer. "Well, hell, I was pretty excited."

"What does that have to do with it?"

He gaped at her. "Are you joking?"

"No, really. Is it adrenal, then, or something?"

"Uh, Doc, I hate to say it, but you seem pretty surprised by the whole thing. Didn't you know that would happen?"

"Of course not. Not in my entire life has that ever happened."

"Great." He ran his hands down his face. "You probably think I'm a pervert."

"What? No. I think you're— How did you do that?"

"Well," he choked, embarrassed. "I didn't, really. You did. You've got great hands, Doc. I've always thought so."

"What are you talking about?"

He hesitated. "What are *you* talking about?"

"Picking me up like that. I'm not exactly a small girl, Daniel. You lifted me right off the ground. Twice!"

He stared at her for another minute, then burst out laughing. Laughed until his stomach hurt. Laughed until his head dropped forward and leaned on the horn, making them both jump.

She punched him in the arm. "What did you think I was talking about?" He raised his brows at her, dipped his chin. "*That?* Oh, my God!" She was laughing now, too. "You are a pervert," she said.

"I know." He shook his head, ran his hands down his face again. "I haven't done that for years. Two minutes in your hands and I went off like a rocket. No control. I don't think I've been that turned on since high school."

She scooted into her pants, took a glance in the rearview mirror and was immediately sorry she had. "I've never done it," she said impulsively, then wanted to clamp a hand over her mouth.

"You were amazingly skilled for your first time." He'd avoided watching her wriggle into her slacks. No sense getting all worked up again. So soon. "What do you mean, you've never done it?"

"I mean, I've never done that specific—act."

"You're twenty-five years old."

"Well, a couple years older than that," she admitted miserably. Here it came. Now that he'd satisfied his curiosity with the town giant, the jokes would start. If he called her a big girl again, she would probably start bawling. Grace scooted herself as close to the door handle as she could get, a self-protective gesture that belied the smile she forced to her kiss-swollen lips. "And, anyway, I know how old I am."

"Don't hunch over like that, Doc," Daniel said crossly. "I'm just surprised."

She ran her fingers under her eyes, belatedly checking for mascara. "Oh, come on," she said with practiced cheer. "Look at me."

He frowned at her. "I have. Believe me." He reached out and tucked a strand of silky hair behind her ear. There was that vulnerability again. She hid it well, he thought, but he was getting used to looking for it. Poor Grace. All that wonderful long length of mouthwatering body and nobody had every taught her to appreciate it. *Thank goodness,* a traitorous little voice in his head whispered. "What the hell is wrong with the men on this planet?"

"I don't know." A corner of her mouth turned up. "You're the only one who's let me get close enough to examine."

He grinned. "Anytime." He opened the door, got out to stand beside the truck, let the chilly spring breeze take a measure of the heat that was rolling off his body. Jeez. What was happening to him? He was aroused again, and he hadn't even watched her put her clothes back on. "Although we might want to actually go inside next time."

A long silence greeted that. "There won't be a next time, Daniel."

He looked up at her, his hand at his jaw.

"Are you nuts? We practically explode every time we're

within a hundred feet of each other. You think this isn't going to happen again?''

Grace took a deep breath, then let it out slowly. Now that she had her clothes back on, she could think a little more clearly. Wasn't that always the case? Didn't women always make stupid decisions in the passionate heat of a naked moment?

Well, that moment was finished now, and it was time for Grace McKenna to use the excellent brain she'd been born with. ''I can't be someone casual, Daniel.''

''You're the least casual woman I know, McKenna.''

She couldn't face him, though she knew he was boring holes into the side of her head with that moss-green stare. ''You know what I mean. You are never going to fall in love with me. I'm never going to fall in love with you.'' Oh, that particular little fib was a hard one to push past the old vocal chords. ''You resent me for being the vet in this town. In your town.''

''That's crap. I don't resent you.'' But he did, a little, and he was ashamed of himself.

Grace didn't believe him, and she let the sting of his small lie strengthen her resolve. If he could hurt her with something as innocuous as that, she was doomed if she ever let herself fall in love with him. She leaned her cheek against the cool window. It didn't matter, anyway. She knew she was using his obvious resentment over the vet practice as an excuse for what she could hardly say out loud. That the real reason he would never fall in love with her had nothing to do with her job and everything to do with herself.

''I'm not willing or able to make love with someone I don't love, and who doesn't love me,'' she explained slowly. ''It's a stupid and disrespectful thing to do with my body, and I'll be hurt at the end of it.''

''Grace, this is—'' He almost said the most awkward, annoying conversation he'd ever had, but he stopped himself. He could tell how difficult it was for her to say this to him, how she'd curled into the seat, her legs tucked under her and her arms crossed on her chest, her head turned to the moon outside the window. "This is hard to even explain."

She looked at him then, her eyes eloquent, defenseless. "Try."

He dragged his lip between his teeth, stalling. "I don't think I can love anyone." The admission was painful, though levelly, honestly said; she deserved the truth. "Look," he continued, his voice softening, "I'm sorry. It has nothing to do with you. It's a decision I made years ago. I loved my wife, Grace. I let my guard down and my world pretty much blew up in my face. I'm not going through that again. But I like you, and I'm attracted to you, and I want to go on seeing you."

Funny, he described falling in love as letting his guard down, Grace thought. She had always looked at it in exactly the same way.

"I like you, too." She smiled. "As surprising as that sounds. But I won't have an affair. I'm not—tough enough." She made a wry face. "You probably think that sounds silly, considering how tough I look."

He had no idea what she was talking about. Right now, she looked about as tough as a baby bunny. "You'll never be with anyone unless they love you? Unless you love them? I don't think it's silly, I think it's damn restrictive."

"Yes, fine, it probably is." But it was also safe, and she so wanted to keep her innocent heart safe. "It's who I am. I can't change anymore than you can."

"Okay. Fine. Do what you have to do." He watched the lights go out at his parents' house, knew they were turning off the news and snuggling into their queen-size bed together. It gave him a hollow feeling thinking of it. He'd allowed his bitterness over a vet school and the divorce to chill his heart. He'd known it long before Grace had pointed it out to him. He didn't believe in love anymore. He believed in sex, he believed in himself, he believed in the ranch and the land and the family. And that was pretty much it.

If he couldn't give Grace his love—amazing, smart and sexy Grace—then it was very unlikely he'd ever share his own house with anyone.

"I do like you, Daniel," Grace said softly.

He squinted up at the moon. "I like you, too."

"Maybe we can be friends."

Daniel snorted softly. "Maybe, Doc." He reached in and shut off the ignition of his pickup. "But I doubt it."

Daniel reined his big horse around another pair of Herefords, mamma and baby, and scooped them into the herd he was moving across one of the north pastures. Fifty or so cows moved slowly, calmly, ahead of him, each cow with a two-week calf at her side.

They'd make a nice profit for the ranch come fall, the calves. Daniel Cash always made a profit. An excellent one. While most of his neighboring cattlemen struggled to make ends meet, Cash Cattle, Incorporated, made every land payment on time, was current on its taxes, and bought new equipment when it needed to instead of piecing things together with baling twine and hope.

And every minute Daniel Cash was working like a madman for that profit, showing everyone in Nobel, Idaho, he wasn't a loser and a cheat, he was wishing he was in the little clinic on Main Street, tending to his life's dream.

She was tending to it, now. Grace. The thought of her brought a strange little constriction to his heart. Last night had been amazing, and if she'd been any other woman, and he any other man, he never would have let her leave. But she wanted more, and was right to. She deserved more. He just couldn't give more.

But, man, the sex. What there had been of it was sexier, hotter, more incredible than anything he'd ever had with anyone. It had been impossible to erase it from his thoughts, and more than once during the sleepless night, he'd brought his fingers to his nose, imprinting the scent of her body into his brain.

Mind elsewhere, he automatically clucked at another pair of resting cattle, watched them pick themselves up, rumps first, and fall in with the herd.

A movement caught the corner of his eye, and he stopped his horse to watch his brother come loping toward him. Frank had always sat a horse well, Daniel thought. He'd rodeoed in high school, but Sara had made him stop when they got married. It scared her to think of him riding broncs, trusting his life to the strength of a cinch and one hand. And Frank had given it up for her. Happily. As he'd done everything for her. As he'd done nothing since she and the baby died.

"Danny," Frank said.

"Hey, Frank." He kept his eye on a balky pair of cattle in front of him. "What's going on?"

"Spy got kicked by the roan mare."

Daniel's head snapped around. Spy was his favorite border collie, a valuable dog to the ranch, and a good friend. "Where is she?"

"I left her in the barn."

"Anything broken, can you tell?"

"I can't tell, but I think you need to go take a look at her."

"You'll head these in?"

Frank blinked rapidly, as though the low spring sun was too bright for him. Another odd little habit he'd picked up lately. Daniel didn't want to think what it could mean, these tics his brother was displaying. Refused to.

"Yeah. Okay."

Daniel swung his horse around and started for the barn.

"I wanted to know if you thought about what we talked about the other night," his brother called out, as if it were an afterthought.

Daniel stopped his horse, nimbly turning it to face Frank again. He knew better. This was no afterthought.

"Hell, Frank."

"Be disgusted all you want, you son of a bitch," Frank said tightly. "Just give me what I want and I'll be out of your hair."

"I don't want you out of my hair, Frank. I just want my brother back."

"Well, Danny, he's not coming back. Get used to it. I have."

"Have you? Seems to me you're fighting yourself every minute of the day."

"No, I'm fighting you every minute of the day. I went to the folks yesterday."

Daniel squinted at his brother. "Sorry?"

"I went to them. I wrote out a proposal and gave it to them, outlining what we could liquidate around here so they could buy out my shares, since you don't want to do it."

Daniel was half out of his saddle before he checked his temper. "I cannot believe this, Frank."

"Well, don't worry. They shot me down."

"Did you think they'd do anything else?"

"I thought maybe they considered me as much their son as you. Evidently I was wrong."

"Don't be an ass. God, listen to yourself, Frank. Is this what you've become? You're whining that Mom and Dad don't love you?"

"It's just a fact, Danny. What you want, they want."

"That's because what I want is for this ranch to continue in this family. Look around you, Frank. This is our legacy. And whether you think it's going to happen or not, one of these days you're going to pull your head out of your butt long enough to realize Sara would hate you for doing this to yourself. She died in that accident, and Cody died, but you didn't die, Frank. Stop trying to convince yourself you did."

"I did die with them, Danny." Frank's eyes glittered with fury, with pain, with unshed tears. "My heart and my guts shriveled up inside my body the day they died. The rest of my body just won't go with them."

"You seem to be making a stab at hurrying it along."

"That, brother, is none of your damn business." He swiped at his eyes with the back of his hand, a rough, angry motion. Daniel thought if they'd both been on the ground, he might have swiped at Daniel in the same way. Maybe it would have done him some good, to have a target for all the pain. Daniel would have served as one gladly.

"Frank—"

"Shut up. I'm done asking you for favors, Danny. I'll do what I have to do to get free of this place."

He wheeled his horse around and followed the cattle that were moving slowly down the hill. Daniel soothed his horse, who had wanted to run with his pasture mate, and sat staring after his brother.

After a minute, he kicked his horse into an easy canter and headed for the barn.

"You could pack hay bales around in those bags under your eyes, Grace," Lisa remarked as she walked into Grace's office. She never knocked. Grace had thought Mrs. Handleman was just stubborn for always doing so, and now she found Lisa's casual attitude toward professional privacy somewhat irritating. She really wanted a happy medium, but doubted she'd find it with these two around.

"I've been preg-checking dairy cattle all afternoon," Grace replied dryly. "Is Mrs. Handleman gone for the day?"

"No. She's on the phone with someone I don't particularly care for, making an appointment. Do you need something?" Lisa sat in the chair Grace kept for consultations, though she hadn't had a single one yet that hadn't taken place in either her examining room or standing in half a foot of fresh manure.

"Someone you don't particularly care for?" Small towns. Grace almost sighed. She might never get used to the intricacies.

Lisa smiled. "Bad boys. Tommy Felcher and Guy Tate. They've got a horse down, I guess."

Grace was already half out of her chair. "Where?"

"Out to their place, I reckon," Lisa said casually, picking at a brightly manicured pink fingernail. "I hear you had dinner at the Early Bird last night with my cousin."

"Your cousin?" Grace said rather stupidly, stalling for time.

"Daniel. Of course." Lisa smiled thinly. "My other cousin does drugs."

Grace stared at her new assistant. "I beg your pardon."

"Frank's doing drugs. Has been for a couple years now. It's why I quit the ranch."

"My God." Grace put a hand to her heart, felt its sudden acceleration. She didn't want to know this. She couldn't imagine why Lisa, who had worked for her only a week, would tell her about such a private family matter. Perhaps everything in Nobel was accelerated; confidences, friendships, love affairs.

Almost as though she could see the question form, Lisa answered it. "I thought you should know the truth. I want us to start out on the right foot."

"Oh. Of course." How horrible for them all. "Does Daniel know?"

"I think he probably does, deep down." Lisa shrugged. "I'm going to talk to Aunt Liz and Uncle Howard about having an intervention. I thought maybe you could tell Daniel."

"Me? I can't tell him. We barely— We hardly— I don't even know him very well."

"Oh? You were out to the ranch last night."

Grace ruthlessly battled back a lethal blush. Had she seen them rolling around in the new grass? It was certainly pos-

sible. Oh, what had she been thinking? Her nimble brain
flashed on an image of Daniel Cash, his mouth wet from
hers, his green eyes flashing and intense. The fact was, she
hadn't been thinking. "How did you know that?"

"Frank told me. I went by the equipment shed before I
left for work this morning."

"Oh." Had he been spying on them? No. Not Daniel's
brother. "How did he know, did he say?"

Lisa's blue-shadowed eyes went sharp. "He keeps close
tabs on what Daniel does. He wants out of the corporation,
and he's pressing Danny pretty hard about it."

"He does?" That explained the shadows in Daniel's eyes
when he'd spoken of his brother. "Well, why doesn't he
just leave?"

"And walk away from a million-dollar investment? He's
trying to get Daniel to sell the place, or at least buy out his
shares. He needs the money to feed his addiction, is what I
think."

She said it so casually, it made Grace's skin crawl. "You
know what, Lisa? I don't think we should talk about this
anymore."

"Oh. You're probably right. Sorry if I upset you." She
rose. "I hear Mrs. Handleman talking. I'd better go out and
see if you have a customer."

She did. Daniel Cash, holding his dog in his arms.

"Thank goodness you're here," Mrs. Handleman snapped
at him as he walked through the door.

He glanced around. "Is she here? Spy's been kicked.
Needs her ribs wrapped."

"As if you couldn't do that your own self, boy," the older
woman scoffed. "You just wanted another look at the new
lady vet."

"Get her, will you, Alice? Spy may need an X ray."

"May?" Mrs. Handleman said, rounding the reception
counter. "I worked alongside you eleven years, Danny Cash,

and I know you can make a better diagnosis than that. Bring that dog in the examining room.''

He followed Mrs. Handleman's wide, familiar waddle down the corridor. ''Why thank goodness I'm here?''

''That Tate boy's called the doctor out for a horse down.''

Daniel grunted as he placed his dog gently on the stainless-steel table. ''She's not going out there. They'll have to trailer the horse in.''

Mrs. Handleman sniffed in approval. ''That's what I thought.''

''What's what you thought?'' Grace asked as she followed Lisa out of her office. ''What happened to this dog?''

''Kicked by a horse,'' Daniel said shortly. ''Hey, Lisa.''

''Hey, Danny.''

''You had a call to go and check on a horse out to Guy Tate's, but Danny here doesn't think you should go,'' Mrs. Handleman said smugly, handing Grace a pair of latex gloves.

Grace examined the dog quickly and efficiently, palpating her sides and looking closely for signs of internal bleeding. It stopped her from shooting Daniel a look of death. ''He doesn't, does he?'' Grace murmured. ''Get me some wrap and tape.''

Mrs. Handleman handed her the supplies. ''No, he doesn't. And I'd take his advice if I were you.''

''Would you?''

She was speaking quietly, but Daniel could hear the vibration in her voice. He stood with his hands in his pockets, watching every move she made. He hated to admit he couldn't have wrapped Spy's ribs better himself. She had on her too short coveralls again, and this time they were covered in a fragrant combination of fresh manure and bovine mucus. He thought she looked beautiful.

''Yes. They can trailer that horse in if they want it looked at.''

"Hard on a horse, if it's suffering," Grace said, stripping off her gloves. She looked at Daniel. "Your dog?"

"You're not going out there, Grace," he said flatly.

She smiled thinly. Not a conversation she wanted to have in front of her two assistants, but here she was. "Yes, I am." She turned to Mrs. Handleman. "Get me the directions."

Mrs. Handleman humphed nastily, but followed orders, anyway.

"Guy Tate's a lunatic and Tommy Felcher's even crazier. He'd been in the county jail three times for assault. It's his horse they've got out there."

"She'll need to be kept quiet for at least a week," Grace said, nodding at the dog. "I'll give you some antibiotics in case she develops an infection."

"I'll come with you."

She stood her ground, no easy task considering he was breathing fire again. "No, you won't."

"Yeah, I will." He turned to Lisa. "Can you put Spy in a kennel until I get back?"

"You're not going—"

"Look, Doc, I know these boys." He shrugged. "I've also doctored the horse. Maybe I can be of some help."

He saw what looked suspiciously like pity slide into those angry brown eyes of hers, and could have strangled her for it.

Pity? Rage bubbled up from nowhere and choked him down. Pity? He was trying to protect her and all he got was arguments and pity? Hell with her, then. Let her take her chances.

"You know what," he said, turning toward the door, "forget it. See you, Lisa." He was gone before Grace took her next breath.

Grace forgot about Lisa and Mrs. Handleman and even the little border collie and rushed out the door after him. His long stride got him to his truck in double time, but she was no stroller, either. She caught his arm as he yanked open the door of his truck.

"Wait a minute!"

"Nope. I got things to do."

"You big baby. Wait!"

He gave her a cool look. *Baby?* "You're pushing it, Grace. Let go of my arm."

"No. Why are you so mad?"

He raised his eyebrows.

"Okay," she said. "Okay. I admit, it makes me nervous that you want to go on calls with me."

"Not calls. Just this call. But you think you're tough enough for Tommy Felcher and Guy Tate, you go ahead on out. I won't ask you again."

"Do you see the position you're putting me in?"

"Yep. I do. Let go of my arm."

She knew better than anyone he could have shaken her off in a blink. It was another measure of the man that he didn't. "You stubborn jackass. I'm sorry if I hurt your feelings—"

"Hurt my feelings." He stuck his tongue in his cheek and stared out the front windshield. He slowly shook his head. "Hurt my feelings."

"Well, didn't I hurt your feelings?"

"No. Now let go of my arm, Grace, before I shut this door on you."

"Well, if I didn't hurt your feelings, what did I do?"

"You felt sorry for me. Didn't you?" He narrowed his eyes, caught a glint of guilty truth in hers. "I don't need your pity."

"No. You don't. I'm sorry."

"Uh-huh. Let loose of me."

She did. Stepped back. "I am sorry. I didn't mean to make you so angry. I didn't even know I could."

"Well, now you know." He closed the door of his truck with a definite bang. "See ya."

She slapped the side of his truck as it moved away from the curb. "Mule," she shouted, and ignored the stares she got from the crowd at the Early Bird.

Chapter 6

The farm, if it could be called that, was a mess. Broken fence lines lay like spaghetti strands along the edges of weedy fields. No cattle in the single, small pasture, and what was utilized as a barn was not much more than a shed. And it stank. Even Grace, who was accustomed to the various smells of the animal world, had to wrinkle her nose when she stepped into the dim building.

The two men, who'd introduced themselves as Tommy and Guy, walked in behind her. Close behind her. Grace struggled for calm.

"He's swolled up in his gut," said Tommy—or possibly Guy, as she hadn't paid much attention during the introductions, busy as she was rethinking Daniel's offer to come with her to this stinking hole.

She ignored the tickle of dread at the back of her neck and examined the horse carefully. He was jumpy and snorted at her.

"Get a halter on him, please, Tommy," she said, and watched which man moved. Okay, she had them straight now. That would be important if she had to describe them to the police. She bit back a bubble of slightly hysterical laughter. "Hold his head. And have you got lights in here?"

"Nope," Guy drawled.

"Let's get him outside, then." She took the halter herself and strapped it on, speaking soothingly to the horse all the while. He didn't calm and she had to jump out of the way when he stamped his wide hoof too close to her boot.

"Settle down," Tommy said sharply, giving the horse a brisk slap on his thick neck.

"Hey!" Grace snapped. "Don't do that."

"He don't behave."

"Probably because he's injured," Grace said.

"He ain't injured, he's just sick," Guy said. "Got the colic."

"This horse does not have colic." What he did have wrong with him, Grace was almost afraid to speak aloud to these two men, who were clearly responsible for his condition. "Which one of you kicked him?"

They stared at her, and then exchanged a glance. "Kicked him? Nobody kicked him," Tommy said. "He was like 'at when we come out this afternoon."

Fury, ugly and vicious, snaked up Grace's throat. She'd dedicated her life to helping animals, and these two slack-jawed yokels had just taken a boot to a perfectly fine horse and damaged its kidney. "There's a toe mark in the hide, from a steel-toed boot. The hide's ripped open, there." She looked down, could see the glint of stamped, ornamental steel at the tip of Tommy Felcher's slim cowboy boot. "I'm taking this horse with me in my trailer back to the clinic. I'm also calling Animal Services and reporting you both for cruelty. This animal is emaciated and dehydrated. How long has he been locked in this shed?"

"He's only been in here a day or two."

Grace gritted her teeth. She could smell something besides

the sick animal and the filthy barn. Human halitosis; a lethal combo of beer and onions, if she wasn't mistaken.

"More like a week or two," she said stiffly. "Excuse me, I'm taking him outside to get a better look at him. Meanwhile, clean out this manure. You're inviting disease."

Guy Tate smiled, revealing a raggedy set of teeth and a wad of chewing tobacco the size of a walnut. "You ain't taking this horse anywhere, Legs."

"I am," she said, pulling herself to her full height. She topped them both by a couple inches, and she was furious, besides. No way they could take her, she thought.

They eyed her, eyed each other. "How tall are you?" Tommy asked, grinning. Grace felt something like real fear slick down her spine. She didn't speak, but braced herself. The horse behind her shifted nervously, sensing the sudden tension.

"Six-three? Six-four?"

Grace narrowed her eyes. She slid her hand over the halter rope, clenched it between bloodless fingers. "Move it. I'm taking this horse."

"You are the godawfulest tall woman I ever saw," Guy said.

"I betcha you're six-three," Tommy decided. "Am I close?"

They were having fun, now, she could see. Her lips thinned "Get out of my way."

"You ain't taking this horse," Guy declared mildly once more. "I don't even know how you find clothes to fit you, with those long legs."

He decided to stare at her legs for a while, or at least at the apex of her thighs, Grace noted in disgust. She took a step forward, leading the horse, but neither man budged an inch.

"I don't know how she finds a bed to fit her," said Tommy.

Guy thought that was plenty clever. He grinned again. "Mine would fit her," he said.

"Okay, I've had enough," Grace said tightly. Fear and fury were rapidly turning to flat-out nausea. "Get out of my way, *right now*."

She took another step forward and found herself pinned between the two men, who shifted to her sides. She acted instinctively, and would later thank her brothers for the years of backyard wrestling matches. She elbowed Tommy in his considerable beer belly and stomped as hard as she could on Guy's filthy shoe.

All hell broke loose, as she suspected it would. She dropped the halter rope just as one of them snaked out a hand and yanked her hair nearly out of her skull. The other slid his hand around the slim column of her neck. She no longer cared which man was doing what. She just wanted out. She began to fight, but almost instantly found her arms clamped behind her back.

"That was a big mistake, Stretch," one of them hissed in her ear as she aimed, and missed, a kick to a shin.

"I will have you both arrested for assault," she threatened between her teeth.

"You started it, honey."

"And I'll finish it." The threat was like the retort of a gun in the dank little barn. Daniel towered in the doorway, blocking off most of what little light there was. The men on either side of Grace froze. "Get your hands off her."

Whichever smelly hillbilly had hold of her hair dropped his hand, but the fingers around her neck just tightened a little at the warning.

"I said," Daniel growled, "get your greasy hand off her, Tommy, or I'll get my ax out the back of my pickup and chop it off at the elbow."

He stepped into the barn, rage pumping through the muscles in his back and shoulders, bunching his fists and pouring into his adrenal glands. He could have killed both of them with his bare hands, and smile doing it. They'd touched her, had their hands on her, put that scared look into her beautiful brown eyes. He wouldn't let them live without the appropriate scars.

"Danny, listen now," Guy started to babble as he backed up. Grace was astonished how quickly his smug sneer had oozed into a grimace of abject fear. "We was just telling the lady she couldn't take the horse. The horse is our property."

"Was that your paw yanking on her hair, Guy?" Daniel asked through his teeth.

"Oh, God," Guy whimpered. "I didn't mean nothing. She stomped my foot."

Not sparing Grace a glance, Daniel reached out a long, mighty arm and grabbed the little man by the collar of his stinking flannel shirt. "She should have knocked you flat for touching her. Looks like I'll have to do it for her."

"Daniel," Grace gasped, but couldn't have stopped the punch that seemed to explode like a cannon out the end of Daniel's arm. Guy Tate landed five feet from where he started out, with his head in a pile of horse apples. He didn't move. He didn't, in fact, so much as groan, though Grace was gratified to see his chest stir in a shallow motion.

Daniel turned the weighty force of his menace to Tommy Felcher, who was in a low crouch, ready for action. "Last words?" he asked blandly.

"She started it."

Daniel almost laughed, it was so absurd. "I'll keep that in mind while I'm beating the hell out of you."

"Daniel, stop," Grace said. "I'm fine. I just want to take this horse and go."

Daniel ignored her, but Tommy thought she had come up with a grand idea, apparently. "Let's just forget the whole thing, Danny. Like the lady says. Take the horse and go."

"I don't think so," was the terse reply.

"Listen, she don't even want your help. Look at her, for

God's sake, Danny. She looks like she can take care of herself."

He didn't so much as flick a glance at Grace. "Yes, she does," he conceded softly. Tommy didn't fly so much as crumple as one of Daniel's massive fists caught him in his stomach. He went down with a bit more noise than did Guy, but in the end the effect was the same. "But she shouldn't always have to."

While Grace stared at the two men lying just about lifeless on the disgusting floor, Daniel grabbed her wrist in a death grip and hauled her close. "Are you all right?"

She was wild-eyed. "Yes."

"Good. Get your damn horse and get out of here."

Grace spoke carefully to the horse and managed to get close enough to grab the halter rope. The poor thing was dancing with anxiety. She led it out of the barn. Daniel watched her, scowling, and Grace had the feeling he was waiting for her to make a mistake so he could pounce on her, as well.

They walked in silence to Grace's truck and trailer. He helped her load the horse without a word and stood like a sentry at her door until she was inside and buckled up.

"Daniel—"

"Don't talk to me right now, Grace."

"I just want to say—"

He gripped the open window. "I don't want to hear what you have to say."

"You were right about coming out here."

"Yes, I was."

"And I'm sorry."

"You should be." He was still fuming, almost as much from the scene at her clinic as the one in that stinking old shed. He'd followed her out here, muttering every mile. He'd known there would be trouble with those two, had known them since grade school and had an excellent idea how they would react to the thrilling sight of Grace Mc-

Kenna. What he hadn't known is how unbelievably insane he would feel when he saw them yanking her hair, pawing her white, slim neck. He was practically vibrating with the aftereffects. If he'd gotten there a minute later, or if she'd had a mark on her, he would be going back into that barn after Grace left to finish the job.

Grace put her hand over his. His fingers were white-hot and rigid.

"I'm sorry, Daniel. I should have listened to you. But I thought—"

"I know what you thought. You thought I was just trying to weasel my way into your vet practice."

Under the anger, Grace saw the edge of a wound. She was ashamed of herself for opening it up again.

"That one man, the one with the big belly, he kicked that horse with a steel-toed boot. Its kidney's bruised, and it may have some internal bleeding."

Daniel's lips thinned. "I guess I'll just go back and hit them again."

"And then when I tried to take the horse out," she continued, "they stopped me. I want you to know I tried not to provoke them. Sort of."

"They're easy to rile, those two. What happened in there wasn't your fault, Grace. But you should have let me come out—"

"And then, you came bursting through that door like—I don't know. Like a hero."

Daniel scowled at her. "Don't get carried away, Doc."

Back to calling her Doc, she noted. Ah, well. She'd get it said with or without his cooperation.

"And all I could think was, Oh, there's Daniel to rescue me. It just popped into my head. I was in trouble, and there you were."

"Okay, that's enough." His anger was sliding into confusion, embarrassment. She had stars in her eyes, silly woman. All he'd done was toss a couple lightweight troublemakers on their ears. He didn't love her, but he would have done a hell of a lot more for her than that.

"Not one man, not one person, outside my own family, has ever done anything like that for me, Daniel." His gaze sharpened on her. "It's always been like what Tommy said. I'm a big girl. I can take care of myself." She met his eyes, smiled. "I just wanted you to know that, while that may be true, I very much appreciate you hitting those guys on my behalf."

He couldn't help it. He had to smile. "You enjoyed that, did you?"

"Very much. Thank you."

He rubbed his thumb across her knuckles. "I just get to where I think I have you pegged as a nice, sensible woman, Doc, and you turn bloodthirsty on me."

"I'm multifaceted."

He smiled. "I can see that. Go back to the clinic, now. I'm going to chat with Tommy and Guy about buying that horse."

She almost warned him, Be careful. But then she took another look at him. His eyes still gleamed from battle, his big, rangy body appeared invincible. "Okay," she said. "I'll see you."

"Friday," he said. Grace looked at him blankly. "You're checking my heifers?"

"Oh, the heifers." For one thrilling moment she thought he'd been asking her for a date. "Yes. Friday. See you Friday."

He waited until she pulled out before he started walking back to the barn. Grace drove slowly, watching him in her side mirror until he disappeared, and did her best not to sigh.

Friday found Grace shoulder-deep into the back end of one of Daniel Cash's herd cows, checking the size of the fetus. Preg-checking was not the cleanest job, and was physically strenuous, as well. She looked like a woman who'd just been given diamonds.

"Seven months," she mumbled, taking a green grease pencil the circumference of a Cuban cigar out of the pocket of her coveralls and marking a large seven on the hide of the cow in the squeeze chute. She smiled widely at Daniel, her face glowing, thrilled with the job. "Okay, let her go."

Daniel popped open the chute, released the head-catch. The cow ambled out, accustomed to the exam and the noise of the chute.

"Bring the next one through," Daniel yelled to his father, who was standing alongside the alleyway where another three cows waited impatiently for their examination. "Keep her," he shouted to Frank, who opened the gate in front of the released cow and let her walk through.

Howard coaxed another cow into the chute and Daniel clanged it closed on her, squeezing her in so she'd stand still long enough to be checked.

Grace squirted the thread of glycerin jelly over the heavy plastic glove she had clamped to the open shoulder of her coveralls and plunged her hand inside the cow. She frowned in concentration.

"Ooops, three months, Cash. This one got away from you." She marked the cow with a big three.

"Sell her," Daniel shouted as he loosened the head-catch again and let the cow go; Frank headed the cow through a different gate. "This is the little bunch I couldn't find in the desert when I A.I.'ed the rest of them last summer."

Grace grunted. "This one's ready to calve." She market it with a nine.

"Keep her," Daniel bellowed, and let the cow go.

"Do you have an A.I. tech?"

"She asks nonchalantly." Daniel deftly caught another cow as she barreled through the chute. Grace tried very hard not to stare at the muscles bulging in his arms as he squeezed her in. Ever since that episode with Tommy and Guy in the shed, Grace had been trying very hard to not even think about his muscles.

"Doc Niebaur always did it for me," Daniel said. "I can't imagine why you couldn't. Even though you're a girl," he added with a smirk.

Grace smirked back. "Shut up."

He looked her up and down. Slowly, as if neither one of them had another thing in the world to occupy their time at that moment. "It doesn't look bad on you, Grace."

She checked the cow, waved her through with a big zero on her flank, and tried not to let her face go hot and her knees go weak. "Thank you."

She preg-checked the rest of the cows Daniel had in the alley, stripped off her glove and went back to her vet box to wash and gather up her supply of syringes and blood tubes.

The wayward cows had only been an afterthought. She'd actually come out to bleed the two-year-old bred heifers Cash Cattle was selling to a ranch across the state line in Montana, checking them, as law required for cattle going out of state, for the deadly brucellosis virus. Brucellosis, or "Bangs," caused spontaneous abortions in cattle, and the livestock industry was unrelenting in its effort to stamp it out entirely.

"We ready for the heifers?" she called over her shoulder.

"You want lunch, first, slave driver?" Daniel yelled back at her.

Grace laughed. "Nope."

"Well, we're hungry."

"That's a shame." She walked back to the chute. "Because we've got work to do, Cash."

He considered her a minute. Her face was flushed, her eyes sparkling. He was the only other vet he knew who enjoyed this part of the job so much. Only, he reminded himself, he wasn't a vet. "Bring 'em in," he shouted to his dad. "The lady wants to work us to death."

Grace finished with the heifers late in the afternoon. Beautiful, sleek creatures, they were current on their brucellosis vaccinations and appeared healthy. Grace smiled at Daniel as the last young cow was released from the chute into a pen where she and her sisters would be fed and watered, separate from the rest of the herd, until the Bangs test cleared.

"They look good."

"They do," he agreed. He was proud of his herd. He wasn't doing what he'd always thought he'd be doing with his life, but he was taking his best shot at success, anyway.

"I don't see any problems. There was a little touch of pinkeye on Number 254, so I treated it."

"Pinkeye?" Daniel frowned.

"Very mild. It'll be gone by the time you ship them Monday."

He grunted, shoved his hands into his back pockets, looked around to see if he could spot the imperfect specimen.

"I'd better get back to town."

He brought his attention back to her. Jeez. He was sick or something, because those coveralls just did it for him. "Guess so," he said after a moment.

"Thanks for lunch."

Daniel nodded toward the house in the distance. "Mom's thing," he said. "She was a little flustered she had to serve it out in the corral, I think."

Grace laughed. "Sorry about that. I like your folks. *Danny.*"

Daniel winced. "Don't call me that."

She grinned at him. So, Mr. Impervious had a sore spot, did he? "Your mom and dad seem very happy."

"They like being retired." Daniel looked around, saw his father shutting gates after the heifers. "Well, semiretired. They're wasting their lives, of course," he added fondly.

"They ran the place alone before you and Frank took over?"

Daniel nodded. "Dad bought his brother out years ago. Uncle Moe."

"Moe?"

"Maurice. It's a family name."

Grace wrinkled her nose. "Thank goodness your parents didn't hate you enough to give you a family name."

Daniel rubbed his chin, decided prudently not to tell her his middle name was Maurice.

"Lisa's father was a rancher, too?" Grace asked.

"Yes, although she took to it a lot better than he did. He was always sort of halfhearted about it. Almost lost the place a couple times to creditors." He chuckled. "Nothing halfhearted about Lisa."

"You can tell that by her eye shadow alone," Grace mused, then put her hand over her mouth, embarrassed. "Sorry."

Daniel laughed. "You think she looks like a harlot at work, you should see her at the Rowdy Cowboy some Friday night."

"I shudder to think." She took in a breath, pushed it back out. She was stalling, wanting to be near him, and she knew it. Foolish girl.

"Well." She stuck out her hand for a manly shake. "Good day today."

Daniel stared down at her hand for a full five seconds, looking for all the world as if he didn't have any idea why it was hanging there, before his shoulders twitched and he jerked his hands from his pockets. He shook her hand briefly, one hard pump, and let it go as if it was burning hot.

Grace's mouth turned up at one corner. She wiped her hand down the front of her coveralls. "You have manure on your hands."

"You have it in your hair. My mother was repulsed, she told me."

Grace clamped her hands over her head. "Aah! Not really. Are you kidding?"

"I wouldn't kid. I'm humorless."

"Oh, for crying out loud, if I really do have manure in my hair, I'm going to murder you for not telling me."

"Well, if we're going for full disclosure here, you don't just have it in your hair." He reached around her with one giant hand. "It's on your butt, too."

She nearly jumped out of her skin. "Hey!"

"Excuse me." Frank's face was carefully blank as he approached them. "That it?"

Daniel turned on his heel, surprised Frank had come almost upon them without him noticing. Maybe if he hadn't been mooning over his veterinarian... "Yeah, I need to throw a few bales out for them tonight, but I can do that."

"I'm going into town, then."

"Thanks for your help today," Grace said as Daniel's brother turned to leave. "I thought that one old biddy was going to run right over me."

Frank barely shrugged and moved toward the little all-terrain vehicle he'd driven up from his house on the north end of the ranch.

Daniel gave Grace a grim, apologetic look, and went after his brother.

"Real polite," he said when he caught up to his brother. "You barely spoke to Doc McKenna all day, and then you can't even say goodbye?"

"I didn't realize I was required to fall all over your girlfriend."

"She is not my girlfriend," Daniel rasped. "We're just friends. Hell, we're barely even that. But she is our vet, and a woman, and she did give you a compliment, idiot. You weren't raised to be such a jackass. What the hell is the matter with you?"

Frank turned slowly to face his brother. He looked past him for a moment to study Grace. "You're just friends with a woman like that, Danny, and you think something's wrong with *me?*"

Daniel poked his finger at his brother's chest. "Watch your mouth."

Frank practically sneered. "Yeah, that's what I thought. You may not be sleeping with her, but you sure want to. She's smart and good-looking and she looks at you like you hung the moon. Well, good for you. I apologize for not being more thrilled about it."

"You sorry, self-absorbed son of a bitch."

Frank put up his hands. "You think I care about your opinion of me, Danny? Those days are over." Frank dropped his chin to his chest, squeezed his eyes tight. "Look, I can't give you what you want." He looked up, allowed all the misery in his heart to show in his gray and hopeless face. "I just don't care enough anymore."

Daniel stood silently as his brother swung onto his four-wheeler and roared off.

"Daniel?"

He turned to Grace, saw compassion in her soft brown eyes.

"Sorry about that," he said, feeling hollow, guilty.

"It doesn't matter to me. I'm just sorry to see how much he's obviously still hurting. Lisa told me about his wife and baby."

"He's determined to never get over it."

"I don't imagine he will get over it."

Daniel's green eyes went hard as he watched his brother ride away. "We all have to face what life dishes up."

Grace studied the back of Daniel's head. "Yes, we do," she said softly. "Maybe he will. Someday."

"Maybe." He turned, noticed she was wiping her hands with an antibacterial wipe. "You heading back to town?"

Grace nodded.

Daniel rubbed the sting from his eyes with the back of his wrist. "Do you need some help loading your stuff?"

"No." She'd already carried the insulated case of blood samples to the truck, placing them carefully into the vet box in back. "I did it."

"Oh. Okay."

"Okay. Well." She pushed a clod of dirt around with her toe. "I'll have the results of the blood tests on Monday."

"Good." Hung the moon, huh? He'd have to think about that. "Thanks."

"I'll call you. Everything looks fine, though. No signs of any trouble. You can ship them out Monday afternoon."

"Good." He toed at the same clod, hit her boot with his own, sending an insane little shiver up his spine. "You have plans this weekend?"

"I was going to set up the blood serum tests tonight."

"Oh. That sounds good." He looked up, caught her watching him. "I've got to come into town later tonight."

"Oh?"

"Yeah, I've got to—" What? What? "I've got to do some stuff." Brilliant, brilliant, Danny-boy. He could have kicked himself. "I was going to eat at the café."

"Oh."

"There's no reason you can't come along."

She crossed her arms over her chest in an automatic gesture of self-protection. Daniel wondered if she knew how transparent she was. "I think we've been over the reasons."

"As friends."

"I thought you said we couldn't be friends."

He shook his head mournfully. "God, you're a mule."

She sighed. He had no way of knowing how terrified she was of him. From his perspective, she was simply being stubborn. She could hardly stand having him think she was immature and unreasonable. She wanted his respect, if nothing else. "We can eat at the café. But you pay."

He grinned at her, a startling flash of white teeth in that

serious and handsome face. "That doesn't sound like friends, that sounds like a date."

"We'll talk cattle." Grace shrugged. "You can write it off as a business expense. Besides, I'm broke until some of my clients pay up. Middle-of-the-night cat examinations are very costly."

He'd laughed when he'd got her bill for that. "All right," he agreed with great reluctance. "I'll spring. But don't order so much food this time. That three-dollar salad you wolfed down last—"

"Wolfed down!"

Daniel rolled his eyes and started for his ATV. "Really, it was pretty appalling. And then you ate half my dinner."

She knew he was teasing her, but she blushed furiously nonetheless. "I cannot believe you'd mention that."

"I'm just saying, I'm not made of money."

"Actually, you seem to be made of the same stuff that's in my hair," she shot back.

"Oh, very nice. Very delicate talk for a lady," he said. "I'll pick you up around seven."

"I could just meet you there."

"All right. Meet me there." He mounted the four-wheeler in a smooth, athletic motion that actually made Grace's throat go dry. "I'll just pick you up."

Grace laughed. "Okay."

He nodded again, and without another word, started his machine and zoomed off.

Chapter 7

When she opened the door, his cool green eyes went on instant simmer. He flicked his gaze down her legs. "I've never seen you in a dress."

And this one was a beaut. Soft material wrapped around her and tied at the front. Not too short, but when she sat he'd bet the ranch it'd hike up her thighs and cling. He was afraid he'd be salivating over it all night.

"I don't have much occasion to wear dresses." But she was glad she had tonight. He was wearing brown chinos and a neatly pressed dress shirt; she'd been as flattered by that as she would have been by roses and champagne. "It's probably a little too dressy for the café, but I don't have anything else clean but jeans. I haven't had time to do laundry since I got here."

"You look good."

She smiled. "Thanks. You, too."

"I'm sorry about my brother's behavior today."

"It's fine." She backed up a good five feet, to keep the

mouthwatering scent of him out of her nostrils. "Do you want something before we go?"

"What have you got?" He watched her turn around the room, touching things, smoothing down her dress, checking her watch. He didn't know what the hell she was so nervous about. He was the one who'd have to look at her in that dress all night.

She blinked. "Oh. Nothing, actually. I meant to buy some wine…" She trailed off, looking a little frantic. "You drink beer, though, don't you? Or whiskey?"

He had to smile. "It doesn't really matter, if you don't have either one."

"No." She twisted her hands together. Oh, blasted shyness. Why couldn't it be a nice, invisible disease, like hardening of the arteries, or nymphomania? Why did it have to manifest itself in such stupid ways? She'd spent an hour getting dressed up in this silly getup so she'd feel confident, and now she was acting like an excitable schoolgirl anyway. A long silence stretched between them while she worried over it.

"Well, did you get the serum tests set up?" Daniel finally said. He had to say something, or her face was going to burst into flames.

"Yes."

"How's Felcher's horse?"

"Oh. Good."

"You want to go?"

"Yes."

She tripped on her high heels when she whipped around to grab her coat off the sofa, and Daniel reached out automatically to steady her, but she righted herself before she actually fell.

"Oops," she muttered miserably.

He chuckled. "I like the way those shoes make your legs look, McKenna, but if they're going to trip you up ever time you turn around, maybe you should put your boots back on.''

She shot him a quick, fierce glower from beneath her lashes.

''I can wear heels.'' She snatched up her coat. ''I'm not a complete klutz.''

He grinned. ''You must have just tripped on the carpet.''

He moved to help her on with her coat. ''Right.''

She jerked away from his touch. ''I can do it,'' she snapped. Nothing in the world could have made her stand there and let him perform such a simple, masculine ritual when he was basically accusing her of being too uncoordinated and unfeminine to walk in a pair of one-inch pumps. He wasn't her date, anyway, was he? God, the dress had been a stupid mistake.

''I know you can do it, I was just being polite.''

''Don't be polite with me. It throws our whole relationship out of whack.''

He stared at her. ''What's that supposed to mean?''

She tugged at her coat. He held the collar in his hand and she wanted it back. ''You know what it means.''

Oh, more than anything in the world, he hated when a woman said *that*. ''Why don't you explain it?'' he said tightly.

She gave him a mutinous look. ''You take every opportunity to say insulting things to me. Give me back my coat.''

He exerted equal pull. ''You tripped right in front of me. I just said if you were uncomfortable in those stupid shoes, you should take them off.''

''You implied I couldn't even wear high heels, just as you have previously implied I eat too much, wolf down my food, and can't bake.''

''I was joking!'' He shook his head. ''And you *can't* bake. You told me yourself.''

Her mouth dropped open. ''Oh. That's just typical.'' She

was dragging with all her considerable strength now on the lapel of her good winter coat. "That is just typical."

"What the hell are you talking about, you crazy woman?"

She glared at him and dug in. "'Crazy woman'?"

"Crazy woman," he repeated. "You hide it behind that quick brain and that incredible body, but you are certifiable." He was shouting now, and hauling in the coat hand over hand, as if it was a rope. "Now, let me help you on with your coat so I can get something to eat."

Her teeth were bared now. "Forget it, Cash. I can put on my own coat. You obviously think I'm a man, so don't treat me like a woman."

It was Daniel's mouth that fell open this time. "What?"

She struggled two-handed, but it was like battling a tree trunk. His muscles didn't so much as quiver under her assault. "You heard me," she groaned. "Give me my coat."

If there was one thing Daniel Cash understood perfectly, it was a battle. She was being an idiot—*he thought she was a man?*—and he didn't want to help her on with her coat any more than he wanted two sharp sticks jabbed into his eye, but he was damned if he'd let her put her own damn coat on now!

He took a last jerk on her coat and caught her arm with his other hand at the same time. "I'm helping you on with your damn coat," he said between his teeth. He slid his hand down to her wrist and started stuffing her stiff arm into the sleeve. "And when I'm done," he muttered ominously, "you are going to apologize for being such an imbecile."

Grace wanted very much to wrestle him to the ground and beat the pulp out of him, or at least wrench dramatically away and stomp off to her room, but she knew both schemes were pretty much out of the question. He wouldn't let her get away with either one and she'd just end up looking even more foolish than she did now. But her face was flaming, with anger this time. She didn't give a single thought to feeling shy.

"You're assaulting me," she said stiffly, her lips disappearing between her teeth.

"I'm not assaulting you," he stormed. He jammed her other arm into its sleeve and jerked the collar up around her neck. "Though I want to, baby. I really want to." He used the lapels of the coat to manhandle her around to face him. He started to do up the buttons.

She started to brush his hands away, then stopped, her hands at her shoulders.

Oh, God, what was she doing? She was mortified. Mortified. She couldn't even lift her chin to face him. All indignation seeped out of her and she wanted to soak into the floor at her feet. Had she really acted like such a lunatic over a comment about her shoes? Was she so insecure and foolish?

Daniel, to punish her a little, was slowly, methodically buttoning every single button on her stupid coat. Making his point. Winning the battle, he decided. Hands down. She'd never again use that mouth of hers to confuse the hell out of him and make him feel like an idiot after—

His knuckles brushed her breasts as he reached the middle button. He heard the slightest intake of her breath as she felt the brief contact. His fingers froze.

He was aroused, and realized dimly he had been for several minutes. It was probably a little twisted, getting turned on while you were wrestling with a woman for the dubious privilege of helping her on with her coat, but Grace McKenna had been giving him the strangest ideas since the day he met her.

He let his knuckles brush her again, then rest on her chest, in the hollow between her breasts. He didn't look at her, couldn't. He had never wanted to want this woman, but knew he'd never wanted any other woman more.

He undid the button he'd just fastened.

Grace sucked in another breath. Good Heaven. She was torn suddenly between tears of embarrassment and something entirely different. What had changed, and when, she scarcely knew.

He watched his own fingers slowly unfasten the rest of the buttons on her coat. Still he didn't look at her. The coat hung open and he slid his hands inside, brushing her waist, smoothing over her hips.

She wasn't breathing at all now, Grace realized. And she certainly didn't feel like crying anymore.

Daniel slipped his hands down the sleek sides of her thighs. Because she matched him so perfectly in height, especially with those troublesome heels on, he could almost touch the backs of her knees if he bent his own slightly. Ah, there. Silky nylons over heated skin. His arousal pulsed upward a notch or two. That, of course, was just a bump compared to the surge he got when he ran his hands back up the backs of her thighs and slipped them under her dress. Stockings, thigh-high, with not a thing between the tops of them and her panties. He slid a finger under the elastic tops of the stockings and made them both moan a little.

"I can't believe you wear these," he whispered.

"I bought them for a friend's wedding," she answered inanely. "They're all I have."

"Thank Heaven."

His head was still bowed, his breath falling heavy on her breast.

"Daniel?"

"Don't say it's a mistake," he whispered thickly. "Please don't say it's a mistake."

She pulled his head up to hers. "I won't," she managed to say before he fused his mouth to hers.

He wrapped his arms tightly around her, then, when he found too much between them, levered his body away long enough to rip the coat he'd so recently thought he wanted on her body right back off.

"Grace."

"I know. Hurry, Daniel."

He scooped her bottom into his hands and she wrapped those impossibly long legs around his waist. He banged her back against the first wall he found. And pressed ruthlessly forward.

She cried out against his mouth, as frenzied as he. She pulled at the buttons of his shirt and found her normally clever fingers numb. So she used brute strength instead, and for the first time outside her job, was grateful for it. Buttons flew like buckshot.

''Bed,'' he muttered when her hands dipped beneath the fabric of his shirt. ''Right now.''

He carried her to her room, his wide, work-worn hands—the hands that just days before he had used to protect her against two men who'd meant her harm, she thought giddily—splayed across her bottom. He dropped her unceremoniously onto the bed and began to frantically yank at the rest of his clothes. His pants got stuck around his boots and he nearly toppled onto her before he managed to toe off the whole mess. He dropped down beside her and would have flipped up that slinky little dress and plunged inside, but he caught sight of her face in the dim light shadowing in from the living room.

That look. His brother had been right. She looked at him as though he'd hung the moon.

''Grace,'' he whispered against her neck. ''Grace.'' Again, just to hear it.

Slowly now, calmer, he slid his hands down to her waist, slipped them inside the wraparound dress. The soft fabric seemed to dissolve under his hands and he found skin. He kept his mouth at her neck, nibbling, kissing, while he unwrapped her. Then he went onto his elbows so he could look at her.

Oh, man, *where* had she got that underwear? Not in Nobel, Idaho. He'd have know about it if there was underwear like that within fifty miles of his hometown.

It was shimmery and see-through, like a tightly woven

gold spider's web. He could see the deep color of her areola through it, and the already tight pucker of her nipples. And the soft, dark down between her legs.

He swore softly, an invocation more than a curse.

"Grace, you're beautiful."

Grace could not take her eyes off him. All her life, from the time she'd been tall enough to look in the bathroom mirror until this very moment, she had never believed a single person when they told her she was beautiful. Not her mother or her father, not the people who loved her, and certainly not any man.

But she believed now. His intense expression was testament to it.

He lowered his face to her breast, took a long, slow swipe with his tongue across her already distended nipple, making her arch off the bed. He ducked his head to watch with ardent concentration as her hips met his briefly, then returned that intense gaze to her breasts. He laved the other nipple through the glistening fabric of her bra, then took the wet, stiff tip fully into his mouth. When he pulled it between his tongue and the roof of his mouth, Grace cried out.

He undid the front clasp, swept the pretty bra aside so he could savor her prettier skin. He plucked at the dark crown of one breast with his fingers while he suckled luxuriously at the other, making her crazy. She thrashed about beneath him, her legs shifting involuntarily, her forehead beading with sweat.

"Daniel," she gasped. "Please."

"I will," he muttered darkly against her damp skin, answering a question she didn't even know how to ask. "Wait."

He dragged his hand roughly down her body, cupped her. The gold webbing that covered her was already wet through. He peeled it down her legs, monumentally sorry to see it go. Whatever had happened to those cotton panties and the sensible bra he'd been fantasizing about for upward of two weeks, he didn't miss them at the moment.

He slipped a broad, rough finger across her, skimming lightly over damp hair. She shamelessly pressed against it, wanting desperately for it to dip inside.

"You're as wet as your mouth," he said, his voice thick.

He was blatantly immodest, kneeling between her legs, and she felt an entirely rational anxiety when she looked at him. She'd had him in her hands, she'd seen him and measured the length of him, but never with the intention of having him inside her. She was not a small woman, but that...well, that would never fit.

He was puffing like a bull in a breeding barn, his breath coming out of his nose in great gusts as he quickly protected himself. He looked down, caught the concern in her eyes, gave her a narrow-eyed look.

"You need to tell me now if you don't want to go through with this, Grace."

"No," She shook her head, but couldn't take her eyes off him. All resolve, all fear, eased from her heart as painlessly as Daniel has eased her clothes from her body. "I want to."

He kissed her mouth, kissed her breasts, and slipped his finger inside to test and stretch her. And when she thought she might explode from that contact alone, he met her eyes, clasped her hands, and pushed inside.

She'd been very careful to shield her body from this final, intimate invasion—almost as careful as she had been to guard her heart—and it protested for a minute against a lifetime of protection. But he moved slightly inside her, and whispered her name against her ear, and she felt herself softening, opening, welcoming.

Daniel felt his vision gray. Every instinct that had formed his sexuality since he'd been thirteen howled at him. He wanted to pump his hips forward like pistons, take her fast, show her the kind of man he was. Strong and virile and ungoverned. But he held himself as still as he could manage, watching her. Sweat popped out on his skin, the muscles in his arms screamed as he held his weight off her. She'd whimpered when he'd joined with her, and it was only just dawning on him what that little gasp of discomfort might mean. She'd told him she'd never... But it had never occurred to him she was... Oh, man. If he hadn't been so monumentally aroused, he would have slipped away from her in pure, male panic.

Her eyes focused slowly on his. And she smiled. "Lovely," she said after a minute, and, impossibly, he managed to smile back at her.

"It gets better," he promised her gently. He'd do anything to make sure it did.

It did. Blindingly, shockingly better. And when Grace reached for what she wanted, her hips slamming into his, he was there to give it to her.

When she was finished, and every little tremor had subsided, he buried his face in her neck and followed her in.

"Dammit."

Grace sighed at the expletive, ran a limp hand down his back. He'd been practically comatose on top of her for several minutes. Only the harsh sound of his breathing at her ear and the movement of his chest against hers gave any indication she hadn't killed him. She opened her eyes. "What?"

"We didn't get any dinner." He bit down gently on her neck. "I know I'm crushing you. I'll move in a minute."

She ran her hand down his back again. "Take your time."

He managed to get as far as his elbows, so he could peer into her face. "You all right?"

She pinched his tight rear end. "Don't ask me stupid questions. You know perfectly well how I am."

His smile bloomed slowly, lit up his face. "Yeah?"

She raised her brows. "Oh, what an egomaniac."

He laughed, rolled with her until she was on top of him. They grinned stupidly into one another's faces for a minute.

"I've never been ravished before," she blurted.

He chuckled. "Me, either."

"Well, I'm a brute."

"You are. It's a damned holy wonder you stayed a virgin this long."

Grace's face fell. He'd known. Oh, dammit, he'd known. She must have done something wrong, something…virginal. Well, she wouldn't blush again. She'd face up to her mistakes like a woman.

"No one ever bothered to use your brilliant seduction techniques on me before," she said, hiding nerves behind a stouthearted chuckle. "I'm apparently a sucker for a nasty snarl and a crabby attitude."

He grunted. "You probably had the major moves put on you a hundred times and didn't know it." He leaned his head forward and kissed her sweaty neck. "Checking the guy's cat for feline ataxia while he was trying to get you into bed, knowing you."

She smiled, flattered in spite of herself. "Feline ataxia is a very serious problem."

"You should have told me, Grace."

"Why?" Shyness battled with contentment.

He smiled, ran his finger down her nose. "It's the polite thing to do. And since you seem to have a thing for politeness—"

"I'm unfamiliar with the etiquette for this sort of thing. I'll do better next time."

He slid her next to him on the sheets, cuddling her, and yawned hugely. "There's no next time," he said, making her heart bump.

No next time? Grace stared at the wall next to her bed, then slowly let her eyes close.

Oh, God. A one-night stand. This was a one-night stand. How could she not have understood that? Of course there wouldn't be a next time. This had been a fluke for him, a fling, a short little walk on the wild side with the freak. No reason to think it had been as amazing for him as it had been for her.

Daniel shifted in the bed, snuggling closer to her. "You do understand that, right?" he mumbled.

Grace swallowed, forcing saliva and tears back down her throat. "Of course I understand. I'm a grown-up."

He nuzzled her hair. She felt his mouth curve against her damp scalp. "Can you imagine?"

"What?"

"Losing your virginity more than once."

She blinked. "What are you talking about?"

He lifted his head. She had tears in her voice, he could hear them. "I'm saying there won't be a next time because you can only have your first time once." His eyes narrowed on her flushed face. "What are *you* talking about?"

She stared at him for a full ten seconds, memorizing the way he looked, just now. The way his sleepy green eyes traveled over her face, the way his mouth looked soft and bruised from kissing her, the way his nostrils flared slightly at the scent they'd rubbed up from each other. The relief that this wouldn't be her last time with him was palpable. "The same thing," she answered finally.

He watched her for a moment more, then dropped his head back onto her pillow and fit himself against her once more. He knew there was more, knew there was something behind that quavery voice, those shining eyes, but he didn't press her. She scared him quite enough as it was, he thought ruefully. No sense asking for trouble.

They were quiet a long time, and Grace listened as Daniel's breathing evened out. She could hear his heart beating under her ear, the strong thud of it slowing into a steady, powerful rhythm. When she was sure he was asleep, she whispered, "I'm glad I waited for you."

Beside her, awake, aroused again already, Daniel let his

eyes close. He felt the strangest lump come into his throat. "I'm glad you did, too," he murmured and felt her startle. He tucked her closer to him and did his best to ignore the stirring he experienced when she slung one of those showgirl legs over his. Too soon for her, he thought, though his body was, miraculously, ready again. She snuggled her cheek into the hollow of his shoulder.

"I thought you were asleep," she admitted shyly.

"I know you did." And he felt such a tenderness for her, knowing she'd only have admitted her feelings when she didn't think he'd hear. He ran his hand down her hair. It felt like satin through his rough fingers. "Are you sleepy? Or more hungry? We could still have dinner."

"Are you hungry?"

He was starving, but couldn't bring himself to say so. She might move, put her clothes back on. He didn't want that. "I'm okay."

She yawned, the day, the anticipation, the man beside her, all catching up with her. "Then more sleepy, I think."

He smiled, kissed her soft hair. "Go to sleep, Grace." He watched the shadows the waning spring moon cast on the ceiling of her bedroom. Go to sleep, he thought.

I'll just lie here and wonder what the hell I'm supposed to do with you now.

The sound of her pager woke her. She could hear it in the other room, where she'd left it on her kitchen counter, buzzing at her.

Stupid thing. She squeezed her eyes shut. She hated modern technology.

"Don't get that," a voice rumbled next to her ear.

Good heavens, she was in bed with a man. She giggled. Would wonders never cease?

"It's probably Spandell with another case of milk fever," she mumbled.

"Spandell couldn't get milk fever," Daniel muttered,

turning his big body in the bed to spoon her. He was deter-
mined to not wake up. If he woke up, he'd have to let go.
He wrapped his arm around her waist, scooted her closer.
"Spandell's a man."

That was funny. Grace giggled again. Everything was
funny.

"I really should get that."

He pressed against her naked bottom. The arousal he'd
gone to sleep with was hammering at him again.

"I'll give you a thousand dollars to not get out of this
bed."

She wriggled around to face him, making him hiss in air
through his teeth. She gave him a quick kiss before she
scooted out from under his heavy arm. "That smacks of
prostitution."

"Two thousand dollars," he mumbled into his pillow as
she padded, naked, into the kitchen.

It was her answering service. She called to get her message, hung up, immediately made another call.

Daniel was sitting up in the bed when she returned to the
bedroom. He'd been listening to her side of the conversation,
and had spent enough time working for Dr. Niebaur, and,
later, as a veterinary resident, to know what was happening.

"Whose mare?" he asked.

"Nick Hollowell's."

"How long has she been in labor?"

"He doesn't know. He checked her about ten minutes
ago. Sounds like she's prolapsing." Grace pulled up her
panties, left the bra where it lay. "You can stay here until
morning if you like."

He gave her a look. "Right."

She yanked jeans out of the dresser, practically jumped
into them. "I'm sorry about this."

"Don't be stupid." He walked, naked, into the bathroom.
She could hear him in there, and again struggled not to
blush. So what if he didn't close the door? She wasn't a

schoolgirl, to be giggling and blushing every other minute. Get hold of yourself, Gracie.

She threw on a sweatshirt. ''I'll—'' What? See you around? Call you later? What was the protocol when you slept with a man for the first time?

He came out of the bathroom, still naked, and Grace tried not to stare. ''You'll…?'' he prompted. He yanked on his shorts, pulled his jeans on over them.

''I'll see you.''

''Yes, you will. I'm going with you.''

''Oh.''

''Don't argue with me,'' he warned.

She took in a deep breath. ''I wasn't going to.''

''Because you're not going out in the middle of the night to foal a prolapsing mare by yourself.''

She grabbed her jacket and her bag as he followed her out to the kitchen. ''All right.''

''Where the hell are my buttons?''

Her eyes went wide. ''I don't know.''

He caught the chagrin in her voice and smiled at her. ''I was in a hurry, too.''

''Not after a while, you weren't.''

He shook his head, a little embarrassed himself now. ''I'm polite that way.''

''I like polite.''

''I know. You liked polite twice, actually.''

''Oh, God. Let's just go.''

He laughed. ''You started it.''

''Yes, I know. I'm sorry.''

He shut the door behind them. ''Not me. It shows another whole new side to your personality. The trampy side.'' He jogged behind her to the truck. ''Grace, I won't get in your way,'' he said as he got in behind the wheel.

''I know.''

''It could be anything.''

''I know.''

"You could need my help."

She turned her head, smiled out the passenger-side window.

"I know."

She'd wanted him to come with her. And there he'd been.

They worked together over the mare until nearly dawn. They got the foal born; it was wobbly, weak, but alive. While the mare's owner wiped the shivery little thing down with towels and kept it warm, Grace gave the mare a shot of Pitocin and sewed up the prolapse. Daniel never left her, using his superior strength when it was needed, to hold the mare, to pull the foal, to hold the prolapse in while Grace took neat stitches.

When it was over, and she'd given her instructions to Hollowell, Daniel kept his hand at the small of her back while she trudged, exhausted, back to her truck. She wasn't sure she would have made it otherwise.

"I'll be back at noon," she told Hollowell through the open passenger window. "Call me if you need me before then. And let that baby suck as much as she can. It'll help contract the mare's uterus."

"Thanks, Doc," the man said. He slapped the side of the truck. "I wasn't sure about a woman vet, but you done a good job."

She smiled. "Thanks."

"You're big and strong, I'll give you that."

"Thanks," she said again, wanting to give Daniel, who was snuffling with suppressed laughter beside her, a sharp jab.

Hollowell stuck his hand through the open window. "Dan, thanks for the help."

Daniel nodded, gave Grace's client a quick, manly handshake. "You bet, Nick."

"You ain't forgot much, have ya?"

Play

The Lucky Hearts Game

and get...

FREE BOOKS & a FREE GIFT...
YOURS to KEEP!

Yes! I have scratched off the silver card.
Please send me my **2 FREE BOOKS**
and **FREE MYSTERY GIFT**. I understand
that I am under no obligation to purchase any
books as explained on the back of this card.

Scratch Here!
then look below to see
what your cards get you...

345 SDL C6KG

245 SDL C6KC

NAME   (PLEASE PRINT CLEARLY)

ADDRESS

APT.#   CITY

STATE/PROV.   ZIP/POSTAL CODE

Twenty-one gets you
2 FREE BOOKS and a
FREE MYSTERY GIFT!

Twenty gets you
2 FREE BOOKS!

Nineteen gets you
1 FREE BOOK!

TRY AGAIN!

Offer limited to one per household and not valid to current Silhouette
Intimate Moments® subscribers. All orders subject to approval.

Visit us online at
www.eHarlequin.com

The Silhouette Reader Service™ — Here's how it works:

Accepting your 2 free books and gift places you under no obligation to buy anything. You may keep the books and gift and return the shipping statement marked "cancel." If you do not cancel, about a month later we'll send you 6 additional novels and bill you just $3.80 each in the U.S., or $4.21 each in Canada, plus 25¢ shipping & handling per book and applicable taxes if any.* That's the complete price and — compared to cover prices of $4.50 each in the U.S. and $5.25 each in Canada — it's quite a bargain! You may cancel at any time, but if you choose to continue, every month we'll send you 6 more books, which you may either purchase at the discount price or return to us and cancel your subscription.

*Terms and prices subject to change without notice. Sales tax applicable in N.Y. Canadian residents will be charged applicable provincial taxes and GST.

Daniel made a sound with his teeth and his cheek. "Hard to say."

"Well, you come on back at noon with the Doc, here. I'll have the wife fix you up some calf fries we saved from fall branding."

"Sounds good. See you, Nick."

"Yeah, see ya. Don't forget about them fries."

"Nope." Daniel waved as he eased Grace's truck down the dirt lane.

She had her head on the seatback, and her eyes were closed. "I'm not eating that."

Daniel smiled. The adrenaline was still pumping through him and he wanted nothing more than to pull over onto the side of this dark country road and exorcise some of it with the woman falling asleep beside him. "Do you even know what they are, city girl?"

"Yes, and I'm not eating calf testicles. I don't care if he thinks I'm a sissy."

"It's a traditional food."

She snorted. "Like blood pudding? Haggis? Tripe? Yech." She made a face with her eyes still closed. "I don't eat disgusting stuff."

"For a woman who regularly does things to animals that would make most people faint dead away, you sure have a delicate stomach."

"Hmm. Hey!" She sat up. "Can we stop at the clinic on the way back to my house? I want to get the Hollowell file. I think I know why that mare prolapsed tonight."

"Fine, but then we're stopping for breakfast. I'm half starved to death."

"Your arteries will clog if you keep eating at that café."

"Well, you can't feed me. You don't have anything in your refrigerator."

"I have cottage cheese. A bagel, I think. I have half an orange."

"I'll risk my arteries, thanks." He smacked his lips. "Besides, there's a woman at the Early Bird who bakes blueberry muffins like you wouldn't believe.'' He kept his eyes on the road. ''Not that I don't pretty much worship that body of yours, Doc, but I could really go for a woman who bakes.''

''Very funny.'' Grace closed her eyes again. ''I liked you better when you were humorless,'' she said.

Daniel drove through town and pulled in beside the back door of the clinic. Grace started to jump out. ''Can I have the keys? I'll just be a second.''

He handed her the keys, then got out and followed her to the door. She looked quizzically at him.

''I'll just be a second,'' she repeated.

''Uh-huh. I'm going to let you go into this building alone in the middle of the night.''

''It's almost six. It'll be light in twenty minutes.''

He just raised his brows at her. ''Aggravating,'' she muttered, then stuck her key in the lock, thrilled to death with this man.

The door opened before she could turn the key.

''Huh,'' she said, frowning. ''I could have sworn I locked this last night.''

He shouldered her aside. ''Go sit in the truck.''

''Right,'' she said, and crept in behind him.

Daniel went straight for her meds cabinet. The lock was undisturbed. People broke into vet clinics all the time; in many cases, drugs for animals were not discernably different than those for humans, and brought decent cash on the black market.

''The lab's still locked, and the kennels and the office are fine,'' Grace said as she came up behind him.

''I thought you said you were going to sit in the truck?''

''You need a refresher course in sarcasm.'' She looked around. ''Nothing's disturbed here.''

They returned to the back door and Grace jiggled the han

dle. "It's still locked. I must just not have pulled the door closed tightly enough."

"Huh."

"Stop grunting. It's nothing. Let's go."

"I thought you wanted Hollowell's file."

She waved it in front of him. "I got it. Mrs. Handleman may not want to touch my computer, but she keeps very good files. So—" She didn't want to ask, was unsure of the procedure. "Breakfast first. Then you probably need to get back to the ranch?"

He pulled the door closed, and checked it. It didn't seem sticky or badly hung. "No."

"No?" Her heart jumped into her throat. "Not at all?"

He shoved at the door. Nothing gave. He decided he'd buy new locks for it anyway. As the landlord, of course. "Frank's feeding the heifers this morning."

"Oh. So, that's…good."

He finally noticed her. Her hands were clasped over her file, bending it. "Do you want me to go home, Grace?"

She shrugged, shook her head. "You can do what you want."

"Because I don't particularly want to."

"Oh, well, whatever," she said nonchalantly, but one corner of her mouth kicked up.

He saw it. "Don't make me go home, Grace," he whispered at her ear, teasing her.

She pretended to consider, while her fingers tingled and her heart raced. "I need my sleep," she said.

"You can sleep. I won't touch you."

She gave him a look that made him laugh.

"Just get in the truck, Doc, before I unlock that door and see how much weight your desk can hold."

"My desk?"

He laughed again. "Your desk."

She stared at him. "You know, I'm growing oddly fond of that imagination of yours."

"Doc, honey, you ain't seen nothing."

Chapter 8

They undressed just as the weak Idaho spring sun managed to send enough light into Grace's small bedroom to gild her pale skin and shoot glimmers of gold into her brown eyes. Daniel watched her intently as she turned away from him to slide into her bed, bashful even after all they'd shared. She hadn't let him undress her, hadn't tried to rip his shirt off him again. More's the pity, he thought.

She was unsure, he could see it. So he battled back the animal that clawed at him, made him want to seize her and take her and send them both screaming into the new day. He'd be gentle, remember it was all so new to her, keep every touch and caress careful and sweet. She was so vulnerable, he thought, standing naked and fully aroused beside her bed, regarding her soberly as she tried to hold his gaze. All that long, cool babe of a body was just packaging for an uncertain, nearly innocent woman. He'd do his best to remember that.

He climbed in after her, fitting himself against her. She shifted her legs to accommodate his thoroughly indiscreet reaction to her and he almost jumped out of his skin as he felt her body against his most sensitive skin. He felt Grace shudder slightly.

"Are you cold?"

She shook her head.

"Tired?" He threaded his hands through her hair. She'd been up with Hollowell's mare all night. Maybe she just wanted sleep.

Grace shook her head again. "I'm not tired." How could she be? She thought. He was naked. Shameless. Huge.

"Are you nervous?"

She cupped his face in her hand. "No."

"You shivered," he whispered, concerned.

Her face went red, the blush starting at her ears and moving to her chest. "I'm not nervous," she repeated. She moved slightly and Daniel felt the brush of her body against his again.

A slow smile curved his lush, too beautiful mouth.

He brought his hands between their bodies, brushed at her stiff nipples. "Are you excited, Grace?"

She moaned, her eyes closing. "Yes."

He pressed his hips forward, sliding against wet satin. She whimpered and so, to his astonishment, did he.

"So am I," he murmured.

She smiled, her eyes still closed. "I can tell."

He fumbled with a condom, barely able to separate himself from her long enough to put it on. He took her hips, guided her on top of him. "I want you to ride me, Grace."

Her eyes flew open. "I don't know how to do that."

"It's not hard," he said, gasping slightly as her damp body stroked the length of his arousal.

She gave a little shimmy. "It feels like it is."

"What I meant was, it's not *difficult*," he muttered. He was close to begging. If she kept sliding against him that way he was never going to make it inside. "Grace, please."

His desperation, deeply flattering, astonishing even,

cleared away all shyness, all reserve. She took him in her hands as he took her hips in his. With a guttural groan he surged upward before she had time to guide him. He knew where he wanted to be, Grace thought, giddy with the still-new feel of him inside her, and he wasn't willing to wait until she managed it. She nearly climaxed from the excitement of being so urgently, recklessly desired.

Daniel pushed up into her body, watched her sink down to meet him, watched her neck arch and her mouth open, her eyes glaze and her breasts tighten. It took away his breath and a good, carefully hoarded measure of his reserve against her.

He had the strangest sensation he was in over his head with this golden-skinned and eager woman. He was suddenly afraid she was going to want much more than he'd bargained for. And that he'd try—and fail—to give it to her.

"What do you want, Grace?" he heard himself murmur.

She misunderstood him. She was not thinking about the future or what she'd want when this was over, what he'd want. She was only aware of sensation, of her body and his. She ran her hands up her torso, cupped her breasts in her palms and offered them for him to suckle. "Move inside me, Daniel," she breathed. "Move—ah, yes, like that."

His brain dimmed at her request and he surged up from the bed to feast on her, indistinct anxiety fading in the strong pull of lust. She bucked violently when he sucked her nipple, hard, into his mouth and he met her downward thrust with an upward one of his own.

She rode him as no woman ever had. He struggled to keep his eyes from slamming shut so he could watch the smooth, strong motion of her thighs, the contractions of her taut stomach, the supple bowing of her body. She might not have done this before, he thought, his fingers digging into the soft flesh of her pistoning hips, but she was clearly a natural.

Grace was certain she would not be able to bear the pleasure, that it would kill her before it fulfilled its promise. But she was wrong. She felt the strongest, strangest building inside her, as if every cell and nerve ending was heating and tingling and pooling low in her belly, as though there was nothing left of her but the one amazing sensation centered where her body met the pounding flesh of Daniel's.

She didn't die. She exploded instead, blew apart, stunning herself and her lover by screaming out loud with the impact of it.

Daniel watched her with slitted eyes, and thought about cattle futures, tried to remember the five-day weather forecast, ran the words to *Yankee Doodle Dandy* inside his head. Anything to keep from following her in. He wanted more. He wanted to give her more.

When she trembled a long, last time and collapsed on top of him, he flipped her expertly onto her back and took her face between his hands.

"I want to see that again."

Grace shook her head, dazed. "I can't," she moaned. "Please, Daniel. I can't."

He smiled ruthlessly. "You can."

She did, and not once more, but twice, before he shuddered and groaned and spilled inside her. She was utterly astonished by the fortitude of her body and by the unbelievable skill and patience and endurance of his.

"You'll kill us both," she commented after a minute, running her hands idly down his broad back. She began to count the muscle structures with her fingertips.

He was a dead weight on top of her, but he managed to chuckle back in his throat. "You're just tired from foaling that mare. Sissy."

She grinned at her ceiling, wondering for the first time since she'd stepped back through her front door how she could possibly be making love in the middle of the morning with as gorgeous a man as Daniel Cash. It was too inconceivable to be real. Yet here he was, sweating all over her, his body twitching and softening inside hers. "No, it's you. I'm terrified by how well you do this."

"Don't be," he rumbled against her neck. "I learned from a manual, I swear."

She laughed. "I don't know whether that's a relief or just really sick."

He placed a wet, sucking kiss on her shoulder. "Which would make you hot?" he asked, leering at her.

"Neither, you pervert," she said, laughing so hard now her chest shook. "Leave me alone. I'm finished with you."

He was enjoying the game, enjoying her. Entirely too much, it occurred to him, but he brushed the niggling thought aside as he watched her pretty little breasts jiggle slightly.

"Come on, Grace. Let's hear it. What would make you hot?"

"Clearly, you already know," she demurred. "You just proved it."

"Three times," he gloated.

She rolled her eyes. "I cannot believe you keep track like that."

"Who's going to if I don't?" He took his weight on his hands and knees. He started kissing her neck, smiling against her damp skin. "Talk dirty to me, Grace. Tell me what would make you hot."

"I will not," she said primly, but then he hit a sensitive little spot and she couldn't help the sigh.

"You like when I kiss you."

"Of course." Of their own accord, her arms wrapped around his neck.

He murmured encouragement. A minute ago he'd been playing around. Now he really, *really* wanted to know. What made Grace McKenna crazy? He so wanted to make her crazy.

"And when I kiss your breasts," he said, moving his

mouth to gently caress the pink tips of her breasts. "And when I suck them."

She lifted half off the bed. "Daniel," she gasped.

He rolled a nipple around his tongue. "You're so sensitive. I touch you and you just go off like a rocket."

"I know."

Daniel heard the chagrin in her voice, decided not to let her get away with it. Even if he had to embarrass her a little. "Like out at the ranch. You were so wet."

"Oh, no," she moaned.

"Oh, yeah." He licked her between her breasts. "I've had erotic dreams about it every night since. You without your pants on, rolling around in my front yard. Those long legs, Grace. I can't get over those long legs."

"Stop it, Daniel," she said breathlessly, aroused by his tongue, mortified by his words.

"I won't stop it, Grace." He made love to her other breast, taking his time. "Because you don't seem to understand how sexy you are."

"I'm not." She was an oddity, a novelty. She understood that perfectly and was, to her shame, willing to be that for him as long as he wanted. When he tired of novelty, she'd join a convent or something.

"You are. You are," he repeated. "I love the way you taste. I can't get enough of the way you taste."

He was trying to, she thought. Her head moved restlessly on her pillow as he brazenly, drowsily licked his way down her body. He took a long, slow detour at her belly button, then went shockingly south.

"Does this turn you on, Grace?" He looked up, saw her eyes squeezed shut, her hands fisted into the sheets. He dipped his tongue between her thighs and took a leisurely swipe. "You can tell me, Grace. I won't be shocked."

"I've never—" She couldn't catch her breath.

"What?" He took another lingering lick. "This?"

She shook her head, unable to beg him but wanting to,

tortured by his tongue, mesmerized by his teasing, sexy voice. She knew, dimly, what he was doing, but she had never imagined seduction could be so carnal, so thrillingly naughty.

"Grace?"

There was a long hesitation, and then she nodded, her face red, her breathing ragged. "I'm just curious, you understand," she managed to rasp.

"And naturally so," he said, smiling. The scent of her was driving him crazy. "I'm a little curious myself."

"You've never done it?"

He wished he hadn't, wished, at least in this, he'd been as innocent as she. He shook his head. "Not with you," he murmured, kissing her lightly at the top of her thighs.

"Do you think I'm perverted?" she asked.

"Yes," he'd said, smiling though his body screamed. He used his thumbs to open her. "Lucky for me."

He brought her to peak again in minutes with his mouth, then, unable to resist the urge, slipped inside her slick and shivering body and rocked with her until he, too, felt the sweet, enervating completion.

They stumbled out of the bedroom a few minutes later, oddly refreshed by the sex and ravenous, their big bodies craving food even more—for the moment—than each other. They scrambled eggs, toasted and split the single bagel she had in her refrigerator, and brewed coffee with silent, single-minded purpose. And left Grace's small kitchen looking as if it had suffered through a small typhoon.

"How old are you?"

He looked up from his eggs. "Thirty. Why?"

She colored. "No reason."

His slow grin of comprehension turned into a self-satisfied smirk. "You should have known me when I was eighteen."

"Oh, brother," she said, but he caught her smile. "That wasn't even what I was talking about."

He laughed. "Sure it was."

She gave him a prissy look, which made him laugh, and looked vaguely back at the kitchen. "I'm still hungry. I'd kill for a delivery pizza."

"Nobel ain't the big city, little lady," he said in his best cowboy voice.

She giggled foolishly, rose from her chair, kissed the top of his head lightly. "It has some advantages, however."

"That's what I've always thought," he agreed smugly. He leaned back in his chair, watched her as she put her dish in the sink and started straightening the mess they'd made of the kitchen.

He was comfortable here, with her. More than he'd been with any woman since Julie, he mused, bringing his coffee mug to his lips and studying Grace's bottom as she bent to scrape eggshells into the trash. Maybe even more than with Julie, because he'd always been slightly competitive with his wife. He didn't feel competitive with Grace. Or, anyway, no more than usual. He smiled slightly to himself. Okay, he felt damned competitive, but he could get over it.

The sex was remarkable, of course. No getting over the sex. He tried to catch a glimpse of the length of her legs in her frumpy terry-cloth robe, and wondered idly if he could untie the belt with one hand.

He liked her. She made him laugh. And he was comfortable with her.

His coffee cup bobbled in his hand.

Oh, hell.

Abruptly, in the same sort of flash of self-preservation he'd felt earlier while they'd been making love, he knew, if he wasn't careful, he could stay with this long, cool drink of water. And staying with her would make him what he was before. Vulnerable, a target for the fates, a man who could be destroyed, right down to his heart.

He was never going to be that man again. And if it meant leaving Grace McKenna and her warm kitchen and her warm bed, well, hell, he'd leave her. He could do it.

He hesitated as she bent to peer into her nearly empty refrigerator, ignoring the low hum in his blood as she slicked her tongue over her lips.

He *would* do it.

"There's nothing here," she rumbled crossly. "How can there be not one single thing here?"

He stood. "I should go."

She turned, blinked. "I could go to the store."

He hardened his already cooling heart against the picture she made. Mussed hair, unfocused eyes, soft, soft smile. "I have to get back to the ranch."

"Oh."

"Frank—" he began, then stopped. He didn't need an excuse. He'd made no promises. "I should go."

"Okay." She kept her face carefully blank. She'd known he would go, of course. No reason to make a scene.

"I had a good time." God, that sounded obscene in his own ears.

Grace nodded. "Me, too. Thanks for helping me with Hollowell's mare."

"No problem." He shoved his hands into his pockets, wished like hell for the buttons on his shirt. He felt suddenly self-conscious, exposed. How the hell had it come to this? He wanted her, sure. But he didn't not want to feel anything for her. He knew if he didn't get out, right now, he would. And he wasn't ever going to risk himself for love again. The first time had almost killed him.

"Grace, listen—" he began.

She shook her head, smiled. "Oh, no, I don't want to do this."

He scrubbed at his whiskered face, at a loss. "It was fun," he said, knowing how feeble, how lame, that sounded.

"I know."

"You were amazing," he offered, then winced when she squinted at him, her mouth pursed in a rueful parody of a smile.

"I'm thrilled you think so."

"I can't stay with you."

She heard a deeper meaning in the statement. Knew as well as she knew her own name and the treatment for canine distemper that he didn't mean just today.

"That's fine."

"I don't mean to hurt you."

"You're not," she assured him, and wished fervently that he'd go before she burst into tears, humiliating both of them. "I'm a big girl, Daniel," she reminded him. And that, she thought bitterly, was the crux of it.

"I'll see you around, I'm sure."

Oh, she hated him for that one. She found some satisfaction that he shifted uncomfortably under her glare. "I'll call you with the results of the serum tests."

"Okay." He nodded curtly. He started down the hallway to retrieve his shoes, stopped dead, pivoted. "You were right, back at the ranch. We're not a good idea. I'm not ready for anything serious." *Nor will I ever be,* he thought, miserable.

Grace nodded calmly. She'd let him ramble, stumble, make excuses. But she knew the truth. A woman like her was an interesting kind of diversion, but no one wanted "anything serious" with a freak, an ambitious giant with a plain face and huge feet. Men wanted a woman who would draw the *right* kind of attention.

She'd been damned careful all her life to not be anyone's novelty, anyone's unique, peculiar distraction. Daniel had been right when he'd generously suggested she'd probably had offers before. She had. But she'd always refused them, knowing them for what they were. She was not going to be any man's "I once had sex with the tallest woman in the West" tavern story. She winced thinking about it. She would kill Daniel Cash if he made her into something so trivial after all she'd felt with him.

But no, he wouldn't. She clearly could not trust him with

her heart, but she could trust him with her secrets. After all, he'd been honest with her from the start, and it was a lucky thing, too. She'd been careful; just her body was involved now, not her heart. It would have been really sort of tragic if she'd involved her heart.

"Daniel, just go," she said as casually as she could manage. "It's ridiculous to have this conversation. We never made any promises. Let's just see this for what it was and be happy."

It was exactly what he'd hoped she'd say. He could not for the life of him figure out why it didn't make him feel better. "I know this was your first time," he said softly. "I just want you to know that it was special for me, too."

Grace smiled coolly. "That's very nice, Daniel. But I'm twenty-seven years old. I had to lose my virginity sooner or later. Let's not attach import to it neither of us feel."

Daniel felt that like a slap. He studied her carefully for a minute, then nodded. He knew it was nobody's fault but his own that she'd gone still and calm and reasonable, when literally minutes before she'd been like a long wand of fire in his arms. He knew the kind of chilly, carefully enunciated absolution she was offering him was just what he was looking for. He simply didn't know why it made him feel like such an ass. "Okay."

"Okay," she said, a little too brightly.

He paused at her tone. "I don't want to leave you angry."

She cocked her head, gave him a dazzling smile that thinned her lips and sharpened her eyes. "But you do want to leave me, Daniel, and that's the only decision you get to make about it."

Grace dropped her laptop and her briefcase down onto her desk and reached for the lab coat on the hook behind her office door. She let herself into her locked laboratory and pulled the blood cultures marked Cash Cattle from their shelf.

Setting them aside, she pulled on a mask and gloves, smiling wryly to herself. God, it was a relief to be at work, where she was sure of herself. She'd wanted to come in Sunday and do this, but had forced herself to stay home instead, doing laundry and other neglected, domestic chores. She'd gone to Nobel's only grocery store and bought a hundred dollars' worth of food, then cooked herself a huge meal she didn't eat. She'd driven out again to check Hollowell's mare and was treated to a hearty platter of fried calf testicles, which she declined as politely as possible by telling her hostess she was allergic to testicles, something that had made both Hollowells howl with laughter. She'd cleaned her house and washed her truck and endured the weekend as though it were a death march, and it was finally over.

Now it was time to get back to work, thank God. Back to the life she'd come to Nobel, Idaho, to make for herself. She was fully resolved to forget Daniel Cash and his mobile, expert mouth and his rough, sensitive hands and his big—

Wait, she was forgetting all that, she told herself sternly.

She'd be a grown-up about the whole thing; grateful to him for introducing her so skillfully to lovemaking, appreciative of his clever mind, mildly fond of his vaguely appealing masculine personality. And that was it. There was no way in hell she was going to have a broken heart. No way in hell.

She smeared a slide with a culture, felt an almost palpable comfort in being back where she belonged. Being a veterinarian was something she knew she was good at, something she was proud of. Being a woman had turned out to be exactly as she'd feared since she hit puberty; embarrassing and ultimately unfulfilling. No more forays into sultry bedrooms with sexy men, she determined, her forehead creasing in concentration. She'd stay in her lab, or with her animals, in her coveralls and clunky boots, and she'd never again try to be a woman she wasn't.

She fit a glass slide into her microscope and checked the

Cash heifer's blood serum results. Frowning, she sat up in her chair. That couldn't be right. She rubbed her eyes, leaned over and looked through her microscope again. No. Not possible.

She made another slide, and another and another. She checked them all, then made a half dozen slides more and checked them, too. Disbelieving, stunned, she went through them all again, dread and dismay deepening at each damning result. It took her more than an hour, closed up in her lab, to be sure. She didn't notice the time, or the tension building at the back of her neck with every passing minute; she wanted to be sure. Had to be.

At ten, she cleaned up, left the lab, walked through the office to say good morning to Lisa and Mrs. Handleman, and then went back and checked the slides again.

They were unchanged. The relief she'd felt at coming back into her office dissolved, and she was left with a sick, hollow ache in the pit of her stomach that had nothing at all to do with heartbreak. The distinctive brucella bacterium was present in the blood of almost every bred heifer belonging to Cash Cattle, Incorporated.

Brucellosis. Grace could hardly believe it. The disease had been completely eradicated in Idaho years earlier, making it a brucellosis-free state. Now she had an armful of blood samples sitting in her lab that could damage the reputation of an entire state of cattle producers, and destroy one of them altogether.

She went into her office, rubbed her eyes until she thought she might push her eyeballs back into her skull, and forced herself to pick up the phone.

She spoke briefly, with professional detachment, to the man on the other end of the line, while her fingers drummed impatiently on her desk and her knees jumped nervously. She had to get to Daniel. As soon as she'd covered the legal bases, she went through her files until she found what she was looking for, and made another call. Her voice was even, but in her head was a litany. She had to get to Daniel. Had to get to him.

She hung up the phone again after several minutes, picked up her briefcase, and without a word, left the office.

Grace drove recklessly out to Daniel's ranch, covering the eleven country miles in far less time than was normally required, and was relieved to see Daniel's broad-shouldered outline near the barn. She wouldn't have to hunt him down, could ruin his life in time for lunch, she thought, furious with the whole insane, improbable situation.

Daniel saw her vet truck come barreling down the road, kicking up gravel on its way. He squinted into the late-morning sunlight, annoyed that the sight of her came as such a profound pleasure.

He knew why she was here. He'd been thinking about her—with regret and lust and fondness all jumbled together until they were a vague sting just under his breastbone—and he wasn't surprised she'd been thinking about him. He'd left too abruptly Saturday morning, had been stunned into a rash departure by the revelation that he was on the verge of making a big mistake with Grace McKenna.

Mistakes were something Daniel avoided. He didn't want another blemish on the record of his life; didn't want another rumor circulated through the Nobel gossip hotline, another pitying look or curious glance shot his way. Professionally, he was a cautious man. He took risks just by being in the cattle business, of course, but manageable risks, ones he could calculate. Compared to his personal life, though, his professional life made him look like a riverboat gambler. Personally, he was as wary as a nun in a honky-tonk. After Julie had left him at the scene of his professional disgrace, he'd had the occasional affair. But he'd never let down his guard, and he wasn't about to with the lady vet. If she'd come to the ranch to have it out with him over that decision, so be it. He wouldn't—couldn't—give her what she wanted.

The passion that had driven him all his life, the emotion and intensity that had swept him along, were stone-cold inside him. They'd started a slow, lingering dissolution years before, in that dean's office, and had dissolved completely when his wife of seven months had told him she wanted no part of his disgrace and left him reeling and lost in some small, pitiless airport in eastern Washington. It had been fatal, he thought. Failure upon failure—unjust, humiliating and public failure—had dealt a fatal blow to passion and emotion and intensity.

Grace still believed in love, he'd seen it in her eyes that morning. She still believed in everything. If he wasn't careful, she'd start believing in him, and his track record had proven beyond a doubt that he was not a man whose future could be trusted.

Grace pulled her pickup up next to him, automatically calculating how long it would take the vets from the Idaho Department of Agriculture Animal Industries Division to get from the local office in Payton out to Daniel's ranch. She had a few minutes yet, to tell him his life was about to be destroyed.

Daniel leaned in her open window, his sleeves rolled up in deference to the uncharacteristically warm, windless spring day. She gave herself a moment before she blurted it out, and stared at those wonderfully muscled forearms.

"Hey," he said. "You're out of the clinic early."

"Daniel, I have to talk to you."

"Sure." He caught the nervous tremor in her voice and steeled himself. He'd made his decision, years before he'd even met Grace McKenna. He'd stick to it, whether her voice trembled or not. "Come on in. I should clean up."

She put her hand on his arm to keep him there. "Daniel, where are you keeping those heifers?"

He narrowed his eyes. "Sorry?"

"The bred heifers you're selling. The ones I bled Friday."

"I know what heifers you're talking about." He felt a greasy chill slide down his spine. He understood foreboding, had understood it for years. "What the hell is going on, Grace?"

They saw the dust boil up at the same time, Grace through her side mirror and Daniel from the corner of his eye. Two more trucks, and a car behind.

"Well, hell." Daniel watched the oncoming vehicles. The hole opening in his stomach was cold, jagged, a damp, rocky little ulcer, and it made him want to double over. He returned his gaze to Grace. "What's happened?"

She grasped his arm, but he pulled it away. She took that as only natural and tried not to be hurt. "I found brucella bacterium in the blood serum tests from your heifers."

He stared at her, unwilling to break eye contact even though the state vehicles were already parking behind hers, emptying of the men who would ruin his life. Again.

"You made a mistake," he said coldly.

"I checked it four times, Daniel."

"Howard Cash?"

Daniel did not look away from Grace. "I'm Daniel Cash. I'm cattle foreman and co-owner of Cash Cattle."

"Well, Mr. Cash, I'm Phil Brown, from the Idaho Department of Agriculture Animal Industries Division. We have a report from Dr. Grace McKenna, the veterinarian of record for the County of Nobel, Idaho, of an outbreak of brucellosis in your herd."

Daniel's green eyes went icy. He did not so much as look at the officious man next to him. "She's wrong. I do not have Bangs in my herd." He couldn't. It was impossible. He could not fail again.

"Daniel." Grace reached for the door handle, would have gotten out to stand beside him, but he pushed against the door, straight-armed. "Daniel, let me out."

"I don't want you on my ranch."

"I'm afraid Dr. McKenna is the vet of record, Mr. Cash," the state Ag man repeated reasonably.

"I don't care. She's mistaken in her diagnosis." Grace shook her head slowly, but Daniel was unmoved. "My heifers were vaccinated at eight months, right after they were weaned. She had the records in her office."

As bravely as she could, she kept her eyes on his. "You're right. I checked them. I even called Dr. Niebaur to confirm. He remembers doing it. He suggested there must have been something wrong with the vaccine. It may have been heated in transport, or mismarked at the animal supply lab. I'd have to do tests on the vaccine to prove that, of course, and that's impossible, but I would have to agree with him."

"I don't care if there was nothing but horse urine in those vaccine bottles," Daniel stated.

Her lips thinned. "I have one hundred and twenty blood serum tests back in my lab that show brucella bacterium."

Daniel stared at Grace for a full minute, the air in his lungs like mud, making it hard to breathe. No. It couldn't be true. This was impossible. Daniel saw all the work of the last three years, all the rebuilding of his shattered life, crumbling. Irrationally, he blamed her. He'd trusted this woman, and she was destroying him.

Well, he wouldn't let her. He was stronger than this. He was certainly stronger than she was. He was Daniel Cash. He turned to the man next to him, ruthlessly turning the frost in his gut from fear to cold determination.

"Have you checked the agglutination tests?" This time, he would not go down. He'd sacrifice everything for it not to be true, including her. "This is Dr. McKenna's first couple weeks in her own practice. There is likelihood her lab procedures are faulty."

Oh, a killing blow. Grace felt it go all the way to the marrow of her bones. She understood why he'd said it. It made no difference. She shoved at the door with all her strength.

"Let me out, you bastard," she hissed between her teeth.

He released his hold against the door. She got out of the truck and stood, not beside him as she'd wanted to, but against him. She knew her job, and her wounded heart meant nothing at the moment.

"They're checking my results in their own lab," she said tightly. "In the meantime, we have to quarantine your herd. And my being in practice two weeks has nothing to do with it."

"I know the drill, Doc," he said through his teeth. "You've made a mistake." He would allow nothing else to be true; would, through sheer conviction, head this all off before it took him down. "Those heifers are in their second trimester, and not one has aborted."

"I can't explain that," she admitted. "But if they test positive, they have to be destroyed. It's the law."

"I know the law," he said flatly, sickened. If his heifers were positive, then likely the entire herd was infected. His whole herd, slaughtered. Gone. His job, his future, the security of his parents' retirement, everything he'd been working for—including his reputation, already savaged once—wiped out. He turned to the men who stood with Grace against him. "Test them again."

"We plan to do that, Mr. Cash," said the man closest to him. "Until that time, however, your cattle are quarantined. They may not be sold, grazed or otherwise removed from this property. We've contacted the Bureau of Land Management office in Boise. You are to remove all cattle grazing on spring range and return them within the next twenty-four hours to your ranch, where they, too, will be tested." He took a deep breath, plunged onward through his official speech. "There will be three blood serum tests on each animal. If all three consecutive tests are negative, your herd will be declared Bangs-free."

He didn't say what Daniel already knew; three positive tests and the financial and professional prospects of his entire family would be destroyed, right along with the cattle.

"Anyone sharing your B.L.M. allotment is also entitled to testing at your expense."

"No one shares my land management allotment," Daniel said curtly. At least he wouldn't have that on his conscience. He forced himself to not look at Grace. He'd trusted her to test his heifers, and she'd screwed it up. Thank God, none of his neighbors would have to pay the price for that. He swung around on his heel and strode off toward the heifer pen. Over his shoulder he shouted, "I'll have the heifers in the chute in fifteen minutes. Be ready."

He moved with chilling competency, and had the heifers in the pen leading to the squeeze chute in ten minutes. He used the extra five to hunt down his father and his brother. He found them together.

"Dad. Frank," he barked. They were in the kitchen of his parents' house, leaned against opposite countertops, arms folded in front of them. An argument, Daniel surmised in the moment he gave himself to observe. "Get out to the chute and help me run the heifers through again."

"Daniel," Howard said, pushing himself from the counter, "what's wrong, son?"

"The state Ag boys are here. They're quarantining our herd. Frank, before you come out, call Doug and Ennis, tell them we need a couple riders to go out with us—" he looked at his watch; by the time he got the heifers run through and tested again, it would be too late to ride the desert tonight "—first thing in the morning. Call Dale, too. And Cal. Have them bring out whoever they can find. Full wages. I want everybody saddled and ready to go before dawn. We have to get the whole herd off the desert before three o'clock tomorrow afternoon."

As an afterthought, a painful one, he said, "And call Barness in Missoula. We won't be delivering those heifers this week. If he doesn't want to wait on us, he'll have to buy someplace else. Tell him—tell him we're sorry.''

Frank lunged for the phone without a word or question, and Daniel was grateful. Barness was one of his best customers. Three negative tests or not, he'd probably never buy from Cash Cattle again. Neither would anyone else who heard of this scare. Even a rumor of Bangs in a herd was enough to ruin a cattle operation. He blew out a long breath.

"Dad, you coming?"

"Why the hell are they quarantining the herd, Daniel?"

"Brucellosis."

"My God, no."

"It's a mistake, Dad. I'd bet my life on it." Daniel hit the door running. It occurred to him, as he saw his vet conferring with the other veterinarians from Animal Industries, that he had already made a bet almost as important as that.

Chapter 9

The lab at the Animal Industries Department confirmed her diagnosis of brucellosis in the blood samples she'd taken from Daniel's heifers. Phil Brown called Grace at home to tell her.

They'd check their own samples after the two-day incubation period, and let her know the results, he said. Would she, as the county vet, please inform Mr. Cash, and check to make certain he was following the quarantine instructions?

Wonderful. The headache that had dogged her since her short but rather intense crying jag on the way into town from his ranch earlier in the evening jumped up a couple notches in severity. One more horrible task today and she'd be blinded by it, Grace thought.

She picked up the phone and dialed Daniel's number. It rang ten times before she hung up and called his parents' house. It rang once, was snatched up.

"Hello?"

"Oh. Liz." The sweet and friendly voice of Daniel's

mother took her back. She'd been expecting the growl of one of her sons.

"Yes?"

"This is Grace. Dr. McKenna. I'm sorry to be calling so late."

"Grace. How are you, dear?"

"I'm okay, Liz. I'm sorry about today."

"I'm sorry I raised such a hothead."

"Oh. It's—" Grace had nothing to say to that, nothing that wouldn't open a wound she was desperately trying to sew shut "—it's to be expected, I suppose."

"I don't think so. I'd hoped I raised him better than that."

Grace felt the tears burning her throat again, felt the headache escalate. "It doesn't matter."

"Oh, Grace, honey," Liz said softly.

The sympathy in Daniel's mother's voice nearly undid Grace. She worked her throat for a minute, digging for the professionalism that had got her through this afternoon. It was almost gone, she knew, but there had to be enough left to see her through one more phone call. "I need to speak with Daniel, please, Liz. Is he there?"

"Yes. And, Grace, what Daniel said today? About not being on the ranch? Well, sugar, I own a quarter of Cash Cattle and you're welcome here anytime. And I know Howard feels the same way."

"Oh. Well."

"I'll let you talk to Danny now."

"Thank you."

Daniel met his mother scowl for scowl as he reached for the phone she held out to him. He covered the receiver with his palm.

"Thanks, Mom."

His mother didn't flinch. "Serves you right," she whispered fiercely.

Daniel put the phone to his ear. "Yeah?" he said, his

word a short, clipped chunk of ice working its way from between his teeth.

That chill was all it took to snap Grace's spine straight. "The Animal Industries lab tested the serum samples I took Friday. They check out."

Daniel pulled his lips between his teeth and took a deep breath in through his nose. He blew it out again. "Okay. When do they test the new samples?"

"Wednesday. I'll call you."

"Fine."

"I have to come out tomorrow."

"Why?"

She fought back the urge to cringe at his angry question. A natural reaction for her, to round her shoulders and make of herself the smallest possible target. But she wasn't doing that anymore, she reminded herself. She bristled instead. "I'm the vet of record. I have to make sure you're following quarantine instructions."

"You don't trust me?"

The bitter little laugh, unprofessional though it was, was out of her before she knew it. "I don't think that's a particularly fair question, coming from you."

"What the hell is that supposed to mean?" he bellowed at her, though he knew perfectly well. He'd been haunted by her face all evening. It was why he was still here, pacing the night away in his parents' kitchen, keeping them awake. He couldn't go home, face the quiet devastation he'd put on Grace's pale, pretty face. The image of her swam in front of his eyes even now, hours later, and he dug his fingers into them, trying to make it disappear.

"I don't want to talk about this with you," Grace said.

"Tough. I think I deserve an explanation for that remark," he shouted, taking the well-traveled path of men everywhere: the best offense was almost always a good defense.

"I think, Daniel, that you certainly know what I'm talking

about.'' She forced her heart and breathing to slow. Her voice was a little quavery, but there was nothing to be done about that. ''I'll be out in the morning.''

''Wait a minute— Dammit!'' He slammed the receiver back into its hook. Then, when that gave him no satisfaction, he took the high road. And punched a hole in his mother's kitchen wall. ''Dammit!'' he shouted again, but this time as much for the useless pain in his fist as anything else. He glared for a minute at the hole he'd just made, his jaw working. Then he turned to his mother. ''I'll patch that.''

''Okay, honey.''

''Look, don't be nice to me now, Mom.'' He dropped his head back, closed his eyes. ''I don't need sympathy.''

She pursed her lips. ''You're beating yourself up enough. I've decided you don't need my help.''

''She's wrong about all this mess. She's got to be wrong.''

''We all hope she's wrong, Danny.'' Howard got up from the kitchen table and poured himself another cup of coffee. ''But that's no excuse for what you did to her out there.''

''If her lab standards are faulty, the department of agriculture needed to know,'' he insisted, though his argument held little heat. ''Those samples could have been contaminated in any number of ways. She's only been in practice two weeks,'' he repeated for his own peace of mind, being stubborn, feeling miserable.

''That's true,'' Frank said from the door. He'd been away from the ranch since they'd fed the heifers, and as always after an evening in town, his eyes were bright, his pupils in pinpoints. He toed off his boots, walked in his socks to the coffeepot. ''And how much of those two weeks has she spent in bed with you?'' he asked casually.

Daniel was across the kitchen in the blink of an eye. He grabbed his brother's collar and twisted it in his fist, shoving him against the wall.

"Say anything like that again, and I'll put your nose through the back of your skull."

"Daniel!" his mother cried, rushing toward them. Howard caught her by her wrist and hauled her to a stop.

Frank wearily met his brother's furious glare. At that moment it occurred to Daniel that Frank possibly didn't care whether Daniel broke his nose or not. The significance of that barely penetrated his self-absorption.

"My point is, Danny," Frank said quietly, "that whether she's been in practice two weeks or two decades, she's something more to you than just the county vet." He raised his eyebrows, his expression contemptuous. "And you turned on her like a dog."

"Hell." Daniel loosened his grip on his brother, dropped his chin to his chest in defeat. "Hell."

Frank nudged him aside, got his cup of coffee. Daniel stood staring at his back for a moment, then started for the door.

"Danny, hold up there, son," his father said.

"I think she's wrong about all this, Dad. I have to think that. The alternative—" He shook his head quickly. "But Frank's right. I should go talk to her."

"Not tonight," Howard said firmly. "We've got about eight hundred head of cattle to get off the range in the next twenty hours, and now's not the time to go tearing off to town." He went to Daniel, put his broad hand at the back of his son's neck and squeezed. "Get some sleep, son."

Daniel shook off the comforting gesture. "I can't, Dad," he said as he grabbed his coat and headed out the door. He wouldn't sleep, he knew. He had to talk to Grace, though he wasn't at all sure what he'd say once he got to her.

He couldn't recant, because he did believe she'd made a mistake in her lab. He had to believe that, particularly now that the Ag department had confirmed the presence of bacterium in the original samples. If he didn't believe it, then all this would become a terrible, crushing reality, rather than someone's blunder. And that prospect he could not—would not—face. Not even for Grace.

Her house was dark when he arrived and he sat in his truck for ten minutes before working up enough nerve to go to her door and knock. He saw a light flicker on in her bedroom, bleeding through to the hall.

"Who is it?"

"It's me," he barked.

There was a long hesitation before Daniel heard her turn the bolt. She opened the door and looked at him. Daniel could tell she'd been crying and was shocked by how contrite those red, puffy eyes made him feel. He'd known she was furious, had accepted that. It hadn't occurred to him she'd cry.

"What are you doing here?" she asked.

"I want to talk to you," he said gruffly, burning sentiment under bluster.

"I told you everything I know on the phone," she said.

"That's not what I— Not about that."

"Go home, Daniel." Grace started to close the door. "I'm not up to easing your conscience tonight."

He put his hand on the door and stopped it. "I don't need my conscience eased," he said stubbornly.

She studied him for a minute. "Fine. My mistake. Go home, anyway."

"I can't go home." He couldn't stop himself. He reached up, ran the pad of his thumb gently under her eye. "You've been crying," he murmured, guilt-stricken.

She shook off his hand. "Don't do that."

Daniel shoved his hands into his pockets. She clearly didn't want him touching her, and he was sure he didn't want to touch her. Sure of it. "I understand you're upset, Grace."

"I'm a doctor, Daniel. I don't get personally involved in these things," she lied smoothly.

He was taken aback by her calm response. "Then what the hell was that all about on the phone? About me not trusting you?"

"Do you trust me?"

He took careful tack. "It's not a matter of that. It's a matter of you being human. Of you making a mistake."

"You think I could contaminate forty blood samples with brucella bacterium and not know it?"

Daniel shook his head, frustrated. "How do I know? I've never been in your lab. I don't know what you're doing in there."

"Well, I'm not trying to ruin you, Daniel." She tried to close the door again but it was like pushing at the gates of the Panama Canal. He held it open with no effort at all. It galled her.

"I don't think that," he said.

"You just think I'm an idiot."

"I don't think that, either."

"Daniel, it's one or the other."

He watched her for a minute, watched those fine brown eyes flash at him and the wide, firm set of her shoulders and the almost imperceptible lines of pain and fatigue around her beautiful mouth.

"I don't trust you," he said finally.

She nodded, turned without speaking and started toward her kitchen, leaving the door open. She'd rather face a town full of burglars than spend another moment with him.

Daniel strode through the open door, catching her in two long strides. He wrenched her around, one broad hand encircling her strong, slender upper arm.

She flicked a glance to his hand and back, giving him a chilling stare. "Get your hands off me," she said quietly.

The look she gave him made him desperate. He couldn't have said why. "I want to explain."

"You don't have to."

"This had nothing to do with you, personally."

"I beg your pardon? Did I hear you correctly?" She went up on her toes, quiet acceptance and the lie of professional detachment falling away like sand. She was furious now. Her lips pulled across her teeth. "Nothing to do with me personally? Are you out of your mind?"

"You're making this about you and me. It isn't."

"No, it isn't about me and you. It's only about you!" she shouted at him. "It's about you being so afraid of failure, you're willing to do whatever it takes to make it so it isn't true."

"It *isn't* true!"

"Yes, Daniel, it is. You have brucellosis in your herd, and it's not my fault. But you're willing to throw me to the wolves, humiliate and hurt me, so you can live a couple more days pretending everything will clear up. As your vet, as your friend, I want to help you, but you never even gave me a chance. You went for my throat the instant you saw a problem."

"This isn't just a problem, Grace!" He took in a great, shuddering breath. It unmanned him, admitting it, but she deserved the truth. "This is my life. If I lose this, there's nothing left for me. The only two things I know, the only things I ever wanted to do, will have been taken from me. Do you think that's an easy thing for me to face?"

"No! I don't think it is. But I'm not Julie. I wouldn't have abandoned you the minute things got tough. You didn't have to push me away. I could have helped you. As a good friend."

"I don't need a good friend, Grace," he yelled at her. "I need a good vet."

If he could have taken back the words, he would have, because he could see the impact of them. She literally reeled on her feet. But he stood resolute, trying to shield himself from shame with righteous conviction.

"I am a good vet, Daniel," she said, drawing professional pride around her again. "But you're too angry and bitter and scared to see it. It's not my fault I'm here and you're there. You've blamed me from the beginning for something that never had anything to do with me.''

''I don't mean to hurt you,'' he said, feeling inexplicably wretched. ''I don't want to hurt you. But—'' his voice caught, disgracing him ''—you can't be right.''

She battled back a fresh sting of tears. She would have sworn she couldn't cry again. ''The instant you were backed against the wall, Daniel, you came out fighting. I expected that from you. I just didn't expect, after…after everything we've—'' She took a moment to pull herself together, staring at the ground at his feet. It hadn't meant as much to him as it had to her, and she be damned if she'd use their lovemaking as a way to shame him. ''I just didn't expect you to come out fighting me.''

She turned on her heel and fled down the hall. Daniel heard her bedroom door close, heard the click of a tiny lock being thumbed into place. He worked his jaw. How stupid of her to think a lock would keep him out.

He strode toward her bedroom, intent on kicking in her door, splintering it into a million pieces, forcing her to stop crying, dammit. Stop looking at him as if *he* were the one ruining everything.

He stood in the hallway, the fist he'd formed sliding silently open on her door. He leaned his forehead against the wood, his eyes closing. It was better this way, he told himself. Better she hate him, better he hang on for dear life to his suspicion and his fear.

If he didn't, God only knew what would become of them both.

The tests that came back from the Animal Industries Department were clean. Negative. Showed absolutely no trace of brucella bacterium in the blood serum.

Grace stared at Phil Brown, who sat across her desk in the little chair she kept there for client consultations.

"You're kidding."

"No. They were clean. I sent a man out this morning to bleed the heifers for the second round of tests, but the first ones are clean."

Grace shook her head, torn between a stunning relief—it was her county, her client, her adopted state, and a brucellosis outbreak would have meant the destruction of all of those things—and the beginnings of a paralyzing self-doubt. "I can't believe it."

"Neither can I. I saw your serum samples. They were loaded."

"Yes, they were. There was no chance for contamination, Phil."

"I'm not saying there was."

"But there must have been," she argued against herself, "if your samples were clean."

"Well, we'll see how this next round of tests turns out. This may be an anomaly."

Grace cocked her head, gave him a skeptical frown. "You know as well as I do, one bunch of samples loaded with bacterium and another from the same group of cattle with nothing is more than just an anomaly."

Phil cleared his throat. 'Do you, uh, keep brucella bacterium samples in your lab?"

"No. How ridiculous."

"If the second and third tests on those cattle come back clean, the only explanation can be that your samples were somehow contaminated."

"Yes."

Phil rose. "You're going to have to figure out how. Have you checked your dairy herds, possibly transmitting the bacterium from an infected cow through the use of a syringe?"

"No, of course not. I know procedure, Phil. Besides, this county is clean. The dairymen around here are like little old ladies about that kind of thing."

"What about manure?"

"Not in my lab. It's impossible."

"Well, I don't know, then." Phil shrugged, his hand on the closed door to her office. "But I'll call you, Grace, when we get these next results."

Grace nodded. "Thanks, Phil." When he opened the door, Grace caught a glimpse of Lisa passing by. "Lisa, will you please get Daniel Cash on the phone for me?"

"Why?"

Grace sighed, would have been embarrassed in front of her colleague, but was frankly too preoccupied at the moment for worries over protocol. "Could you please just call him for me?"

Lisa raised her shoulders. "Okay," she said.

A moment later the phone in Grace's office buzzed.

"Daniel."

"I heard." He gripped the cell phone in his hand. He was elated, but the sound of her voice took the blush off the victory.

"They'll take the second tests on Friday. If those are clean, they'll take more blood before the weekend. You could be clear to end the quarantine by Monday."

"That's fast."

"Everyone wants this over as quickly as possible."

"I know."

"I'll call you Friday as soon as I hear anything." There was a pause. "Congratulations, Daniel."

"Grace—" The small phone buzzed in his ear. She had a tendency to hang up on him, walk away before he was finished talking. He closed the phone, stuck it back into his pocket and restarted his four-wheeler. That was probably for the best.

Grace spent an agonizing two days waiting for the results of the second test. On the one hand, she wanted more than anything to have been wrong. On the other, she could think of no explanation why that should be so. Her lab was spotless, her procedures faultless. She'd never made a mistake like this; couldn't remember many mistakes at all. When a woman looked the way she did, she drew enough attention. There was an overwhelming need to be meticulous in everything else, so as not to draw any more.

But she must have made a mistake somewhere, because the second tests were negative.

She began searching for answers in her lab. She went over both her recorded and written notes, and could find no aberrations. She called in Lisa and Mrs. Handleman and together the three of them went over everything. The tested the autoclave, they took swabs from equipment to see if it showed signs of bacterium, they even tested slides, petri dishes, syringes, anything Grace could think of that might have made a difference in her testing procedures. And they found nothing.

"Maybe the state department of agriculture is doing something wrong," Lisa offered helpfully. "Maybe their tests are wrong."

Grace dismissed that as too slim a possibility, and continued her search for what had gone awry. When the third and final tests came back negative from the Animal Industries two days later, releasing Daniel's herd from quarantine and proving that Grace had, in fact, been wrong in her diagnosis, she knew something terrible had happened. She just for the life of her could not figure out what it was.

She took the drop-off in business over the next few days as perfectly natural, as was the fact that Daniel did not call her. He'd been right all along; she had made a horrible mistake that had almost cost him and his family generations worth of work and financial security. And everyone in the county knew it.

Her dairy calls, the mainstay of her practice and, she knew, the only way she'd survive in Nobel, declined until no one was calling at all, not even Spandell. The vet from Payton called her for records several times, and she knew her reputation had been destroyed. She visited with the occasional sick dog over the following week, spayed a couple cats, vaccinated the animals brought in by Animal Control, and spent the rest of her waking hours and sleepless nights trying to determine what had gone wrong.

Daniel came to her little house a week after his cattle were cleared from quarantine. She answered the door, already sure it was him. She was a pariah now; the few people she knew, except for Lisa, wouldn't have anything to do with her. And no one at all besides Daniel Cash would come to her house at eleven at night.

He looked amazing, and she felt the pain of that come all the way up from her chest to lodge in her throat. He looked as strong and handsome and tall as he had the first time she laid eyes on him, and she was overcome by how lonely she was, how much she missed him. Funny, she thought as she stood looking at him. She'd been alone all her life, and it had never particularly bothered her. In the weeks she'd known him, he'd somehow made that familiar sensation unbearable.

"Hello, Grace."

"Daniel."

"May I come in?"

She debated, he saw. Too bad. He couldn't go another minute without seeing her. He stepped past her before she could answer.

"We need to talk."

"Probably," she agreed, and shut the door. She folded her hands in front of her, then met his eyes squarely. "I should have called you after the final tests came back, but Phil Brown told he sent someone out to notify you. It wasn't very professional of me."

He shrugged that off. "I know why you didn't"

"I didn't think you'd want me to. I imagine you were angry I'd put you through all that."

He had been, of course. But he'd gotten over his anger.

He just couldn't seem to get over this strangling need to see her, be with her. He shrugged again. "You made a mistake. It happens."

"No, Daniel. Not to me."

"I don't want to talk about it, Grace. Let's just put it behind us."

She moved into the room, folded her arms in front of her for protection. "My practice is in a shambles, which is to be expected. I'll be leaving as soon as I can sell it."

"Leaving?" His heart stuttered against his chest. He'd been almost faint, big old boy that he was, with it pounding as it had when he'd finally got up the nerve after ten minutes on her front porch to knock on the door. But now it threatened to stop in his chest. Sell her practice? Leave Nobel? Never see him again? These past two weeks without her had nearly driven him crazy. And now she wanted to make that madness a permanent thing? "Why?"

She stared at him, incredulous. "Why? I nearly ruined you, Daniel. A diagnosis of brucellosis in a herd is a deadly serious thing." She frowned. There was always something there, at the back of her mind, when she thought of it. If only she could pull it up. She shook off the self-doubt, the anguishing recriminations she'd been plagued with for a week. "Do you think any of the dairymen around here are going to trust me after this? I've been here less than a month and I've already made a false diagnosis of one of the most serious diseases in the livestock industry."

"They'll get over it."

She laughed shortly. "No, they won't. You know that as well as I do." She studied him. "Why are you trying to talk me out of this? You've made it very clear all along this was my mistake, my fault."

He pushed a hand through his spiky, short hair. "I don't think you should give up on a whole practice because of one stupid mistake."

"It wasn't a stupid mistake," she insisted, though all evidence and even a good deal of her own self-confidence was against her. "Something happened to those serum samples, and someday I'll figure out what it was. Meanwhile, I have to make a living, pay back my parents. I clearly can't do that here, so I have no reason to stay."

He stared her down. "I can't believe you'd go."

"I can't believe you think I'd stay."

"What about us?" he shouted at her, furious, and regretted the words the instant they came out of his mouth.

"What about us?" she asked flatly.

He didn't have an answer for that, so he just kept yelling. Whatever came into his head. It seemed, at the time, the right thing to do. "You're just going to pack it in and not give this relationship a second thought?" he accused.

She stared at him. "This relationship? Are you insane?"

"What's that supposed to mean?"

"Figure it out."

He balled up his fists in frustration. "Oh, my God!" he bellowed at her. "Why do women say that?"

"Get out, Daniel."

"I'm not leaving until you talk to me."

"I'm done talking to you," she said calmly.

He glared at her, lost. "Fine," he muttered, raking his fingers across his scalp. "Fine with me." And he grabbed her by one slender wrist and yanked her against his chest. Right before his mouth slammed down onto hers, he glared at her a last time. "No more talking."

Chapter 10

She pulled back, astonished both by the fact that he'd kissed her, and by how desperately she wanted to respond. Pull him to her and forget he didn't love her, didn't trust her. Forget the humiliation and pain she'd known since she met him, and give in.

"Don't kiss me, Daniel," she whispered, wiping her mouth with the back of her hand. "We did this last time. Let an argument get out of hand."

"Is that what we did? I remember different." He kissed her again, more persuasively this time. "I remember everything."

"No." She shook her head, pushed at his chest, but her eyes stayed tightly closed. "You can't do this. Not the way you feel about me."

"How do I feel about you, Grace?" He really wanted to know. He certainly couldn't have answered that simple question himself.

"You hate me."

"My God, I don't hate you, Grace."

She searched his face. "How could you not?"

"One thing has never had anything to do with the other. I realized that the first day I met you, standing in your clinic that was supposed to be mine." He pressed against her. "I was furious you were there, but I wanted you, anyway."

"I don't understand that," she whispered.

"Well, I don't, either." He bent, hooked his elbow under her knees and lifted her into his arms. "And right now I don't care. I need you, Grace. Just let me love you."

Not love me, she wanted to correct him. But she couldn't say anything. He was kissing her, touching her, making her remember everything he'd awakened in her just a short time before.

He knew everything about her, and he used the knowledge mercilessly. He took her into her bedroom and came down on top of her on her bed. They began to work at each other's clothes. When they were skin to skin, and he had fastened his greedy mouth at her breast, the exquisite flooding of her body, the perfect arousal of her heart, scared her to death. This was more than she could contain, this feeling, and if he was here, in her bed, in her heart, for any reason other than an honest need, she knew it would destroy her.

"Daniel," she whispered desperately, a last chance to hang on to sanity, dignity. "Listen to me. Please."

He raised his head. He was dazed with the lust coursing through him, didn't want to listen to anything she might say that would make him stop.

"What, Grace? Tell me quick."

She closed her eyes, ashamed, but compelled.

"Daniel, people have looked at me all my life, and seen one kind of person. But I'm not the person people see. Just because I'm a big girl, just because I'm tall and strong doesn't mean I can't be hurt." She was speaking quietly, frantically, as though she had to get the words out but against her will, and he had to duck his ear to her mouth to hear her. "If you're doing this to humiliate me, for revenge, you will hurt me.'' Her voice hitched, her head moved back and forth on the pillow as she looked up at him. ''So badly, Daniel. So badly.''

She destroyed him. Utterly unmanned him, and he felt unfamiliar tears burn at the back of his throat. ''Grace,'' he whispered. ''No. No.'' He buried his face at her neck, breathing deeply the smell of her. ''I don't want to hurt you. I never wanted to. I wish I could tell you why I'm doing this,'' he murmured, half to himself. ''Mostly it's because I think I'm going to die if I don't.''

He kissed her then. He kissed her, Grace thought dazedly, very much as if he loved her.

Daniel wanted to reacquaint himself with her body, had spent two weeks' worth of restless nights dreaming about that very thing. But something he didn't understand drove him, and, almost before he knew it, he found himself inside her.

He clutched at her outstretched hands, stared down at her. She watched him, too, but when he began to move inside her, her chin lifted, her neck bowed, her mouth fell open and her eyes closed. The sight of her, the surrender implied by such simple movement, unhinged him, and he began to pound into her. Steadily, ruthlessly. She wouldn't leave No-bel. She belonged here, belonged to him. Why couldn't she see that?

He didn't wait for her, couldn't have if his life depended upon it, but she went with him, anyway. He spilled inside her in a long, almost painful flooding while she clenched around him like a vise. And only when he was sure everything he had, everything he was, was spent within her, did he allow his eyes to close.

He stayed until he was soft inside her, his face at her throat. He didn't want to untangle himself from her limbs, her body, her life.

''Am I hurting you?'' he whispered.

Yes, she wanted to cry out. *You're killing me.*

"No." Nevertheless, she scooted out from under him.

He flipped onto his back to stare at the ceiling with her.

"I didn't use anything. Protection. I didn't come here thinking this would happen."

"I know." She knew her body well. "It's all right. It's a safe time for me."

He felt inexplicably sorry about that. "Good."

They were quiet a minute.

"You have to go now," she said at last.

He nodded, his jaw clenching. "I know I do. What I don't know is why."

"Because I love you. And you don't love me." She closed her eyes, pitilessly fought back useless tears. "And if we do this again, I will never, ever recover."

He turned onto his side to stare down at her. "Grace—"

She met his eyes, told the truth with them. "I'm begging you, Daniel."

He watched her for a moment longer, then got out of the bed. He dressed quickly and was gone. Grace heard the front door close, but it was only after she heard his truck start in the driveway and ease into the street, that she turned her face into her pillow.

The phone was ringing when she woke. Her head was pounding and her eyes were gritty and stinging. She didn't even bother opening them as she grabbed blindly for the phone.

"Dr. McKenna," she mumbled groggily into the receiver.

"Doc, it's Frank Cash."

"Frank." She sat up in bed, wishing she'd put on a nightgown after Daniel had left, so she wouldn't be naked, his scent still clinging to her warm skin. She glanced at the clock; it was nearly noon and she hadn't even called the clinic. No matter. Her pager was on, and she didn't have a single appointment to keep. "What's the matter?"

"We got a big problem out at the ranch. Is Daniel there?"

"No."

"You better get out here."

"Why, Frank?"

"Because I have a dead cow out here. And from the way she died, I think it's pretty damn serious."

Grace closed her eyes. No, this couldn't be happening. "I'll be there in thirty minutes. Find Daniel."

The news hit the sale yard harder and faster than the twister of 1969. In five minutes—no, less than that, everyone knew.

A Cash Cattle, Incorporated, cow had just tested positive over to Doc McKenna's. And because of that whole Bangs mess, she'd had it confirmed by the Idaho Department of Agriculture Animal Industries Division.

She'd called the sale yard, spoken the word through the phone, and, faster even than bad gossip traveled or news of a lottery win hit the poor relations, everyone knew.

Anthrax. The very word was almost as deadly as the disease itself. It stopped the sale like a plug from a double-barrel shotgun. The cowboys wrangling the cattle froze, the cows bunched and clogged the slick alleyways. It stopped the auctioneer, who stood with his gavel stuck in the air and his rapid-fire voice stuck in his throat. It stopped the murmur of voices in the ring, the crack of the whip, seemed even to stop the swirl of wood shavings and dust coming from the selling floor. And it stopped Daniel Cash's heart in his broad chest.

He'd left his house before dawn, too restless even to lie in his bed and brood, and he'd decided to take the bred heifers, which, predictably, his buyer in Montana had passed on, in to the Friday sale. It had taken him all morning to transport the forty fat heifers into town, taking four loads in his horse trailer to avoid trucking costs. He never saw his brother, never saw the dying cow in the pasture.

Anthrax. No disease more deadly, none more dreaded. It

made headlines when it appeared. People died, stock was slaughtered. Whole industries fell. Entire countries were quarantined. And any man who found it in his herd was ruined.

Daniel Cash was ruined. He knew it instantly, instinctively, like he knew the sound of his father's voice and the scent at the base of his lover's throat. She'd ruined him. Not the first time, with her carelessness, but this time certainly.

He got up from the bench where he'd been sitting with the same men he'd sat with for years at these Friday sales; the same men his father had sat with. They didn't say a word to him as he passed, just pulled in their knees and let him by. No one spoke at all, in fact. The cows bawled at being separated from their calves, the calves bawled from missing their mamas, and all the odd buck goats and dry sows and stud colts that ran through a Nobel County Friday stock sale made their own noises to signal their dissatisfaction with the whole mess, but there wasn't a human voice to be heard. The fates had annihilated Daniel Cash yet again, and everyone knew it.

Several men reached up, stood, clapped him on the shoulder or slapped him on the back, lending silent support or commiseration, but no one offered assistance. No one offered solace. They were ruined, too, perhaps. Likely. Their cows were here, penned next to Cash Cattle. Or their cows were out there, running the desert just over a fenceline from Cash Cattle, cheek-to-jowl at salt licks and watering holes. They would suffer along with him.

Daniel didn't notice the rough contact of wide male palms on his back and shoulders. Didn't notice the dead quiet or the averted faces of his friends or the sick, hard, cold lump that his heart had become at this final, killing twist of fate. He wanted only to get to Grace, to find out why she'd done such a thing.

He took the steps leading from the ring one at a time, in no hurry. No answer she could give would start the cold thing in his chest beating again. As he pushed his way through the door that led to the holding pens, he heard the auctioneer's voice behind him, speaking slowly so there'd be no mistaking it.

"Cash Cattle are in the pens, boys. Place is quarantined until the feds clear your stock. That's all." Daniel heard the bang of the gavel after the door shut behind him.

Grace knew he'd come to her before he did anything else. She cleared the office of everyone but Lisa, who was on the phone with the state boys, screaming and being screamed at. No one wanted an outbreak of anthrax in Idaho, Grace heard some bureaucrat shout through the phone lines as Lisa held the phone away from her ear. As if they all didn't know that.

She saw him through the glass door. He stood outside for a minute, watching her. She remembered how he'd done that the night he'd first kissed her, the night they'd met. He'd stood on the other side of that door and looked at her as no man ever had.

Again, that was so. No one had ever looked at her as he was looking at her. No one had ever had the same measure of disgust and pain and disbelief in their eyes. She pulled in her shoulders, a self-protective motion that came to her automatically, and waited until he had looked his fill.

She was afraid. It registered somewhere in his dead heart that she was afraid of him. He didn't feel any joy in it, any thrill, though he probably could have killed her with his bare hands at that moment. He stood a minute longer, watching her watch him, until the urge passed. He'd thought from the start it was better to resist the urges this woman gave him.

He pushed open the door, ignoring Lisa and her phone call, and walked slowly toward Grace until the toes of his boots were nearly touching hers. His eyes did not narrow, nor his jaw clench. He was totally expressionless. Grace was terrified.

"Come into my office," she said, her voice shaking. He followed her back, closed the door very softly behind them.

"Anthrax." The word passed through his mouth to her ears, but she would have sworn his lips didn't move.

"Yes."

"Where? How?"

"Frank called me. A cow went down this morning with the symptoms. It was an old one, he said. You'd left her in the pasture when you moved back onto the range." She took a breath. "I know what you're thinking."

"I don't think you do."

"You're thinking I've made another mistake. But I haven't. I tested blood smears, taken separately, transported separately. They were positive. I checked the brain tissue, to make sure. I found the spores. I don't take this lightly, Daniel."

"It's impossible. It's impossible for me to have something like anthrax in my herd."

She had nothing to say to that. She'd argued the possibility before, when it was brucellosis she'd found, and she'd been wrong then.

"You checked for anaplasmosis, leptospirosis?"

"Yes. And anemia, bracken poisoning, lead poisoning. I know what I'm doing, Daniel."

"You were wrong about the Bangs."

She swallowed thickly. "I don't think I was wrong about that. I think someone tampered with the blood. It came to me this morning, Daniel. This kind of thing doesn't just happen. A Bangs scare, then anthrax, of all things, in the space of two weeks. It's impossible."

"You think someone's trying to sabotage me? Destroy my business and kill off my entire herd?"

"I know it sounds implausible—"

"It doesn't sound implausible, Grace, it sounds insane."

"You don't have one enemy? No one who would do this to you?"

He looked at her, those horrible expressionless eyes boring into hers.

"Just you."

She thought she'd been ready for that. "Not me, Daniel."

"For last night," he said.

She shook her head, clenched her teeth. "No."

"Well, not anybody else."

"What about your brother?"

Oh, he'd thought he was dead inside, but the swipe she took at his little brother was a fresh pain. He was ashamed that the thought had flickered, however briefly, through his mind the instant she'd mentioned sabotage. But he would never believe it.

"No. Not Frank."

"Come on, Daniel," she said, unbelievably frustrated. "Do you believe this can all just be some horrible coincidence? Animal Industries confirmed the brucella bacterium in the heifer samples. I didn't make them up. They've tentatively confirmed my diagnosis of anthrax from a description of the bacilli in the smears and the symptoms of death. I don't believe this could have happened without someone tampering with your herd and my lab. And no matter what you say, no matter how big a bastard you are, you don't believe I did it to take you down."

She was furious, terrified, taking in huge gulps of air as she shouted at him. She forced herself to calm, realized that although the door was closed, her chatty assistant could probably hear every word she was saying.

"Do you remember the night we were—the night we spent at Hollowell's barn? We came back here, and the door was open. Locked, but not closed. Remember?"

"Yes."

"I can't explain that. Lisa and Mrs. Handleman say they didn't come back into the office."

"It's pretty thin, Doc. A theory like this one needs something a little more substantive than that."

"I know. But it's all I can think of."

Daniel ran his hands down his face. He understood why she was making this kind of wild accusation. He remembered exactly how it felt to realize he wasn't going to make his living as a veterinarian. After this second mistake, neither would Grace. But he couldn't buy it. There was nothing short of an eyewitness or a signed confession that would make him believe his brother would do this to him, to the family. Not one unlatched door, certainly.

"Where's the cow?"

She sighed in exasperation. He wasn't listening to her. Well, she'd just have to find the proof on her own then. "Burned. Frank did it, under my supervision. We tried to find you."

"I was at the sale. Did you keep the head?"

"Yes. It's bagged, waiting for Animal Industries. Frank's taking care of the manure disposal, the disinfection of the barns, all the rest."

"Before the Ag department even checks your results? I'm tried and convicted and paying the penalty on just your word?"

She stared at him. How could he think she'd take the chance of being wrong again? How could he think she'd do that to him? Didn't he see this was as hideous for her as it was for him? That if she was wrong—again—she'd never work as a vet in any county, must less this one. She kept herself from bowing her head, capitulating as he wanted her to.

"Yes."

"I want to see the smears."

"No."

"I want to see them, Grace."

"I can't let you, Daniel. You know that. They're sealed now. It's dangerous for you, and completely illegal. They have to stay sealed until Phil Brown or someone from his office gets here."

"Listen, Dr. McKenna—" he growled from between clenched teeth.

"No, you listen, Daniel. I understand how upset you must be—"

"Upset?" He said it as though it was wonder she thought so. "You've just shut down the Friday sale. You've announced to my fellow cattlemen and the damn Idaho Department of Agriculture that I have the most deadly disease in the livestock business, just two weeks after you told them, erroneously, that I had Bangs.

"My ranch is under quarantine for the second time in a month and it is unlikely that, even if your diagnosis is wrong, I will ever be able to sell another calf, or lease my farm ground, or sell my hay. And now you're telling me I can't even see the slides that you say have set all this destruction in motion. I'm supposed to take your word for it?"

It took everything she had not to crumble in the face of his quiet rage.

"Don't do this, Daniel."

"I want to see those slides."

"You have to trust that I know what I'm doing."

"I don't trust you, Grace," he said bluntly, and watched dispassionately as she flinched slightly. "I want to see the slides."

After a moment she nodded, then left her office and walked back to the lab. He stalked silently behind her, snapping up a pair of latex gloves from the box on a countertop, taking the chair in front of the microscope before she could offer it to him. She handed him a mask, took one for herself. He methodically, with clinical expertise, went through every slide.

Anthrax. He could see the bacilli, stained blue with the polychrome methylene she'd added; their distinctive, irregular shape marking them as clearly as if penned there.

"Where are the tissue samples?"

"They're sealed, ready for the state lab. I can't let you open them, Daniel. It's against—"

"Fine." He didn't need to see them. She'd been right. Somehow this virulent, lethal disease had infected at least one, and—knowing full well the contagion rate of the disease—possibly dozens of his cattle. They'd have to be shot, burned or buried deep, the rest of the herd quarantined and treated with antibiotics. His reputation was in tatters already, with the Bangs scare; there would be no getting it back now. The land would be tainted, too; not clinically, not actually, but in everyone's mind.

He would no longer make his living in this community.

He raised his eyes from the microscope, got slowly to his feet and stripped off his gloves.

She moved past him to reseal the slides in their metal container.

"I'll be out at the ranch when the Ag boys come out."

She nodded, sliding the metal container into its case, sealing away, just for a while, the infamy of it. She pulled her surgical mask below her chin, left it tied because she simply didn't have the will to reach behind her and untie it. She was so tired, suddenly.

Daniel untied his own mask, tossed it into the bio-hazard receptacle. He stood with his chin on his chest, his jaw working slowly, as though, with an effort, he could push all his teeth into the bone. Then, without another word to her, he scrubbed his hands at the deep sink, dried them carefully, and walked out of the lab.

His cousin was waiting for him, and when she opened her arms, he walked into them. A little comfort was what he needed. He'd always turned to family for that.

"Danny, how awful for you," Lisa murmured against his chest as she hugged him.

He nodded, but his arms didn't close around her. After a moment, he pushed gently at her shoulders, extricating himself.

"We'll get through this, Lisa." He squeezed her shoulders, reassuring her with words he didn't come close to believing. "The Cash family is tougher than anybody knows."

"That's true, Danny," she said, wiping tears from her eyes. She watched him walk out the glass door and get into his pickup. "That's so true," she whispered.

Phil Brown was at the clinic an hour later, having made record time in from Payton. He followed in his own government sedan, a midsize, refrigerated van staffed with technicians in full bio-hazard gear. Grace, similarly attired, oversaw the loading of blood smears and the severed cow's head into the van, then spoke at length with Brown.

At five o'clock, Grace locked the front door of the Nobel County Veterinary Clinic. There was nothing more she could do for Daniel there.

The Animal Industries people had gone back out to Daniel's ranch to repeat the quarantine process they'd lifted just a week earlier. Grace's phone had not rung all day, her pager hadn't buzzed, not a single client appeared. The stigma was irreconcilable; it was as though she had a vial of anthrax spores and was carrying it around in her pocket, waiting to infect every animal in the county.

"I can hang around, Grace," Lisa said helpfully. "In case anyone calls."

Grace looked around at the empty reception area. Not even the little boy with the pet rat who'd asked her if she played for the Utah Jazz would come in today. Or ever again.

"No. I'm having any calls to the office forwarded to my pager." She smiled weakly. "Not that there will be any."

"Well, where are you going? Out to the ranch?"

"No. I don't think Daniel particularly wants me out there right now, and the state boys said they don't need me. They're taking over. The recent press about anthrax has put the fear of God into everyone. They want to handle every aspect of the quarantine themselves.''

"Okay, well, I'll see you in the morning, then.''

"Lisa, I talked to Mrs. Handleman earlier, while you were going over those animal supply receipts. I'm not opening the clinic tomorrow.''

"What?'' There was a look almost of panic on Lisa's face. No wonder, Grace thought. She'd left her job at Cash Cattle to come here. Now there would be no job here, and very likely no job to go back to at the ranch. Decent employment was hard enough to find before Grace McKenna had come to Nobel County, Grace thought ruefully. Now it was downright scarce.

"I'm so sorry, Lisa. I'm closing down the clinic until further notice. I'm selling the practice.''

"No!''

"Lisa?''

"Wait. I'm fine.'' Grace watched her assistant pale before her eyes. She'd shown amazing aplomb during the last month, admirable even, considering it was all happening within her own family. But now she looked as though she might vomit from stress. Odd, Grace thought.

"Fine,'' Lisa repeated. "I just never thought you'd close the clinic over this. What about the rest of your clients?''

"What clients? I haven't had a single call in days, since the Bangs tests came back negative. No one is going to trust a vet who makes mistakes like that.''

"Oh, God. I never thought of that.''

"It's all right, Lisa. Please don't take this so hard.''

"I just—I just don't know what I'll do now. I can't go back to the ranch. I can't.''

"Well, no,'' Grace agreed, surprised at her vehemence. "Probably not now. I'm so sorry this has happened to your family, Lisa.''

"What? Oh, yeah.''

"Look, I'm going to leave town for a couple days. I want to go up to Washington, see what I can find out."

"Find out about what?" Lisa asked, the color back in her face, the fear over her job apparently fading.

Suddenly, though she'd intended to, Grace did not want to tell her the reason she was going to W.A.S.U. She didn't want Daniel to know; she certainly didn't want Frank to know, and it was unfair to ask Lisa to keep such a secret from her family.

"I'm from there," Grace hedged. "I'll probably go back up there to work when this is all finished."

"Oh. Huh." Grace could practically see the thought forming in Lisa's head. "Will you need an assistant up there? I mean, I have no ties here anymore."

"No ties?"

"I mean, no work ties. I'll always have Aunt Liz and Uncle Howard and the boys."

"No, Lisa, I won't be needing an assistant."

"What's going to happen to Danny and Frank now?"

Grace shook her head. "It all depends upon what the state boys find out there. If it was just an isolated case, they'll quarantine the herd and begin antibiotic treatments. If it's an epidemic, they'll shoot the herd, incinerate the bodies."

"Either way, Danny won't be able to sell anything? No matter what?"

"No. Not for a while."

"So they'll go under."

"That's what Daniel has said. I don't know their financial situation."

"I do," Lisa said thoughtfully. "They'll go under. No rancher could survive this kind of thing, no matter how tough he thinks he is. No matter how much he bounces back from things."

"I hope you're wrong, Lisa. More than anything in the world, right now, I hope you're wrong."

Chapter 11

The snow came in from the west, surprising all but the cattle. They'd been bunching up for hours before the spring blizzard hit, and if he'd had his mind on his business, Daniel thought, he would have noticed it. But his mind hadn't been on business. Not for days.

He wanted so badly to be over Grace, and really, couldn't figure out why he wasn't.

He didn't love her. He didn't feel guilty for hurting her. The cool and barely beating lump in his chest wouldn't allow for such tender emotions toward any woman, he was sure of that. But he missed her, found he missed her more every day, and it confounded him why that should be so. He missed the staggering sex her long, powerful body was capable of. He missed sparring with her, talking with her, missed her quick mind and sharp tongue. Missed the way her brown eyes went cloudy when he kissed her.

But the loneliness seemed deeper, more important, than just missing her company of her body. She was a nagging, aching hollow in his gut, like a hunger pang that never went away, reminding him every minute how empty he was.

He eased his horse down a rocky slope behind a small bunch of cows and late calves. The going was slow; the cows knew the storm was coming and were not anxious to move out of the little canyon, and the calves were small, too young yet to be wary of his big gray horse and his booming voice. Flakes hit them and stuck on their long lashes, making them blink, their already bewildered-looking faces appearing even more baffled.

"Get up," he rumbled at them. He wanted them off this exposed slope before the snow came in earnest, and back on home pasture. He'd been planning to drop them down through the wash onto the edge of the property—where they'd be legal, he mused bleakly, his gloved hands tightening on his split reins—but the snow was thickening by the second, and he knew this bunch, with the youngest of his calves, would need the hay and security of a close pasture until the storm blew over. In Idaho, in March, that could mean tomorrow, or a week from tomorrow. "Come on, now, girls, get moving."

The lead cow took a path through the gathering snow on the ground, and Daniel let his horse have its head to follow along the narrow trail. "Good girl," he murmured to the cow. She knew where she was going now, and would take the rest of the bunch with her. They'd be home in a couple of hours.

Daniel would be soaked through by then and freezing, but the prospect didn't much seem to matter to him. He ducked his chin into the collar of his slicker and brooded over the landscape.

He'd never been empty before. When he'd been drummed out of school he'd been furious, frustrated, unimaginably defeated. When Julie had left him he'd felt betrayed, and so disgusted with her, with women in general, that he'd vowed to never fall in love and open himself up to such treachery again. But he hadn't felt empty. He was Daniel Cash, and the only person he needed to feel whole was himself.

That was still true. It had to still be true. He wouldn't be able to live with himself if it wasn't. But when she'd whispered that she loved him, there in that soft bed with her body still quivering faintly from their lovemaking, he'd felt a loosening in his chest he hadn't felt for years. A hope. A wonder. A woman like Grace McKenna loved him? It was something of a miracle.

He'd wanted desperately to tell her the same thing, to tell her that he loved her, too. But it wasn't true, couldn't be true. He simply could not love her, no more than he could go back to vet school, no more than he could admit he had anthrax in his herd. He was not going to risk failure again. Not for her, not for anyone.

He didn't need her. He wasn't empty without her. He was Daniel Cash, dammit.

Daniel watched his cows head down the disappearing trail and absently rubbed the heel of his gloved hand into the depression at the base of his sternum.

Then why did he ache?

Grace found him at home, his zippy little all-terrain vehicle parked almost at the door. She parked her truck in the short drive and hurried through the gathering snow to pound at his door.

Frank opened the door after a minute and stood staring down at her.

"What?" he said, terse with her more as an automatic reaction than with any real animosity.

"I need to talk to you."

"What about?" he asked.

"May I come in?"

He stepped aside to let her in, his stocking feet making no sound on the old linoleum. His wet boots had left a damp place on the floor by the door and he kicked them aside as she came over the threshold.

"You want coffee?"

"No." She was shaking, but not with cold. She was terrified of this confrontation, but determined. Daniel would never believe her if she didn't have proof. A confession. And it was desperately important, vital, even, that Daniel believe her.

"Did you go up to W.A.S.U. when Daniel was there?"

He appeared not to have heard her question. "You want to sit down, Grace?"

It was the first time he'd called her by her name. Stupid, but she hadn't even been sure until that moment he knew it.

"No, thank you. Frank, did you go to see Daniel before he was kicked out of school?"

He focused on her feet. "Your boots are wet. Do you want to take them off and put them in front of the fire?"

"No." She felt a burst of frustration, of apprehension. She'd driven straight through from Washington, after spending three revealing days and two sleepless nights there. She was on the fine edge of exhaustion, and the man in front of her helped calm her not at all. The pain behind his moss-green Cash eyes was palpable. "Frank, please. Answer my question."

When he didn't, Grace reached out a long, slender arm and grabbed him, squeezing his bicep. "Frank, are you high right now?" she asked sharply.

"No."

She let loose of his arm at his suddenly intense expression and stepped back. "Was the week Daniel got caught cheating the same week you went up to visit him at W.A.S.U.?"

"Yes."

"Why?"

"Why?" Frank repeated dully. "Why was I there?"

"Yes."

"Well," he answered slowly, "I told him I was up there because I wanted to talk to him about selling the ranch."

He went to the fireplace to shove another log past the chain screen onto the fire; a spark popped onto his hand and he brushed it away, not seeming to notice its heat.

Grace stared at the back of his head. Despite her suspicions, her mistrust of him, she could see how beaten he was, how his wide shoulders seemed to bow, unlike Daniel's, under the weight of destiny. She fought back pity, brought forward the doubt and distrust that had pushed her from Washington. "But that wasn't the real reason, was it, Frank?"

He turned, straightened. "No, it wasn't."

She felt that apprehension again; this time it shivered up her spine and lodged at the back of her neck. She reached up to rub there and realized her hands were freezing. The storm had taken her by surprise; she'd had nothing but a light spring jacket with her when the flakes had started hitting her windshield.

She did not take her eyes off Frank's. They were almost of a height, and she tried to take courage in that.

"You went up there to frame him for cheating on his exams."

He gaped at her. "What?" he managed to strangle out after a moment.

"You went to W.A.S.U. to frame him. I spoke with all his professors. I looked up a couple of his classmates who were still practicing in the area. They told me he was an exemplary student, gifted and scrupulously ethical. They also told me his brother visited him the week he was suspended for cheating. That you were clearly loaded the whole time you were there, that you even hit some of them up for drugs."

Frank nodded, his mouth twisting wryly. "I don't remember much about that time in my life, but that sounds like something I might have done."

"He didn't cheat on that exam, Frank. You and I both know that. Someone framed him. All these years he's thought it was one of his classmates. But they investigated his classmates after he left, on order of the dean. They didn't find anything." She frowned at him. "He never considered it was you. When he told me about it, he never even mentioned to me that you were there."

"I was there. But I didn't frame him."

She searched his face, found it difficult to not be swayed by that intensity, that anguished passion. But what other explanation was there?

"Then why were you there, Frank?"

Frank pushed his fingers through his hair, a gesture so habitually Daniel that Grace was a bit taken aback. He slumped onto the short, plump sofa, worn to the stuffing at the armrests. He rested his elbows on his knees, put his head in his hands. Grace stood over him, unable to determine her role. She'd come on Daniel's behalf, as an avenging angel, to find the truth for him as one last gift before she left.

But now she was uncertain. She didn't feel much like an avenging angel at the moment; she felt very much more as if she were the aggressor and Frank the victim.

"I was married." He spoke into his hands. "Did Danny ever tell you?"

"Lisa did."

"That figures. My wife and little boy—" His voice pitched, and Grace felt sudden, unexpected tears sting at her eyes. He couldn't even speak of his child, three years later, without that hitch. How terribly sad. Frank cleared his throat. "They'd died a few months earlier. Danny had left school, of course, when it happened, but he'd gone back. I missed him. I needed him. When he was scheduled for spring break, I went up there so I could be with him."

"Frank—"

"The whole family was pretty worked up about it, wor-

ried about me. I didn't want to worry Daniel any more, so
I told him I'd come up to talk about selling the ranch."

"Do you want to sell the ranch?"

Frank barked out a small, bitter chuckle. "Not much
chance of that now, is there? But yeah, the idea grew on
me. I don't want to be here anymore. This is where Sara
and Cody and I lived. I wanted out. I still want out."

"Badly enough to frame your brother?"

"No, Grace." He looked up at her. "Not badly enough
for that. I was there when it happened. I could see what it
did to him. Danny was always the confident one, the one
with all the gifts. It was damned hard on him to fail out of
school, and for such an unjust reason. Then, when Julie left
him, it nearly destroyed him. Not that he loved her so much,
as far as I could tell. It was just another betrayal, another
failure."

"You didn't do it."

"I didn't do it, Grace."

"And you didn't sabotage the cattle?"

He was quiet for a minute. "You know what's funny?"

"What, Frank?"

"I can't even be angry at you for thinking it. I've let my
whole life go to hell. Sara would be so mad at me." He got
up, took her hands in his, tried to rub some warmth back
into them when he found they were ice-cold. "I didn't sabotage the herd, Grace. I want out, but not this way. I would
have left it all behind, the money, the security, before I did
this. I love my brother, Grace."

"So do I."

"I know."

"I'm sorry."

Frank nodded. "Okay. Grace?"

"Yes?"

"Did you know I went up to W.A.S.U. that weekend with
Lisa?"

Grace stared at him, felt the air leave her body. Of course. *Of course.* "No. She wasn't on the visitor registration log."

"She drove up with me. When Danny was suspended, she drove the ranch pickup back. I stayed with Danny for the inquiry, then came home with Danny and Julie after he was expelled." His eyes narrowed. "Well, with Julie until we got close enough to an airport."

"Oh, God."

"Does she have access to your laboratory supply company?"

"Mrs. Handleman does. She's been training Lisa to take over."

Grace's mind was spinning scenarios like a movie pitchman, and every one of them was possible, doable, with Lisa the center. "But she's smart, Frank. Mrs. Handleman told me she picked everything up in a couple days. She could very well have figured out how to do what she needed to do."

"Could Lisa have got hold of whatever the hell it is that's been showing up in our cattle?"

"The anthrax, yes. It's not too difficult to get with a vet lamp. It's used for research, and my lab is licensed to receive it because I'm the official vet for Nobel County. They could have shipped it if she forged my signature, gave them confirmation over the phone. Yes."

"What about the brucellosis?"

"That's easy enough to get, too. Does she have access to the cattle?"

Frank shrugged. "She lives out here, Grace. No easier access than that."

"But the cow. She must have injected it, because if she'd put anthrax in a water tank or in the feed, it would have spread. I called the Ag boys on my way home today. They said so far the rest of the herd is clean."

"It's easy enough to run a cow in. All she'd have had to

do was wait until both Danny and I were off the ranch, ru
it into the catch pen and shoot it.''

Grace chewed on the inside of her cheek, considering
''She must have gotten into my lab, that Friday night afte
I set up the cultures, and contaminated the blood serum re
sults on your heifers.''

''And when the state cleared us of that,'' Frank said, fir
ished her thought, ''she infected the cow with anthrax.''

Grace slumped to the couch this time. ''But would sh
have?'' She shook her head. ''I can't believe this. Wha
could be her motive?''

Frank sat beside Grace. ''Grace, I have a drug problem.

Grace turned her head, surprised by the turn in the di
cussion. She nodded slowly, watching his grim, gaunt pr
file. ''I know.''

''Lisa is my supplier.'' At Grace's blank look, he sighe
impatient. ''My dealer.''

Grace was stunned. ''What?'' she whispered.

''I got high with her the first time about three days aft
the funeral. She came to the house. I could barely get o
of bed. I was still in shock. She told me it would help m
make it all seem less painful for a while. She was right
He bit his bottom lip. ''The last time was the night you car
out to quarantine the ranch. Before that, I'd been clean f
a couple weeks.''

''But she doesn't display any symptoms of drug abuse

''She doesn't use, really. Just recreational. She mos
deals. It's how she had enough money to make an offer
my shares of the ranch.''

''With money you gave her.''

Frank lifted his shoulders. ''I wanted what she had to se
Pretty much had to have it, in fact.''

''Does Daniel know this?'' Grace shook her head, sigh
''No, of course he doesn't. Why the hell didn't you tell h
any of this?''

''I've just about disappointed him as much as I can sta

Grace. And I honestly didn't think about whether Lisa had any connection to any of this until you mentioned our trip to W.A.S.U.''

"Why would she have done it? Not for the money, because the way she went about it all, *none* of you will have any money when it's all finished. And what possible motive could she have had for framing Daniel for cheating all those years ago? What possible motive can she have had for any of this?''

"I don't know.''

"She seems so cheerful, so open and…ingenuous.''

Frank's lips thinned. "Part of her charm,'' he said shortly. "Where's Daniel?''

Frank grabbed her arm as she shot off the sofa. "He's on the spring range, rounding up some strays we haven't been able to get to yet.''

"Let me go. I have to talk to him.''

"Forget it. It's snowing like a son of a bitch out there. Besides, Grace, you don't have anything in the way of proof. All you have are a couple people who told you Daniel wouldn't cheat on his exams and a school investigation that turned up nothing. If Daniel was going to suspect Lisa or me of framing him, don't you think he would have brought it up by now? And this whole thing about the cattle is conjecture.''

She wrenched her arm out of his grasp. "Do you know what he thinks now?''

"That you're incompetent. Or worse.''

"Did he tell you that?''

"No. But that man looks just about sick every time he sees you, and I see his lights burning all night long. I know, because I'm not sleeping much, either. He's trying damned hard to stay away from you, and the only reason I can think of for him to do that is he thinks you've screwed this up ten ways from Sunday.''

"Yes. He does.''

"Maybe you have."

Grace took a deep breath. "Maybe I have. But maybe
haven't. And I can't live with myself, not knowing."

Frank rose, seemed to take her measure. "He took the b
gray up to Catbird Spring. He was going to head from the
to The Wash, at the northwest corner of the ranch. Do ye
know where that is?"

"I know where The Wash is. And I have a B.L.M. ma
in my truck."

"Start from there and you'll find him." Frank shot a bri
glance out the window. "Do you have chains?"

"Yes. And four-wheel drive. I'll be fine."

"Why don't you just wait until he gets here?"

Grace straightened her shoulders, pulled herself up to h
full height. She saw Frank take in her determination. "I
a good vet, Frank. If this was all done to ruin yours a
Daniel's ranch, I have to find out. Because it's ruined m
too."

Where the hell was Catbird Springs? She'd been drivi
this winding, godforsaken desert road for hours. At Fran
suggestion, she had started out from The Wash and driv
slowly north, looking for Daniel and the sight of his pre
brown Herefords against the deepening snow.

She hadn't found them; hadn't even found tracks, thou
that was no surprise. She could barely see the depression
the snow where the deep ruts of the old road had kept
mounding snow from completely obscuring her path.

The sky, little help to her in the first place, with its d
flat, snowy light, grew less cooperative as evening fell. S
hitched up the heater a notch and stared blearily ahead.

Damn.

She stopped the truck. It was hopeless. She'd never f
Daniel now. He must have veered off, taken a different ro
home.

She shoved her gearshift into reverse. Shame she wa

as smart. She'd never make it back to the ranch before nightfall. She could only hope the snow wouldn't obscure her tracks before she could get back at all. A cold night sleeping in her pickup did not appeal to her much.

She made just a mile or so in thirty minutes. As the temperature started to drop, the snow became denser, colder, heavier. Thirty minutes later it was dark and her windshield wipers could no longer keep up with the flakes. The tracks she'd made coming in were almost gone. She stopped the truck, afraid if she didn't she'd go flying off a cliff or end up in Seattle or something.

She didn't relish it, but it didn't worry her overmuch, being stuck out on a night such as this. She'd lived in eastern Washington all her life. Sudden spring snowstorms were notorious there, as well. Mostly for dumping piles of snow one day and turning off warm as June the next.

She'd wait for daylight and get herself out of this mess. In the meantime, she had a blanket and water in her emergency pack in the vet box. She'd be uncomfortable, but she was in no real danger. Not her body, anyway.

Her heart, if Daniel didn't trust her this last time, was a different matter altogether.

Frank came into the barn as Daniel was unsaddling the gray.

"Where's Grace?"

Daniel hefted the saddle from the horse's back, lugged it over to the saddle tree. He was wet through, and his saddle stunk from the snow and the sweat from his horse. He wanted a shower and little quiet so he could obsess about his vet; he did not want to have to deal with Frank tonight.

"I don't know. Where's she supposed to be?"

"With you."

Daniel's hand stopped in midair. He'd taken a curry comb off a hook in the old barn wall but he didn't so much as give his gray horse a whisk with it.

"What?"

"She came out today, needed to talk to you. I saw you ride in a few minutes ago. Where is she?"

"Stop asking me that! I haven't seen her."

"I told her you were coming in through The Wash from Catbird."

Daniel dropped the comb on the floor of the barn. "I didn't. Rub down my horse."

Frank caught him at the barn door, swung him around. "I'll help you rub down your horse, then we'll both go after her."

"I can't look for her and worry about you at the same time, Frankie."

Frank set his jaw. "You won't have to."

Daniel studied him for a second. "Fine. And after we find her, remind me to beat the crap out of you for letting her go out in a storm like this."

Frank grinned fleetingly. "You don't know your girlfriend very well."

"She's not my girlfriend," Daniel growled. "And what's that supposed to mean, I don't know her very well?"

"It means, Danny boy, that she's not the type to allow any man 'let' her do anything."

Grace was freezing when she woke. Shivering from her boots to her hair. In her exhaustion, she'd curled onto the bench seat of her truck fetal position, and tucked her hands under her arms. She unbent herself now, not an easy task considering the disparity between the length of the seat and the length of her legs.

"Ow, ow," she muttered between chattering teeth. She was stiff as a corpse and nearly as cold. She considered starting the truck to warm it up but decided since she had no idea how long it would take her to get back to the ranch, or anywhere else for that matter, in the morning, she'd better conserve the fuel she had left. Besides, she had the emergency blanket in the back. All she had to do was step out, unlock the vet box and get it.

She shoved at the door. It stuck, frozen shut, and she had to kick it open with both feet, bracing herself against the dash and the seat. When it opened, she stumbled out into the snow. It didn't seem to be coming down with that impenetrable density anymore, but damn, it was cold. Her fingers could barely work the key into the lock of her vet box, and she realized the lack of coordination indicated more than just shivers. She was looking at hypothermia if she didn't warm up soon. Well, fuel shortage or not, she thought as she gathered her supplies and shut the box, she'd start the pickup again and warm up. She could wait until Frank realized she was missing and sent someone after her if she ran out of gas.

She clutched the emergency supplies with one hand and grabbed the steering wheel with the other to hoist herself into the cab of the truck. But as she stepped up she put her smooth-soled boot on the ice that had kept the door stuck hard to the frame of the truck and fell backward into the snow

Wonderful, she thought. Soaked to the skin now. Just great.

She propped herself up on her elbows and snagged the blanket and water and started to rise, disgusted with herself and her whole stupid predicament.

But she found she couldn't rise. Because when she stepped on her ankle, it sent a shooting pain through her leg all the way up to her skull.

"Hell," she muttered. She bent double, palpated the ankle through her boot. Sprained, at least, she thought as she hissed out a breath. Dammit.

What had begun as nothing more than an inconvenience was fast becoming something of a situation, Grace decided. She was now stuck overnight in a spring snowstorm with at least a sprained ankle and no one around for twenty miles.

Very poor planning, Dr. McKenna, she chided herself. Very poor planning.

She shifted to her hands and knees, ignoring the howl of distress her ankle put up. With the blanket clenched in her hand—the water was something she'd think about in the morning—she crawled the few feet to the cab. It took her several minutes to haul herself inside and once she was in she lay prone on the seat, her feet sticking out into the cold, trying to catch her breath, trying to overcome the dizzying pain in her ankle. Maybe not a sprain, she diagnosed with a strange sort of clinical detachment. Maybe worse.

Finally, and only because she understood she had to, she shifted in the seat, brought herself to a sitting position and closed the door. She was wet from head to foot, and her rear end felt numb from where she'd sat in the snow. With frozen fingers, she wrapped the thin, silver emergency blanket around her and lifted her ankle onto the seat. It was already swelling inside her boot.

And the instant she thought again about starting the truck, she realized she no longer had the keys to it in her hand.

Chapter 12

He was wild to get to her. Every minute that went by, he went a little crazier. He was going to kill his brother for letting her come out here in this damn storm. He was going to kill Grace when he got to her. What the hell had she been thinking?

He could hear the faint drone of Frank's ATV behind him. They'd never have gotten this far in a pickup, and a horse would have taken forever and provided no light to track her.

He could see her tracks in the snow, barely, in the narrow tunnel of light the headlights of the four-wheeler provided. They were almost filled over with new snow, but he'd spent his life tracking stubborn cows through thick spring storms and he was confident those slight depressions were hers. They had to be.

The sick feeling in the pit of his stomach negated any thoughts of invincibility he'd talked himself into during the last few weeks. There were some things he didn't think he could live through. Finding Grace McKenna frozen to death on this godforsaken desert was one of them.

He was cold despite his heavy coat and his insulated coveralls and the long underwear he'd been wearing all day. His hands, encased in thick gloves, were half frozen around the handlebars and his face, though protected by a length of wool scarf, stung from the chill wind. He ignored the discomfort and wiped blowing snow from his goggles. His brother pulled up beside him, teeth chattering, as Daniel slowed to a crawl beside the disappearing tracks.

"It's getting pretty bad out here," Frank screamed over the sound of wind and machine. "Can you still see her tracks?"

"Barely," Daniel shouted back. Without another word, he pulled ahead again. He registered dimly that he was probably kicking up a face full of snow on Frank every time he went on ahead, but they both knew it was important not to ride together and risk crossing Grace's faint tire tracks.

Daniel had no idea how long they'd been searching when he finally saw the indistinct outline of Grace's truck through the dense snowfall. They were nearly upon it, in fact, before either of them noticed it. Daniel shot forward, gunning his ATV to full speed and sliding to a stop next to the truck. His heart was hammering, his mouth was dry.

The door was frozen shut and when he couldn't open it, he began shouting her name. There was no answer and the clubbing inside his chest increased tenfold. "Grace," he bellowed over the sound of the wind.

Daniel began to kick at the door to loosen the ice that stuck it to the frame. His boot left great indentations in the metal but he didn't notice. He was mad now with the need to get to her. If he hadn't been afraid of hurting her, he would have jumped onto the hood of the truck and kicked in the front windshield. The fact that she hadn't answered them, hadn't shouted back when he yelled for her, set a vast, nauseating dread turning in his gut.

No, he told himself. She wasn't frozen to death. Impossible. A smaller woman, perhaps. A weaker, frailer, less consequential woman. But not Grace. Not Grace with her long legs and her strong heart. Not Grace.

The door came open with a crack of ice and she spilled backward into his arms. Her lips were blue, her eyes closed, the fine veins of her eyelids showing faintly in contrast to her dark brows and lashes. Her face was as pale as the snow and Daniel felt rather than heard the moan that twisted out of him.

Frank shouldered up next to him. "Check her pulse, for crying out loud," he yelled.

Daniel held out his hand and Frank yanked the glove from it. His hand was cold, but it was warmer than Grace's skin.

Daniel dug frantically past the silver emergency blanket, the light spring jacket and the thin, useless blouse Grace wore. He nearly wept with the relief of finding her pulse.

"She's alive," he said

"Thank god," Frank breathed. "How do you want to do this?"

"We'll take her out in the truck. You drive, get the heater going. I'll go ahead on my four-wheeler. Follow my tail-lights."

Frank nodded in agreement, but when Daniel began to rip at the outer snaps of his coat, he stayed his hand.

"Don't be stupid, Danny."

"I've got to get her warm."

"You'll freeze to death without your coat, you moron."

Daniel held his brother's gaze for a moment. Then he eased Grace into a sitting position on the seat, her head lolling against the back window. When her feet hit the floor of the cab, she whimpered quietly, sending twin shafts of alarm and hope through Daniel, but she did not awaken.

"Get in," Daniel snapped at his brother, "get the truck started. Crank up the heat."

"You go with her in the truck. I'll lead you home."

"No. I know this mountain better than you do, Frank. I can get us home faster."

It was, in fact, an entirely correct argument, and Daniel had just enough wildness in his eyes to keep Frank from arguing with him.

"Let's get going, then."

Daniel nodded, but was reluctant to let go of Grace's shoulder long enough to let his brother scoot in beside her. "See if you can get her to wake up," he ordered unnecessarily. Frank was already crooning softly to her, though Daniel could not hear what he was saying over the sound of the wind and his own ragged breathing. "Wrap your coat—" Frank was twisting out of his jacket. "Good. Now your hat. Okay, follow as close as you can."

"Daniel!"

"What?"

"No keys."

They stared at one another for a moment, then began a mad scramble for the lost keys. They searched for them while snow piled around them, obscuring the tracks they'd made as they'd come in. Every minute they lost, both of them understood perfectly, brought closer the possibility that none of them would get off the mountain that night.

"Where the hell—"

"Get out." Daniel yelled.

Frank scooted out of the truck, stood with his arms wrapped around him and watched his brother dig his hands between the cushions of the bench seat. Daniel was muttering a string of swearwords that would have made even the lowest of the lowlifes his brother had met in the past three years widen their eyes.

When he couldn't find the keys after another minute of searching, Daniel crawled into the truck, heedless of the snow that fell from his clothes to dampen the upholstery. He gathered Grace into his arms and slapped gently at her pale cheeks. That she hadn't awakened during all the shouting and cursing worried him.

"Grace, honey, wake up. Grace."

She didn't respond.

"Grace, we need to get you off the mountain. Honey, wake up. Where are the keys to the truck? Grace!"

"She's not going to wake up until her body temperature comes up, Daniel."

"I know, dammit!" He took Frank's coat from her, and his hat, and flung them carelessly out the door to his brother. He took the glove he had tucked under his arm and pulled it onto Grace's bare hand; yanked the other one off his hand and repeated the process. He ripped his wool cap off and tugged it over her short, dark curls. Then he pushed an arm under her knees and cradled her in his lap.

"Oh, hell." He shuddered as her bottom nestled into his lap. Her clothes were wet. He made a decision in an instant and began to claw at the clasp of her thin slacks.

"What the hell are you doing?"

"Her clothes are wet."

"We've got to get her out of here!"

Daniel struggled to peel the wet fabric down Grace's long legs. "You might want to stop stating the obvious, Frankie," he grunted, "before I come out there and pound the crap out of you."

"Sorry." Frank buttoned his coat as quickly as his gloved hands would allow. "I'll go back down, get help."

"Go."

A moment later Frank was off into the night on his ATV. Daniel sent up a prayer that he'd make it down and back before morning, but he wasn't optimistic.

"Okay, honey," Daniel murmured, maneuvering Grace's limp, cool form so he could pull off her boots. His breath came out in white gusts, worrying him; but at least in here they were out of the wind and relatively dry. "Let's get you warmed up."

He dragged off her right boot and slid her pant leg over her—thankfully—dry sock. But when he tugged at the other boot, she cried out, stopping his thundering heart in his chest.

He palpated her foot, her ankle, through her boot, watched her mouth drop open, a sobbing, unconscious breath wrenched from her as he touched the slight swell at the crease of her boot.

He swore viciously under his breath. Her ankle was obviously sprained, or broken, and if he took the boot off it would swell further, causing her even greater pain. No matter how cold, how unresponsive she appeared to be, the grimace on her face was enough to make him reluctant to do anything more to hurt her.

"Okay, Doc. Okay. We won't do that." He left the boot on and dug into the front pocket of his coveralls for the knife every cattleman worth the name carried at all times.

"I won't hurt you, sweetheart. I won't hurt you anymore." He muttered softly, reassuring her, reassuring himself, while he slit her trousers at the inside seam and wrestled them from her damp legs. Grace was a tall, unconscious woman and they were in a small, frozen pickup cab, but he finally managed to drag off the rest of her clothes, leaving her naked on his lap except for his coat, which he'd awkwardly kept wrapped around her. He then tore at the long front zipper of his wet coveralls, inching them to his hips. He took off his scratchy wool shirt and pulled it around her shoulders. He whipped his long underwear shirt off and dried her legs with it, then tucked it around her lower legs. He pressed her against his chest then, gathered as much of her long body inside the warm circle of his arms as he could, and wrapped the blanket around them both, tucking it close against her bare thighs. Her breasts were cold, her nipples beaded against his bare chest. He pressed kisses on the top of her head, and prayed and cursed and waited.

After a minute or two, she began to shiver again. Violently. He could barely hold her in his lap as she regained enough warmth that her body began to react to the cold. She shook in his arms; he had to clench his freezing fingers around the coat and blanket to keep them on her, and her teeth chattered until he thought they might chip. He held on, rubbed whatever spot on her body he could reach, and prayed Frank would make it home, would come back for her soon.

"Grace," he said, his own teeth clenched against the cold. "Grace."

It registered somewhere that she could hear his voice, that she'd been listening to it rumble at her ear for some time. His body was like a furnace; it was burning her and as the fire hit her extremities, the fingers and toes and arms and legs that had been blissfully numb, she whimpered.

Everything hurt. One foot was freezing, the other felt as though someone was banging on it with a hammer. Her fingers stung as they warmed from the inside out, a million pins and needles poking at her from within her own skin. The shivering, furious and unstoppable, made her bones ache. Even her lips, pressed against his warm neck, throbbed as they thawed.

Her arms came slowly around him, clutched desperately, her hands meeting at his back.

"Hold me," she said, her mouth barely able to form the words. She tasted blood, and realized she'd bitten through the tip of her tongue with her clattering teeth.

He tightened his grip on her. "I am holding you."

"Closer."

He couldn't get any closer, but he tried anyway. Her shivery little voice made him want to cry. "I'm holding you, sweetheart. You'll be all right now."

"The keys—"

"Where are they, Grace?" He didn't want to loosen his grasp on her, so he tilted his head back so he could look at her face. Condensation from the back window dripped down his hair onto his neck. "Where are they?"

Her eyes were still closed, but tightly now, as if she were fighting against consciousness. He couldn't blame her.

"Grace," he spoke sharply, and watched her eyelids twitch. "Grace, where are the keys?"

"'Side. Dropped 'em."

"Can you feel your extremities?" He shook her, which was rather redundant, considering how hard she was trembling in his arms. "Can you feel your fingers. Toes?"

She nodded, buried her nose back into his throat, like a mole burrowing into warm ground. "Yes," she answered, though between her swelling tongue and the chill that threatened to consume her, it sounded more like "yeth."

"Good." He wanted to keep her awake, keep her talking. The shivering was a good sign; it meant her body was struggling to warm itself. "Are the keys near the door?"

She managed to nod her head again, no easy task. The shivering, along with the heat from Daniel's big, healthy body, had warmed her, but it had also sapped whatever had been left of her strength.

"Don't fall asleep, honey."

"Have to."

"No. Listen, I'm going to look for the keys. Don't fall asleep." He reached up a hand and Grace winced at the chill of it against her face, heated now from his body. "Promise me, Grace. Don't fall asleep."

She opened her eyes finally, looked into his. "I promise."

He unwrapped her arms from around him, tucked them into the wool shirt and buttoned it. He then shoved her arms into the coat, as well, and zippered it.

He slid out from beneath her, left her sitting sideways across the bench seat. She instinctively rolled to her side in a fetal position, tried to tuck her bare legs to her chest. Pain washed over her, making the cold superfluous for a moment. She bit down on her lip to keep from crying out.

Daniel wriggled clumsily back into his coveralls, zipping them over his bare chest, and kicked open the re-frozen door.

He dropped to his knees in the snow, slamming the door shut behind him. It was a terrible risk, looking for the keys, he knew. The snow had nearly stopped, but only because it was now too cold now for any sort of precipitation. He felt that cold in every breath he took. The air froze in his lungs, snapped the moisture in his nostrils to ice, immediately numbed his hands.

He smoothed deadened fingers across the crisp surface of the snow, working his way outward. He knew he had just minutes more before the cold overcame him and he succumbed to the hypothermia he already felt wearying him. He would, as Grace had done, slowly slip into unconsciousness, escaping the cold in a kind of imagined, paralyzing warmth. Only there would be no one to help him, and as a consequence, no one to save Grace.

He didn't feel the sharp points of her keys under his anesthetized hands so much as understand there was something there. He grasped the keys clumsily and stumbled to his feet, wrenched open the door and fell face-first into the truck. After a moment he managed to drag himself the rest of the way up into the seat. He forced his fingers to unclamp from around the frozen keys and shoved the ignition key into its slot.

The sturdy, Detroit-built pickup started on the first turn. Frigid air shot out of the vents, making him swear, but after a minute or two fiddling with the controls and gunning the engine, a faint warmth flowed over them. Daniel turned, found Grace's naked bottom at his hip. She was asleep.

She was in his bed. Daniel was stretched out, on his belly, next to her. His head was turned to her, and one of his tree-trunk arms was slung protectively across her waist. Naked, both of them. Grace could almost laugh at the irony of being naked in bed once more with the gorgeous Daniel Cash. Almost.

She still had her left boot on, against the swelling she

surmised correctly. The events of the night came back to her, and she remembered the sound of Frank's voice through the snow and wind. It was not quite dawn, and she wondered whether Frank had made it back, as well. She gazed at the rugged, ragged-looking, beautiful giant snoring softly beside her. Of course he had. Daniel would never have allowed himself to sleep if Frank hadn't been safe and warm in his own bed.

Daniel. He had to stop coming to her rescue, Grace thought, watching him sleep. It broke her, made getting over him impossible. She needed to return to the place in her life where she could count on no one but herself.

But first. Oh, Daniel, first… Her hand hovered over him for a moment before she gave in to the unreasonable longing to touch him. She smoothed back the hair from his forehead, lightly traced those thick, mobile brows, that strong nose and chin. She took a last look down his long, lovely body. She needed to remember everything about him for the time when she was old, and alone, and yearning for him still.

When she made it back up to his face, she found him watching her.

"How do you feel?" His low voice was a growl, his vocal cords strained from cold and shouting. She looked so sad, so beautiful. Daniel felt every cell in his body react to her, wondered if it would always be this way between them.

She swallowed tears. "My ankle hurts."

"You need to get to a doctor. As soon as they plow this morning, we'll get you into town."

"It's my left foot. I can drive myself."

He didn't even bother disputing that ridiculous suggestion. "Are you thirsty?"

She was, terribly, and she nodded. He levered himself up with a groan and left the bed. He padded into the kitchen without a thought to his nudity, and Grace was astonished to see he was almost fully aroused. She knew men often awakened…in that condition. She simply thought Daniel would be too tired for anything close to a sexual thought. Not only was he apparently *not* too tired, he was also not shy about her knowing it.

Grace was not so sanguine. Somehow, the scratchy shirt that had kept her warm last night had been discarded on the floor next to the bed. She wore nothing now. She had no idea where even her underwear was, and she needed to be dressed for what was to come.

"Do you want coffee?" Daniel asked as he came back into the room and handed her a glass of water.

"No." She drank deeply. "Thanks. Uh, where's my underwear?"

He regarded her steadily. "On the floor of your truck. You were wet through. I took them off you."

"Well. Thank you."

"You're welcome." He'd been expecting a bit of trouble over that. Women were unpredictable when it came to underwear, and its removal, he'd found. "Do you want some clothes?"

"Yes, please."

He went to his dresser, not bothering to so much as wrap a towel around himself, and gave Grace an excellent view of his excellent butt as a reward for such a difficult week. She took in every muscle and shadow with greedy, lonely eyes.

"Here." He turned, tossed her an old W.A.S.U. sweatshirt and a pair of sweats. He decided to pull on a pair himself, if for no other reason than to get her to stop looking at him. Those round brown orbs boring into him were doing nothing to calm the restless feeling he'd had since he'd awakened to find her touching him. "I'd like to get that boot off you and have a look at your ankle, if you think you can stand it."

Grace nodded and slipped the oversize sweatshirt over her head and tucked it around her hips. Only then did she allow the sheet and blanket she'd been clutching virginally to her chest to drop to her lap. She whipped back the covers to her knee, exposing her booted foot.

Daniel took a multi-use tool from a drawer, flipped open a pair of leather shears. "This is going to hurt, honey," he said, using the endearment absently. Grace stared at the top of his head. If he called her that one more time, she was going to drop to her knees and beg him. For what, she couldn't quite decide.

Daniel's breath hissed out as he peeled back the leather, easing the boot from her heel. The ankle was the black and blue and sickly yellow of damaged flesh, and swollen, but not as badly as it might have been had she taken the boot off earlier. He ran a hand under her heel, another over the ankle. It was her turn to hiss.

"That hurt?"

She bit down on her lower lip. "Pretty much."

"It's broken."

"Of course it is," she sighed. "First a little case of anthrax, then hypothermia and now a broken ankle. I've had a terrific week."

Daniel leaned over and snagged a couple pillows from his side of the bed. He gently elevated her ankle. "We'll get you to a doctor as soon as it's okay to drive the roads."

Grace nodded. "Okay." She was humiliated, angry with herself for making this all so difficult for him. She hated being helpless, hated being nearly naked in his bed, hated what she had to tell him, what he probably wouldn't believe. "Daniel, I need to tell you something before we go anywhere."

He sat on the bed with her, his heavy body making a dent in the mattress, and she almost pitched into him. She held herself upright, unwilling to have even that much contact, he noted grimly.

"Good." With unconscious gentleness, he tucked a strand

of her hair behind her ear. "I've been wondering what could be so important, Grace, that you'd risk your life."

"Someone's been poisoning your cattle, Daniel. And I think I know who."

Chapter 13

Daniel braced himself. If she said it had been Frank—his own brother, the destruction of the family—he needed to be ready. Not to accept, but to dispute. He'd never, ever believe it. Even if it was Grace telling him it was so.

"Who?"

"Lisa."

He laughed; couldn't help but laugh. "Come on."

Grace stiffened. How many times was she going to allow this man to doubt her word? A dozen more? A hundred? She narrowed her eyes, reminded herself yet again that despite the fact that she was practically naked in his bed, this was not a personal issue between them; she was the Cash Cattle, Incorporated, vet, and for the safety of this herd and the rest of the cattle in Nobel County, Idaho, she was obliged to tell him what she suspected. He could believe her or not, no use feeling hurt over it. He'd made it very clear she was the only one who thought he ought to believe what she said because she loved him. Would never lie to him.

"You don't believe me."

He got up, paced the room. "Lisa isn't capable of pulling off something like this."

Grace shook her head in disgust. "Think, Daniel. For once, stop acting like you have control over everything that goes on in your life, refusing to allow there might be a couple things you can't bully your way through. Think."

"About Lisa? I've known her all my life. We grew up together. She'd never do this." He shook his head. "She wouldn't even know how."

"I think she does know how. And I think she did it."

"You thought Frank did it."

Grace met his gaze without flinching. "I went to the university. Found out Frank had been there with you the week you were suspended for cheating."

"So?"

"What I didn't know was that Lisa was there, too. Don't you think that's a suspicious coincidence?"

"No. I think it's just a coincidence."

"Well, it isn't." Grace ran her hands over her face, was shocked by how tired she felt. When this was over, when it was all out and Daniel had decided one way or another how to handle it, she would sleep for a week. Then she'd go home, to Washington, and start her crazy life all over again. "I know you think I'm grasping at straws, Daniel. I know you think this has all been some huge mistake I've made. I know you think I'm not a good vet, certainly not as good as you would have been."

He said nothing, knew she was waiting for him to deny it. He wanted to, if for no other reason than to take the hurt from her eyes, the hurt she was trying so valiantly to hide. It buckled his knees, that betrayed, wounded look. He would have done almost anything to not have put it there.

But if he did deny it, then he would be as good as admitting this situation *was* out of his control, and he would never be in that position again.

Grace sighed and gathered her considerable professional

confidence around her. Her personal confidence was shot, but she still had resources. She'd use them to convince him.

"I don't know what happened at W.A.S.U. I don't have any evidence, only suspicions. Take them or leave them. I think Lisa framed you for cheating. And I'd bet my license that Frank thinks so, too."

"You talked to Frank about this?"

"He was the one who told me Lisa was there with you."

"What did he say?"

"He said it was possible. She had opportunity. He doesn't know, for certain, either. But I talked to some of your classmates, Daniel. They've sworn there wasn't a reasonable way for anyone else to have done it. You were well-liked, a model student, nearly finished with the program. You didn't live on campus, so someone had to have had access to your apartment. There was an investigation after you left, and they came up with nothing on any of the students. It almost had to have been done by someone outside the school. You've ruled out your wife, and I don't believe anymore that it was Frank."

"You talked to my classmates?"

"The ones that were still in the general area, practicing locally. Just a few. But everyone gave the same answers, Daniel."

"Why would she have done it?"

"I don't know."

"And now, three years later, she's out to get me again?"

"You don't have to believe me, Daniel. I'm only presenting you with a theory."

"And no empirical evidence."

"No."

"Grace, look—"

She put out a palm, stopping his words. "I'm not doing this with you again. I know—" Her voice broke in spite of herself, and she cursed herself for it. "—I know you don't trust me, and I don't care." It was a lie, and they both knew it. "But you have to listen to me. It's my duty as your vet to tell you."

Daniel nodded, barely kept himself from going to her, reaching out. The hitch in her voice was an agony.

"Lisa has been working closely with Mrs. Handleman. She's been ordering not only drug and office and kennel supplies, but laboratory supplies, as well. You've seen the slides I took from that dead cow. You saw the anthrax bacilli. And the state lab confirmed my initial diagnosis of brucella bacterium in the heifer samples. Daniel, think. How else could those samples have been contaminated? How else could you have a false outbreak of Bangs one week, and a cow dead from anthrax the next? It's statistically and medically implausible, if not impossible. Unless I made a mistake, I know." She held his gaze. "But I didn't. I don't make mistakes like that. Personal mistakes I seem to make in abundance, but not mistakes in my lab."

"Grace—"

"No. Shut up and listen. Lisa has keys to the clinic. She has had every opportunity to order both anthrax bacilli and the brucella bacterium as lab testing supplies. You know as well as I do, all it takes is a signature from a licensed vet. You've watched the news, Daniel. It's how terrorists get the stuff. The night we found the door to the clinic open, she could have gone in and contaminated those samples, and she could have injected your cow anytime after you brought it in from the range."

He made no commitment. "Have you gone to the police?"

"No." Grace sat back against the pillows. "It's all conjecture. I haven't been back to the clinic to check the order records, I haven't called my suppliers. I only just put it all together after I talked to Frank."

Daniel shook his head. "What does Frank have to do with this? Why would he think this could be true? He and Lisa have worked together half their lives."

"I can't tell you that, Daniel. You'll have to ask him."

He said nothing for a while, just jammed his hands into the pockets of his sweats and studied the worn carpet.

"Daniel," Grace said softly, earnestly. "You can trust me on this or not. It doesn't...it doesn't matter anymore." His eyes whipped back up to hers, but she had them cast down now, unable to bear the doubt she knew she would see on his face. "I may have done it all. I may have made horrible mistakes, or I may have done it for spite. I *may* have, but I didn't, and I can't do anything to convince you of that until I get those supply records. Until then, you have to consider, for the sake of the rest of the cattlemen in this state, that I'm right.

"Mrs. Handleman had access to the laboratory supply forms and my signature and the clinic. But she has not had access to your cattle, nor was she at W.A.S.U. Frank was at W.A.S.U. and he's had access to your cattle, but he could not have ordered those supplies without my vet stamp, nor could he have got into the clinic easily. If they didn't do it, and I didn't do it, that only leaves Lisa."

"I know." He raked his hands across the crown of his head, spiking his hair. "I know it."

"But you still can't trust me."

He came again to sit beside her on the bed. She wished he hadn't. She could smell him, count the fine hairs on his wrist, see the tortured aspect in his sharp, beloved face. In the distance she heard the rough sounds of a snowplow clearing the gravel roads.

"I want to believe you."

"But you won't. Not really."

He looked away for a minute, watching the gray sky outside his bedroom window. "You have no evidence, Grace. This is all just speculation, based on what you want to be true."

"No, Daniel," she said softly. "Even if I laid a stack of evidence two feet high on this bed right now, you'd never trust me, never believe me. Because it isn't in you to trust anyone. What happened to you at W.A.S.U., and with Julie, was horrible. A looting of your life and your dreams. But I didn't do it, Daniel. And you can't keep blaming me for doing with my life what you were kept from doing with yours." She'd been tired before, but now she was drained of everything but the desire to leave him with his doubts and his pride. She no longer had the strength to battle against them. "I hear the plow. I need to go home now."

"No."

"Take me home."

"I'll take you to the hospital, and then we'll talk about all this."

"I'm finished talking to you."

He ran a frustrated hand through his hair. "It isn't that easy, Grace. There's something between us."

She looked up at him. "There's nothing between us," she said, her voice low and steady. "You don't love me, Daniel," she said. "And I don't love you anymore. I just want to go home."

While Daniel took a shower, Grace called Frank. Within minutes she was in the front seat of his truck dressed in Daniel's soft sweats, and heading for the hospital. Neither of them spoke on the way to town; the creak of newly plowed spring snow under Frank's tires was the only sound.

The emergency room doctor put a pretty, purple cast on her ankle, to cheer her up, he said. Frank drove her home and helped her into her house. They stood awkwardly for a few minutes in her living room.

"Do you want me to help you into bed?" Frank asked finally.

"No. I need to do some work."

"You look pretty beat, Grace."

"I'll feel better when I have something in my hands to take to the state boys. If I'm going to salvage anything of my professional reputation and you guys are going to save anything of your ranch, I need to get to work.''

Frank nodded. ''Do you want me to take you to the clinic?''

''Not right now. I need to do some research here first. Besides, last night took a lot out of me. Out of you, too, I'll bet.'' She smiled.

''Nah. By the time I got Dad up and Mom had made coffee and gathered some stuff together to take back up with us, you two were back.''

''I wondered where you were. I didn't think Daniel would have gone to sleep without knowing you were home.''

''No. He wouldn't have. He would have done anything to make sure I was safe. Just as he did you.''

''I know.''

''He'll come around, Grace.''

She took a deep breath. ''It doesn't matter. I only have to prove it to the Idaho Department of Agriculture so they don't shut down the county.''

''How are you going to do that?''

''I'm going to go through the computer files on my laptop first, try to get hold of my lab supply company from here.''

''What will happen to Cash Cattle?''

''If Lisa put the anthrax into the water supply, or on the ground or into the feed, every cow will have to be treated with antibiotics whether they're infected or not. The sick ones will have to be shot and burned or buried.'' Grace shuddered at the thought. ''If she injected the single cow, which is what I think she did, and the rest test out clean, they'll keep the herd off the range for a time, and you won't be able to sell stock for a while, but you won't have to destroy them.''

''How will you know?''

''The state's taken water, soil and manure samples. They'll be able to tell how far the contamination went. And we'll need to talk to Lisa. See what information we can get out of her.''

"Did you tell Daniel everything? About me, about Lisa?"

Grace shook her head. "No. It wasn't relevant enough to compromise your confidence. He wasn't going to believe me anyway."

"He's an idiot."

Grace smiled sadly. "I know."

"But you love him."

"No," she said. "No."

But the lie, though necessary, was so agonizing she could stand against it for only a minute or two. Her face crumpled finally and she burst into tears. She leaned against her crutches to keep from falling as sudden, wrenching sobs shuddered through her body. In a moment, maybe less, she was enfolded in the arms of her lover's brother, and she took what small comfort she could from him.

"Shh," he said quietly, stroking her hair. "Shh. Don't cry, Grace."

She clung to him, wetting his shirtfront, weeping out exhaustion and grief. He held her for a long time, just running his hand down the short cap of her curly hair, over her back and along her shoulder blades. When she calmed a little, he took a clean, worn bandanna from his back pocket and handed it to her. He smiled when she blew into it heartily and then debated handing it back to him.

"I'll wash it," she said hoarsely.

"Okay."

"Thank you, Frank. For coming to get me last night. For everything."

"It's been painful for me, Grace," he admitted slowly.

"I know. I'm sorry."

"But it's the first time in three years I've felt anything much at all. I guess feeling bad is better than feeling dead."

Grace nodded, sniffed. She hoped so. Because she felt awfully bad right now.

Frank smiled again, his mouth working around the unaccustomed expression. "You may have to have all the faith for a while, Grace. Daniel doesn't have much left. Neither of us do."

"It doesn't matter," she whispered again, her voice cracking.

"You're a terrible liar."

She nodded, wiped her nose indelicately on the back of the sleeve of Daniel's sweatshirt. "Always have been." She sniffed again, tried a lopsided smile. "My family calls me Gracie."

"Well, it suits you." He bent his knees, swept her into his arms.

She let out a horrified gasp. "You guys have to stop doing that," she squeaked as he hauled her down the hallway and into her tiny bedroom.

He grunted dramatically as he gently placed her on the bed, then gave her a brotherly buss on her forehead. "We do. You weigh a ton."

She smiled. "Thanks a lot." Oh, the bed felt wonderful, and she snuggled in. She was at the end of her rope, emotionally, physically.

"Say good-night, Gracie."

Grace settled into her pillow, her eyes already closed. "Good night, Gracie."

Daniel leaned against Grace's dented vet truck, his arms crossed belligerently across his broad chest, looking ready to rumble.

"She all right?" he growled as Frank walked up to him.

"Exhausted. She's in bed."

Daniel looked him up and down.

"You put her there?" Daniel asked, his eyes narrowing to slits.

Frank gave him a disgusted glare. "God, what an idiot."

"I want an answer."

Frank got into his face. "No, you don't," he said. "You want a fight. Too bad. You screwed up. I'm not going to make you feel better by pounding the guilt out of you."

Daniel stood nose-to-nose with his younger brother for a minute, his fists vised down, then settled back against his truck. He blew out a breath, pulled his lower lip through his teeth. He *was* being an idiot. But she didn't love him anymore. She didn't love him anymore. He couldn't get past that one pertinent, devastating fact.

"How's her ankle?"

"Why didn't you just come into the emergency room and find out? I saw you tailing us all the way in."

Daniel shrugged, sucking in his cheeks. "She obviously wanted you there instead of me."

"Why do you suppose that is?"

"Do you believe what she said about Lisa?"

"Yeah, I do."

"Why?"

"I have my own reasons."

"Well, I don't have the same reasons."

"You have a better one."

"Which is?"

Frank came close again. "She'd never lie to you, you moron," he said softly. "Not to save herself, not to save her practice, not even, probably, to save your sorry cattle operation for you. She's not Julie, but you've acted from the beginning like she is. Grace is not responsible for your screwed-up life. She loves you."

"No." Daniel shook his head, felt that peculiar constriction in his throat again. "She doesn't. Not anymore."

Frank ran his tongue over his teeth. "You know, Danny, you better figure this out. And do it quick. Because that woman in there?" He jerked his thumb toward Grace's little, forlorn-looking house. "She's great. Amazing. Better than you deserve. And I'm already half in love with her myself."

Daniel couldn't help the lethal look that shot through his narrowed eyes. Frank practically sneered at him.

"That's what I thought. Fix this, Danny." He shoved his hands into his pockets. "I got nothing more to say to you."

Daniel watched Frank walk back to his truck. He turned as his brother drove off and took a dozen involuntary steps toward Grace's door before he remembered she was already asleep.

She was probably exhausted. He was on the ragged edge himself, and he hadn't had a case of hypothermia and a broken ankle.

But, God, he wanted to see her.

He tossed the keys to her truck onto the front seat and started off down the street at a jog, his fatigue forgotten. He'd fix it. His brother had told him to fix it and fix it he would.

He wasn't losing this time.

Daniel didn't have the key to the back door and told himself, as he proceeded to kick it in, it really wasn't breaking and entering, as the deed to the building did have his name on it. The door splintered easily enough under his size thirteen boot.

He shouldered his way past the broken door and walked down the dark back hallway. The kennels were empty and the place was quiet; no caged dogs to set up an alarm. It occurred to him he should have a real alarm installed along with the new door. If Grace had to come into the clinic late, he wanted her to be safe.

He started with the paper files he knew Mrs. Handleman kept of all transactions with the veterinary supply companies. Nothing. He then went into the client files. Nothing. He rummaged through the desks and cabinets, scoured the lab, the kennel area, the examining room. Nothing, nothing, nothing.

Daniel rolled the tension out of his shoulders, unbelievably frustrated. Not one piece of evidence that would point to anyone—Lisa or Frank—having tampered with the results of the bangs tests or the cow that was contaminated with anthrax.

He forced his ingrained cynicism aside, though. Just because there was nothing here didn't mean Grace was wrong about the tampering. He just had to look harder.

"Daniel!"

He rammed his head on the underside of the meds cabinet when he heard the shocked female voice. He was nearly wedged into the cabinet up to his shoulders, so it took him a moment to disengage himself and look up at the woman.

"What the hell are you doing here?"

He rubbed at the small sore spot on his cranium. "Hey, Lisa."

"What are you doing here?" she repeated in that high voice of surprise. "What happened to the back door?"

"I kicked it in."

"You—you—?" She couldn't get her mouth around that one.

"Kicked it in," he assured her calmly. "What are you doing here?"

"I saw the back door as I was driving by."

"You were driving by the back door? In the alley? Why were you driving down the alley?"

She looked nonplussed. "What? Why would you even ask me? What the hell are you doing here?"

"I'm looking for evidence," he said, rising to his feet.

Lisa's eyes widened. "Evidence of what?"

"Of tampering. Someone contaminated those Bangs samples Grace took from our heifers, and someone also came on to the place and exposed that cow to anthrax."

"Oh, God."

"Yeah."

Lisa groped for the desk behind her, rested her hip there. "Oh, God, Danny."

"You got something to tell me, Lisa?"

"I don't— Oh, this is terrible."

"It's pretty terrible," he agreed, watching her, his voice and his face utterly expressionless.

"Do you have any proof?"

"Yes," he lied coolly.

"Did you find it on him?"

Daniel's mouth barely twitched. "On him?"

"On Frank."

"Frank didn't do this, Lisa."

Her eyes clouded with tears. She was either damned sincere, Daniel thought, his heart beginning to race, or she was a hell of an actress. "No," she said quickly, her hand out in supplication. "No, of course he didn't. I shouldn't even have said that."

"Then why did you?"

She took a deep breath. "Forget I did. What kind of proof do you have?"

Daniel took a chance. "We have confirmation from the laboratory supply company that they shipped both anthrax spores and brucella here for examination purposes."

Lisa's eyes sharpened imperceptibly. "You do?" Her lips flattened, her brows knit. "How could he—how could someone have done that?" she asked.

"It wasn't Frank." Though he wasn't nearly as sure as he sounded.

"Danny—"

Daniel took a step toward her, using his height, the stretch of his shoulders, the menace in his eyes, to intimidate her. But she'd grown up with this giant, knew he didn't have it in him to touch a woman in anger. She didn't even flinch.

"If you have an accusation to make," he growled at her, "you'd better just make it."

"Your brother has a drug habit."

He said nothing.

"You don't believe me?"

He shrugged, though the casual gesture cost him. His guts had knotted into a clump at the accusation. "I don't know."

"Oh, Danny," Lisa said sadly, compassionately. "Everyone else does. Even your parents. They've been trying to get him into rehab for months."

"No."

"Yes, Daniel. Call them and ask them. He's been fighting them tooth and nail. Haven't you noticed the tension between them?" She ran her hands down her face and clasped them at her chin, sighing sadly. "He's come to me for money a hundred times. And I'm not the only one. Ask almost anyone in town. He has a supplier here, a woman who hangs out at the Rowdy Cowboy."

"You're lying," he raged. He wished fervently he was a different kind of man; he would have liked to wrap his hands around her throat and stop the words from coming. "You did this."

"I did what? This tampering thing?" She shook her head. "No, Daniel. I didn't."

"You had opportunity. You had access to everything you'd need."

"Ha! Mrs. Handleman barely lets me answer the phone. And besides, what could possibly be my motive?"

"To ruin Grace? To ruin me?"

"Oh, that makes a lot of sense. I ruin you and Grace, and then I have no job here and no job at the ranch. Get a grip, Daniel."

She came off the edge of the desk, reached up and took him by the shoulders.

"I love the ranch. I love you and the folks. After Daddy died, they became my parents, too. I even want to buy into the business with you all, if you'll let me. Frank is the one who wants out. You won't let him out. What better way than this to pay you back for that?"

Daniel took a step back, stared at her, his mind spinning.

Lisa did not take her eyes from his. And, damn her, he could see no hint of guile or malice in her.

"No, Lisa," he said slowly. "You're lying."

Her hand fluttered up to her mouth, and a single tear tracked down from her green eyes.

"No. God, Danny, no."

"Yes, Lisa," Grace said from the doorway. "You are."

Chapter 14

Lisa whirled. "Grace!" She quickly composed her features and pulled her hand from the pocket of her coat. "Oh, thank God, you're here," she said, her voice cracking. "Frank has— Oh, I can't even explain it. Frank has been the one behind this whole thing, and Daniel and I just figured it out."

Grace hobbled through the door on her crutches. She looked magnificent, Daniel thought. Tall and angry and beautiful, like an avenging angel. He moved toward her.

"Are you all right?" he asked.

"Fine." She didn't so much as glance at him. She stared at Lisa, who looked as ingenuous and amiable as ever. Grace could have smacked her. "You're lying, Lisa," she repeated slowly, and watched with some satisfaction as the color drained from the smaller woman's face.

Lisa's hand dipped again into her pocket.

"Grace," she pleaded with a good measure of confused warmth, a last-ditch effort, "what happened to your poor leg?"

Grace shook her head. "It hardly matters."

"Will you please tell me what the heck you're talking about, the both of you?" Lisa asked, looking between them. A hint of menace had seeped through the honeyed tones, and Daniel moved instinctively closer to Grace, protecting her.

"I'm talking about tampering with the blood serum tests in my lab, a criminal offence. About illegally ordering anthrax, forging a doctor's signature, exposing the people and livestock of this state to a deadly disease, all federal offenses."

"Grace, please," Lisa sputtered with shock. "You can't possibly believe I'd do something like this."

The sincerity in her voice wasn't even cloying. It was as convincing as the dawn. She was an excellent liar, pathological probably, Grace thought. It'd be work to convict her in front of a jury.

"I do believe it," Grace said, unruffled. "And I have proof. I called the lab supply company. They confirmed my vet stamp on both the bacilli and the brucella. They'd authenticated the order by telephone, and when it was delivered to the clinic, I apparently signed for it myself. They have verification from the courier. They even e-mailed me a scan of the order, and my forged signature."

Lisa took one look at Grace's forbidding expression and appealed to Daniel instead. "I don't even know what that stuff is."

"I think you do," Daniel said slowly. He pinned Lisa with those deadly green eyes. "I think you forged an order from Grace's lab, and I think you confirmed the order with the supply company."

"I didn't!"

"They said you did," Grace stated flatly.

"You're lying," Lisa said, turning to her. "They didn't say that."

"They did," Grace insisted. "They even described your voice."

"My voice? My voice?" She was incredulous now, vigorously annoyed and provoked. "How could they have possibly described my voice? It wasn't even a woman who—" She stopped midsentence, her jaw clamping shut.

"It wasn't a woman who spoke with them, was it, Lisa?" Daniel said. "You had them talk to a man."

"I didn't have them—"

"Shut up," he ordered bluntly, and Grace was somewhat surprised to see Lisa obey. She may be nuts, Grace mused, but she knows an irrefutable command when she hears one. "You had them talk to a man because you were planning all along to frame Frank for this," he said. "Just as you framed me three years ago at the university."

That really did stun her. The wide-eyed candor and persecuted surprise fell away like a mask from her face, and she stared at him, astounded.

"What?" she breathed.

"You framed me for cheating while I was at W.A.S.U." He shook his head. "Grace figured it out. You know, I never suspected it. Not once."

She squinted at him, furious. "But of course you do now. You've both decided this is all my fault. With no proof at all, you're tried and convicted me. That's typical."

"We have proof," Grace said. "We know it was you, and you're not going to get away with it. Did you think you could? The state would have investigated my clinic, Lisa. They would have found out in a matter of days that someone ordered both the brucella and the anthrax spores through here."

Lisa chuckled acidly, and Grace felt a chill go up her spine. Daniel felt her shiver and stepped between the two women, shielding Grace from whatever was to come.

"How much evidence did you plant at Frank's place, Lisa?" Daniel asked.

There was long silence in the room. The frosty bite at Grace's backbone doubled and her shoulder blades clenched involuntarily. She could practically hear the other woman running through her options. Fight or flee? Deny or admit? She peered over Daniel's shoulder, saw Lisa smile, slowly. Grace felt the dread of that small smile all the way to her toes.

"Well," Lisa said with a palpable quantity of satisfaction in her voice. She pulled a small vial from her pocket and watched their eyes go wide. "Another vial of this, for one."

Daniel's first, overwhelming instinct was to charge her, wrest away the threat to himself and Grace, but Lisa was watching him closely enough to see his muscles tense for attack. She raised the bottle in the air. "Uh-uh," she scolded, grinning.

"If you drop it, Lisa," Grace said, hobbling her way around her protector, "you'll be exposed to the spores, as well."

Lisa shook the vial of deadly anthrax. "That would be a shame," she agreed. "But I won't die from it. They have antibiotics now that can control it. You will die, though." She reached into her pocket with her other hand and brought out the small handgun. She raised her eyebrows, grinned. "What do you think? I brought it in from my pickup when I saw the back door kicked in. Pretty dramatic ending to this whole thing, huh?" She pointed the gun at Grace, stopping Daniel's heart. "You're exposed to anthrax through the lab." She moved the gun to Daniel. "You're exposed from the cow. You're both found in the desert a couple days later, having started walking home after the vet truck broke down, dead as doornails."

Daniel snorted derisively. "That's not very plausible," he sneered, and Grace pinched him, hard, on his rigid upper arm. No way to treat a lunatic, she wanted to hiss at him.

The smug smile was wiped from Lisa's face in an instant

She glared at her cousin. "It's plausible. I hate to break it to you, Danny, but you're not in charge here."

"He's right, though, Lisa," Grace said, trying her best to be persuasive, though her voice fairly shook. "Who will believe this?"

Lisa scowled at Grace. "Everyone will," she insisted. "You're a screwup, Dr. McKenna. Not a single person in this county doesn't believe you botched this whole thing from the beginning. I've helped them along, with some scary stories about the way things are run around here. The fact that you exposed both of us to anthrax through shoddy lab techniques won't surprise anyone."

"And you," she continued, smiling at her cousin, "are even easier to explain. Everyone knows what a failure *you* are."

"If you planned all this with the anthrax," Grace asked quietly, "why did you tamper with the blood samples from the heifers?"

"I had to make sure he didn't sell those bred heifers. The money they brought in would have kept him afloat too long."

"You could destroy the livestock industry in the whole state with this, Lisa," Daniel said, watching her roll the tiny bottle rhythmically across her palm, the fragile glass making a clicking sound as it hit the trio of silver rings she wore. "Why in God's name unleash something like anthrax?"

"Because you couldn't squirm out of that, Danny. No blood tests would clear you. You have one cow dead on your place of anthrax, you're screwed. That's what I was going for." She grinned at him. "I wanted you to be screwed so bad you'd never recover."

Daniel looked at her for a long moment. "I should kill you for this, you psychotic little bitch," Daniel said calmly.

Lisa laughed bitterly. "You see what I mean?" she said to Grace. "You see that? I have a *gun!* A big-ass gun, that *he* taught me to shoot!" She shook the vial at them. "And enough of these anthrax spores to exterminate him and half this town. And he's threatening to kill me?'' She raised her hands as if in supplication, the gun turning on its side as she did. ''Do you see what I mean? He's got the biggest damned ego.'' She shifted her attention back to Daniel. ''Well, I have news for you, Danny,'' she snarled. ''I have done all of this to you without you even knowing it.'' She laughed again, low, back in her throat, and Grace thought it sounded like a growl. ''Without you even suspecting! You never would have figured any of it out if Grace hadn't. How smart does that make you?''

''I never would have suspected you, Lisa. You're family.''

Lisa took in a sharp breath, her eyes narrowing to slits. ''That's right,'' she whispered. ''I'm family.'' She stepped forward, pushed the gun to Daniel's nose. Grace let out a sobbing, terrified gasp and reached out, but Daniel caught her hand in his and squeezed. ''I am a Cash. But am I a part of Cash Cattle, Incorporated? No. I wanted in, Daniel, and I was willing to buy my way in, but you wouldn't let me.''

''Your father sold his shares, Lisa, before you were even born. The ranch belongs to my parents and Frank and me. And our children. It doesn't belong to your side of the family, and hasn't for a generation.''

''Because Uncle Howard stole the ranch away from Daddy and left me with nothing,'' she spat, flecks of saliva spraying from her mouth onto Daniel's composed face.

''My father kept your father from going to jail, Lisa.''

Lisa's head jerked back. ''That's a lie.''

''No, it's not.'' Daniel coolly met her wild eyes over the barrel of the gun. ''Uncle Moe and Dad were once equal partners in the ranch. But back before any of us were born, Uncle Moe forged Dad's name on federal farm relief applications, about a hundred thousand dollars' worth, that the ranch didn't legally qualify for. When the government guys figured it out, they put a lien on the ranch and issued a warrant to arrest Uncle Moe for felony fraud. Dad went to his in-laws, scraped together enough money to pay off the lien and the fines and kept him out of jail. In return, Uncle Moe signed over his shares in the ranch. It left Dad about six thousand in equity short, but he managed.''

''You *liar!*'' Lisa screamed.

''It was what Uncle Moe wanted, Lisa. I've seen the papers. Didn't you ever ask him?''

''Of course I did! He spent hours talking to me about it. How he wanted to pass Cash Cattle on to me when he died, but Uncle Howard had stolen that dream from him to give to you and Frank. Because you were boys. Sons! Because I was just a girl.''

''He lied.''

''Daddy didn't lie,'' Lisa said. ''Daddy never lied.'' Her hands were shaking now, and Grace was terrified the gun would go off in her hand, and the little bottle of death would pop open on the cold linoleum. They were thrust in front of Daniel's face now like the twin heads of a striking snake. ''Daddy was an honest man.''

''Lisa,'' Grace said. ''Pull yourself together. Give me the gun and that vial before you make this any worse on yourself.''

But Lisa kept her wild gaze pinned on her cousin. ''You think you're smarter than everyone. But I'm smarter. Both you and Frank are ruined now, and nothing can save either one of you.''

''What have you done to Frank?''

''You should see yourself, Danny. You're white as a ghost.''

''What have you done?''

''I told you. He's an addict, Danny.'' Lisa smiled wickedly. ''I started dealing to him right after his wife and kid died. Just a little something to help him get over the pain, at first. But, God, it was easy to get him on the stronger stuff, Sara and Cody dying like they did. He took to drug abuse like a calf to the bottle.''

Daniel moved then, so fast that later, when Grace was alone, she could not even reconstruct it. His hand came up as a raw, deadly sound erupted from his throat. The noise was guttural, paralyzing, but Grace forced herself to move, too, and grabbed at the vial in Lisa's hand as Daniel twisted his cousin's wrist.

Grace heard the distinctive sound of bone snapping at the same moment the gun went off, deafening her, burning her nostrils.

Both Daniel and Lisa dropped to the floor. Grace didn't scream, though it occurred to her she should. If Lisa had put a bullet into Daniel Cash, that deserved some significant screaming. But she was busy now, she thought absurdly. She'd scream later.

''Daniel!''

''I'm okay, Grace.''

''Oh, my God.'' She went to her knees beside them, slipping the vial of anthrax safely into the pocket of her coat as she dropped.

Lisa sat back on her butt, holding her wrist. The look on her face was one of complete surprise. She stared at Daniel. ''You broke my wrist,'' she whispered.

''I should do more than that for what you did to Frank,'' he replied. He had the gun now, was holding it against his thigh as he knelt beside Grace. He glanced at her. ''Did you get it?''

Grace nodded. She was certain she'd never been so frightened in her life, was sure she would be unable to speak coherently for at least a week.

''Call the police.''

Grace nodded frantically again. She crawled over to the desk, pulled at the cord until the phone came clattering to the floor.

''And call Frank and my folks.''

"Okay."

"Uh, honey?"

Grace looked over at him. "What, Daniel?"

"Before you do that, could you come get this gun?"

Her pretty brown eyes went wide with apprehension. "Why?" She asked, scrambling over to him. He had his free hand at the base of his throat, checking his own pulse.

"Because, evidently," he said evenly, "I'm about to pass out."

He handed her the gun, and went down like a redwood.

Grace wasn't there when Daniel woke up in the hospital bed, but everyone else in Nobel was, or so it seemed. He saw his mother's face first, of course; it hovered inches above his and she was whispering frantically to God, to him, to everyone she could think of who might help.

"Mom," he said, his voice sounding hoarse and weak to his own ears. "I'm awake now. You can stop praying on top of me."

"Oh, Danny," she wailed, and he was saved from her catapulting herself over the bed rails only by his father grasping the waistband of her trousers and yanking her to her feet.

"You'll smash the boy," he said, then shouldered past his wife to peer into his son's eyes. "Daniel," he said slowly. "Can you hear me?"

He moved his head so he could see past his loitering parents. Where was Grace? "From the pain in my shoulder, Dad, I'm assuming the bullet didn't hit my ears."

"Well, you've been out for over an hour, and the doctor said you lost a lot of blood," his mother said, grasping his hand.

"He said 'some' blood, Liz," Howard corrected. "Not a lot."

"Well, how much do you think is a lot when it comes to our own children, Howard?" she asked huffily. "Doesn't he look pale enough? You want me to stab him with my hatpin so he can lose enough blood so you can take it seriously that your own son has been shot?''

"You don't wear a hatpin, you deranged woman," his father muttered in response.

"Uh, Mr. Cash?" A deputy of the Nobel sheriff's department squeezed in beside his parents, further blocking Daniel's view of the room. Daniel knew Grace had to be here somewhere. She wouldn't just leave him here with these crazy people, would she?

"Oh, go away, Delvin," Liz scolded. "He doesn't want to talk to you now. Can't you see how pale he is?"

"Liz, the man's just doing his job. Daniel's tougher than to let some old bullet wound slow him down, aren't you, son?"

"Does anyone know where Grace—" Daniel began, but his mother was too busy chiding her husband to pay attention.

"Yes, John Wayne. I'm sure you're right. Why don't we just tie him to his horse and let him ride off into the sunset? Would that be tough enough for you?"

The deputy, reluctant but determined, tried to interrupt. "I just need to take a preliminary statement. Dr. McKenna gave me one downstairs—"

Daniel frowned. "Is she still here?"

"Delvin Shutte, you're not taking this boy's statement. He's too weak," his mother insisted.

"He isn't weak," Howard shouted. "You think the boy is weak?"

"Oh, for crying out loud. Just shoot him again! It seems like that's the only thing that will satisfy you!"

"That's not what I'm saying, Elizabeth—"

"Frank," Daniel barked when he saw his brother standing in the doorway. Frank grinned at him sympathetically and then maneuvered his way past the protective trio. They didn't notice, but continued to argue rather loudly regarding Daniel's ability to speak at the moment.

"You okay?" Frank asked.

"Where's Grace?"

"She left the hospital about ten minutes ago. She's gone out to the ranch to talk to Phil Brown and his buddies from Animal Industries."

"Dammit, she shouldn't be walking around on that ankle."

Frank shrugged. "Can't tell the woman anything, Danny."

"I need to see her," he said. Lord, that was an understatement. He needed her to get through a day, to breathe, to live. He was only just realizing it. "Can you find her, bring her back here?"

Frank shook his head. "I don't think so. She's pretty well determined to get this all cleared up."

Daniel frowned absently at his now fully engaged parents. Between them, they'd soon have half the hospital staff in here arguing over his stupid shoulder. "She's too tired to go out to the ranch tonight. She needs to go home, get some sleep."

"I'm not her daddy, and neither are you."

"I've got to talk to her," Daniel said. He ignored the burning in his chest and shoulder and tried to raise himself up off the bed. His parents and the deputy did not notice, but his brother put a wide palm across his forehead and pressed him back into the pillow.

"I don't think so."

"It's not that bad," Daniel said, biting back a groan.

"You got hit point-blank with a .32 slug about two inches above your heart, fool. The back of your shoulder looks like hamburger where they dug it out. You're not getting out of bed."

"Well, *hell!*" Daniel closed his eyes, chewed for a moment on the inside of his cheek. The frustration of not being able to see her burned worse than the bullet wound. "Hell," he rumbled again.

"I'll go to her house in the morning. Haul her back here."

"Why did she leave me?" Daniel asked, barely managing to not whine. His shoulder hurt, dammit, and he needed Grace.

Frank made a sucking sound with his tongue and teeth. "Reckon she wanted to get this all cleared up before you got out. She feels pretty responsible."

"She isn't responsible."

"You've been telling her for weeks she was."

"God," Daniel muttered miserably. "I am a fool."

"True, but it was her vet stamp, her employee."

"Our cousin." Daniel met Frank's eyes. "Did Grace tell you everything?"

"Yeah." Frank shook his head. "I didn't have a clue Lisa resented us so much for having the ranch. She's crazier than I thought, and I thought she was pretty crazy."

"Where is she?"

"They have her in custody. After they patch up her arm, they're taking her in."

"I regret that. I didn't mean to hurt her, I just wanted to save Grace."

"You did, she said."

Daniel dragged at his cheeks. "Then why isn't she here?"

"You'll have to ask her."

"I will." Daniel nodded, squinted up at the fluorescent lights above his bed. "I don't think I can take it if she doesn't stay with me, Frank."

"She will," he said. A corner of his mouth kicked wryly. "She has to do what you say. You're Daniel Cash."

Chapter 15

Grace carefully positioned her surgical instruments in their carrying case and put the case in the small cardboard box on the reception counter. She wasn't taking much with her; the advertisement she'd placed in all the national veterinary magazines said the clinic came fully stocked. She wouldn't be opening her own practice again. She could leave almost everything behind.

Oh, God. She leaned against the counter, closed her eyes. It was almost as painful giving up the practice as it was leaving Daniel.

She sighed heavily and pushed herself away from the counter, reaching for her crutches. One last look around, she decided. Make sure she hadn't left anything behind but her heart.

She hitched her way through the front office, running a hand over the file cabinets she'd straightened that morning. She'd barely had a chance to meet any of the clients those files represented. Now, never would. She regretted that bitterly.

She checked the lab, locked it. The kennels had hardly been used, but she'd had them cleaned again in any case. Mrs. Handleman had come in to oversee it when she'd found out about Grace's broken ankle. She'd been questioned by the police, was mortified beyond consolation to realize she'd let Lisa's deception and gross misconduct slip past her watchful eye.

Grace shut the kennel door. The next dog or cat she doctored would be kept in someone else's kennel for recovery and observation. She regretted that, too. She'd loved running her own show.

Her ankle throbbed as she made the final run-through. She'd rested it as much as she could stand, had been off it nearly all day yesterday as she'd slept off the effects of the hypothermia, the strain of the encounter with Lisa, and the aftermath of dealing with the Idaho Department of Agriculture Animal Industries Division. It had taken some persuading and half a dozen frantic phone calls to the state capital, but she was satisfied with the outcome of it all. Daniel's ranch would be under scrutiny for a while, but he wouldn't lose it.

Grace stopped in the hallway and stared unseeingly at the cool, clean linoleum floor. He'd been released from the hospital this morning. She hadn't been able to keep herself from calling, checking on him. But she'd always spoken to a nurse, never to Daniel or his family. She didn't think she could have stood it. They told her this morning that his brother had taken him home.

It was over. All of it. Her practice, her place in this community, her relationship with Daniel Cash. It seemed woefully unfair.

Well, she thought, straightening to full height, life was famous for being unfair. She'd have to find some way to go on.

Daniel watched her through the glass front door. She didn't see him, and he speculated about what she was thinking. Him? Could she be thinking of him? Well, damn her if she wasn't, he thought, scowling in at her. Because he'd been able to think of nothing but her since he'd awakened two days before in that hospital bed, shot through and miserable.

She came forward again, but didn't notice him through the glass. What a pair they made, Daniel thought. He was bandaged from his shoulder to halfway down his chest, his arm in a sling, and he felt like hell. She was staggering around like a war victim and the shadows under her eyes made him think she hadn't had nearly enough rest, no matter that he'd sent his brother out to spy on her and had been reassured she'd spent most of yesterday at home.

She picked up a roll of tape from the reception counter and pulled out a long piece. Daniel's mouth dropped open as he watched her fumble with a box, barely managing to hold her crutches in her armpits as she secured the tape across an open box top.

If he didn't know better, he'd swear she was packing.

Packing!

Well, hell. That was just great. He'd concede he'd been something of an idiot the past few weeks, but he was reasonably sorry about that and ready to admit it if pressed. It was no reason for her to be packing in any case.

Furthermore, he'd only come to the conclusion a couple days ago that he loved her more than his own life, more than anything, and that he very probably could not manage to exist on this planet without her, and here she was *packing!* The woman, damn her, had a lot of nerve taping up her life in a box and moving on.

Daniel had the strongest urge to kick in this door, as well. He'd take that stinking little box she was worrying over and toss it out into the street.

He didn't do it, of course. He was trying to resist some

of the baser urges this woman gave him, wasn't he? He pounded on the glass with his fist instead.

Grace's head snapped up and her eyes met his. Oh, dear, she thought, her heart leaping to her throat. There he is again.

She crutched her way to the door, twisted open the dead bolt.

"Daniel."

"What the hell are you doing here?" he demanded.

"I called your house, left a message for you."

"I've been in the hospital," he said, trying to keep the accusation out of his tone but not quite succeeding. Nothing in the world would have kept him from her side if *she'd* been shot, he thought, still cranky over it.

"I know. How's your shoulder?"

As if you care, he almost whimpered, but kept himself from it at the last second, fearing he'd sound churlish. "It burns like hell," he answered roughly, hoping she'd be impressed by his macho tone, "but no permanent damage."

"Good." She balled up the tape she'd been holding. It had stuck together when her hands had started to tremble.

"Nice of you to stop by," he said testily. That one just slipped out.

She kept her head down. "I'm sorry. I've been very busy."

"I can see that. What are you doing, Grace?" he repeated, spacing each word carefully to keep himself from shouting.

"I'm packing a couple things. I'm selling the practice. I told you that last week."

"That was last week," he said tersely, a buzz of alarm humming through him. "Things have obviously changed since last week."

She couldn't help the sideways glance she shot him. "Not really." She worked more tape from the dispenser.

He picked it out of her grasp and threw it against the opposite wall with enough force to crack the plastic into a dozen pieces. "I think it has," he replied conversationally while Grace stared at the shattered dispenser on the floor. "Lisa's been charged, everyone knows the truth about what happened. Your reputation is totally cleared."

"That's good," she said slowly. "It'll be easier for me to get a position somewhere else."

Oh, he was frustrated beyond endurance with the woman. And scared to death. "Why do you need a new position?" he asked as casually as he could manage, thinking perhaps smashing her tape dispenser had not been such a good idea, as she couldn't seem to stop looking at it.

"We both know why," she said, then continued before he could interrupt her again. "I talked to Phil Brown about your herd. We agreed that since the cow Lisa exposed was separated from the rest of the herd, the waiting period can be lifted sooner. All the cattle will have to be tested and inoculated before you can sell them or put them back out on public lands, but you won't be quarantined past that point."

"Fine," he said shortly. He was relieved, of course. That solution fit perfectly with his plans, though, if it hadn't, he would have simply adjusted his plans. He was, after all, a very determined man. "Because I plan to sell them."

"You plan to sell them?" Grace finally looked over at him. Daniel did all he could do not to brush back the hair that fell against her cheek. "You're going to sell the whole herd?"

He nodded once. "As soon as they're cleared."

She searched his face for a moment. "Daniel, those cattle are your whole life." She knew that better than anyone. She'd been in his way when he'd had to prove what he would do to save them, in fact. "Why would you sell them?"

"My whole life, Grace?" He frowned at her. "I don't think so. I think I know what constitutes my whole life, and it isn't a bunch of cows."

"I just meant—"

He held up his hand. "I know what you meant. You meant I was willing to sacrifice everything for that herd, including you."

She turned back to her packing. Where was her tape? Oh. Right. She bent the cardboard top to fit together as an alternative. "I don't want to go over this again, Daniel."

"Well, we're going to have to go over it, because there are obviously some things you don't understand, but for the moment I'd like to explain why I'm selling the herd."

Grace faced him again, nodded slowly, wary. The man always seemed to put her on her guard. She remembered thinking the first time she saw him, lifting that unwieldy meds box as though it weighed no more than a pile of feathers, that she'd better watch her step.

"Okay," she said. "Tell me."

Daniel ran his hand down his face, pulled at his bottom lip with his thumb and index finger. How to explain? How to make her understand? He frowned thoughtfully at her. Oh, hell, he told himself, take a shot. You're bigger than she is; if she doesn't understand this explanation, you'll just have to keep her here until you can come up with one she does understand.

"Frank is going into rehab," he began.

Grace's wide and pretty mouth went soft with sympathy. "I'm glad."

"I realize a lot of Frank's problems in the last few years have been because of me."

"Daniel, you can't—"

He held up a hand to stop her. "He came to me a dozen times since his wife and baby died in that accident. He wanted out of the ranching business, wanted to leave Nobel, get away from the ghosts here. But I was too stubborn to let him go. I thought I knew what was best for him, what was best for all of us. I didn't want to fail again, and I kept Frank here through money and family ties. Because if he left, I'd have had to admit everything I put a hand to, the vet thing, my marriage, the ranch, was bound to fail. I let him take the fall for my pride.''

"Frank's a grown man, Daniel. He could have walked away anytime.''

Daniel shook his head. ''I made it too hard for him to do that. He was already hanging on to his life by a thread. He would have had to leave here broke and estranged from his family, and I just don't think he had the strength to do it. I didn't want to see that.''

She stayed silent, and Daniel took a deep breath. So far, so good, he thought. She was still standing there.

"I don't know what he's going to want to do after he gets out of rehab. But I do know the folks don't want and shouldn't have to pick up the slack.'' His mouth twisted into a wry smile. ''And obviously Lisa is out of the picture.''

Grace nodded. ''Phil Brown is out for blood.''

"I reckon he is. She could have destroyed the stock cow business in Idaho.''

"So what will you do without them?''

"I'm going to sell the cattle as soon as the state clears them. The then lease out the farm ground until I get back.''

Grace stared at him. ''Get back? You're leaving Nobel?'' She couldn't imagine it. He was as much a part of this town as the cracked sidewalks and the Grange and the sprawling dairies. She couldn't imagine Nobel without Daniel Cash. Of course, she couldn't imagine much of anything without Daniel Cash. Including the rest of her life.

Daniel screwed up his courage. Speaking the words out loud was clearly more difficult than thinking them. If she discouraged him, or laughed at him, he'd lose his taste for it altogether. He needed her approval, needed her encouragement. Needed her.

"I'm going back to vet school,'' he said.

Grace's hand flew to her mouth, but he rushed on before she could speak.

"I called the university yesterday and got through to the dean. I talked to him about Lisa, about what she told us in the clinic about framing me for cheating. He said if I could get a deposition stating that she was responsible, he'd go to the board, try and have me reinstated."

"Oh, Daniel," Grace breathed.

He grinned. "Yeah." The impact of it hit him for the first time, as though telling her had made it real to him. His dream, his lifelong dream. It was coming back to him. "I'll have to take refresher courses, obviously, because I've been gone so long. I've probably forgotten half of everything I ever learned, but he thinks I could finish in two semesters."

"You haven't forgotten anything," she insisted loyally.

He laughed, reached out with all friendliness and wiped away the tear that had streaked her cheek. "Maybe not. I keep my Merck in my bedside table, next to the girlie magazines," he joked, absently rubbing the tear along his fingertips.

"Daniel, I'm so happy for you."

He smiled at her, could see the truth of that in her shining eyes. "No one but you can understand what this means to me."

That made her breath catch, and Grace had to duck her head and wipe at her eyes.

"You'll come back here, then," she said, already knowing the answer. She worked up a smile. "Dr. Niebaur will be so proud of you."

"I hope so. It's always been a sore spot for me that he thought I cheated on an exam." He hadn't touched her except to wipe that tear away, but he needed to now. He gathered her hands in his free hand. He noticed hers were cold and he chafed at them gently with his thumb. "You know, I've always wanted his clinic, his practice."

"I know," Grace nodded, swallowing the rest of her tears. She squeezed his hands, tried to release them. "Well, it's good that I'm leaving. You belong here."

"So do you, Grace."

She smiled gently. No hard feelings, right? Wasn't that the way it was supposed to be? "No. It was always your place."

He pulled her closer, looked down at her. Tall girl, he thought. Pretty, warm, wonderful woman. "I think it's our place," he said. He rubbed his thumb rhythmically across her knuckles. "I was just waiting for you to get here."

She was certain she hadn't heard him correctly. But she pulled her hands free, in case she had. "Don't do this."

He felt cold without her close, and pulled defensively at the jacket that was slung across his wide shoulders. "I have to. I don't want you to go."

"Don't, Daniel," she said, shaking her head. "I won't be able to forgive you if you do."

"If I do what? Ask you to stay?"

She gaped at him for a moment. "You want to be partners?"

I want to be married, he almost blurted, but decided he'd better hash this out with her first. She wasn't taking his declaration the way he'd hoped.

"Yes," he said stubbornly, and waited for the explosion.

It came instantly. "You jerk," she said, keeping herself from cracking him across the face through sheer willpower. "You blamed me for everything, and didn't trust me for a minute until Lisa told you the truth herself."

"That's not true."

"That is true!" she shouted. "You fed me to the wolves the minute something went wrong. You never believed in me, in my abilities and ethics as a vet."

"Of course I did. I'm just an idiot! I can't say anything in my defense, Grace. I was wrong and stupid and scared. I knew it all along."

"But still you blamed me, accused me in front of my peers."

He nodded shortly. "Yes, and I'm ashamed." Oh, it was intolerably harder to admit it than he'd hoped it would be.

"You should be!"

He stood in front of her, defenseless. He didn't even try to offer an excuse. He loved her, and she deserved to be angry with him for his betrayal. He wondered if she'd ever understand that he hated himself far more for it than she would ever hate him. "I am, Grace."

"I can't forgive you."

He battled back the surge of panic the words brought. "Yes, you can," he asserted mulishly. "I know you."

"If you knew me, you would have known I could never do this kind of thing, made this kind of mistake. You would have known I'd have done anything to not have allowed it to happen."

"I do know that. I did all along. I just fought against it because the only other explanation was that I had failed as a cattleman just as I'd failed as a veterinarian. Just as I'd failed as a husband. I couldn't live with it."

"Clearly."

"But I was here, Grace, when Lisa came through that door with her little gun and her vial of anthrax. I was already here."

Grace stared at him, her chest rising and falling heavily. "What?"

Ah, that stopped her, he thought with a small rising of hope. "You're wrong when you say it took Lisa coming here and spilling her guts to make me believe in you."

"What are you talking about?"

"You sat in my bed, naked except for that old W.A.S.U. sweatshirt and told me my cousin, whom I'd known all my life, was responsible for everything. It's true—" he said quickly when he saw she was about to interrupt him "—I didn't want to buy it at first, and I'm sorry for that. But you didn't even give me five minutes to come to grips with the idea before you called my brother and went tearing off to town.''

She narrowed her eyes. "You'd better not even try to pawn this off on me.''

"I'm not," he said, frustrated. "I'm just saying I'm not the only one who has trouble with faith in this relationship. You left me looking at an empty bed that still had the print of your head on the pillow!" And that had hurt, more than he could explain. "You said you didn't love me anymore. You didn't have any faith in me, either.''

"Did you expect me to? I fell in love with you, Daniel, and you couldn't run fast enough from me. I've been so careful to not let that happen until you, and I tell you, Daniel, I was right to. It was a terrible mistake, opening my heart to you. Did you expect me to limp along after you professionally, as well, until you decided what was right and what was wrong.''

"No," he admitted. He rubbed hard at his eyes. "No." He looked at her. "But you hurt me.''

"You hurt me, too," she whispered.

He could see that, and it tormented him. He pulled her to his chest with his undamaged arm, thankful she went, however stiffly. He held her close with his right hand between her shoulder blades. "I know I did, Grace," he whispered into her soft, brown curls. "And I'm sorry. I'm so, so sorry.''

She held herself like a stone, not allowing her heart to be moved by the misery and remorse she heard in his deep voice. "Who broke my door?" she asked after a minute, her voice even and strong again.

"What?" he murmured, so grateful, finally, to be holding her again. His shoulder ached where hers met it, but he didn't care.

"Who kicked in the door? You?''

"You think Lisa could have?''

"You have a key," she argued, but of course he was right.

Lisa could never have kicked in that door. She'd never considered what that meant, was too busy getting Daniel to the hospital, clearing the mess with the Animal Industries Division.

"I left it at home. I drove your vet truck in."

She eased herself away from him, careful of his shoulder. "You were here first?"

"Yes. Lisa saw the door and came in after me. I confronted her."

"Why were you here, Daniel?"

"I was looking for some evidence against her. Records or order copies or something in the lab that would implicate her."

Grace watched his face, those beautiful, lichen-colored eyes. "Why?"

"Because I believed you. When I saw you driving away with Frank, I knew you'd been telling me the truth. I knew how unforgivably stupid I'd been."

She shook her head. "I don't understand."

"I love you, Grace. And I realized, way too late, I admit it, that if you loved me half as much as I loved you, you never could have lied to me."

She never expected those words. They blindsided her. She expected an apology, because he was the man he was. But those words. She'd have given anything to hear them a few weeks ago, now they made her want to double over in pain.

"No," she whispered hoarsely. Fresh tears sprang to her eyes and she despised them. She warded him off when he advanced on her. "It's too late."

"No. I love you." And God, how amazing it felt saying it out loud. "I love you," he said again, just for the joy of it, "and I realized I'd loved you probably from the first minute I saw you."

"Daniel, don't."

"You've got to stop telling me don't when I have to," he said, smiling gently at her. The vulnerable woman was in front of him now—no Amazon stature or traditionally male profession or a lifetime's armor separated them—and he had to be so careful to not hurt her again. "You're everything I've ever wanted. You're beautiful and strong and smart and I have been a little bit out of my mind since the day you came to town. You make me mad, you make me laugh, you make my eyes cross every time I look at you. How could I not love you?"

She was hyperventilating, she was almost positive. She could not take in enough air. If not for her traitorous ankle, she would have fled. Because the bittersweet pain of it was too much to bear. If he was lying, if it was a joke or a mistake, she wouldn't be able to live through it. And if it was true, it was the first time in her life she'd heard it said outside the small circle of her family. The impact was stronger, more brutal than she could have anticipated.

"And how," he continued thoughtfully as he watched her face change, watched the apprehension build in her eyes, "could I not believe in you? What happened these last weeks was all my fault, Grace. I was terrified of failing again, and so determined to not let anything stand in the way of my success that I forced my head to ignore what my heart already understood. I came here after I left your truck for you because I knew you were right. I wanted to prove it for you, to you. I thought if I could find what you needed to clear your name, I'd lay it at your feet and you'd be able to forgive me for doubting you." He was embarrassed by her silent regard. "That sounds stupid."

It sounded noble and dear, she thought. The idea of it chipped at the last fragments of the hull that covered her tender heart. "It sounds like you," she said simply.

He frowned at her slender, straight back. "Does that mean you think I'm stupid?"

He saw her shoulders tremble, saw her raise her hand to her mouth. God, he was shaking himself. She wasn't going to forgive him, wasn't going to love him again. He could feel it.

He pressed his body against hers in desperation, fitting himself to her bottom, taking her hips in his hands and flexing his fingers into her flesh. He heard her gasp, felt her shudder.

He put his face to her ear, closed his eyes. "Grace," he whispered low, fervently, "don't tell me you don't love me anymore. I won't believe you. I'll believe everything you ever tell me from now on, but not that." He buried his face at the side of her neck, but not before Grace heard the curious hitch in his voice. "Not that," he mumbled.

She reached up without thought and cradled his head in her palm, pushing her fingers through his short hair. "No," she whispered after a minute, "not that."

He stood at her back, trying to pull himself together. Nothing scared him as much as this did. He finally turned her so they were facing each other. He kept his hands at her hips, digging in, holding on. "I can't do anything without you, Grace. I can't go back or go forward without you."

She shook her head. "No. You don't have to." She reached up, wiped the dampness from under his eyes with her thumbs, then kissed him gently on his mouth. "I love you, Daniel."

He searched her eyes, their noses nearly touching, their breath falling hard upon one another. Then he smiled slowly, that killer smile, and she knew she was lost, forever. "I believe you," he said, and made her laugh.

He took that laugh into his mouth, kissing her deeply. He wanted both arms wrapped around her, but contented himself with crushing her between his body and the reception counter. And while his mouth moved and his heart healed, he realized how grateful he was for the last few years, whatever pain they'd brought. They had also brought Grace to him.

He hugged her, kissed the crown of her head. "I'm sorry, Grace," he said against her hair.

She pulled his face to hers. "Don't say it again, Daniel. Don't say it again. It's nothing compared to this."

"No," he agreed, kissing her face, her neck. "No, it's not."

He wound his right arm around her neck, head-locked her, clutched her close. He leaned back far enough to meet her eyes. "Will you stay? Will you stay and let me buy into the practice? It's big enough for both of us."

She grinned. "If you promise to do all the dairy preg-checking, I'll stay."

"Deal. And I want to get married. Will you marry me, Grace?"

"Yes." Grace laughed. "But you really should have asked that one first. Your priorities are showing, Daniel."

"You're my priority, Grace," he said, kissing her nose. "My first priority, always. We'll have very tall children, you know."

"And we won't make them play basketball if they don't want to."

Daniel laughed again. "No, honey. No basketball." He hugged her tight, felt her damp cheek against his. It amazed him still how she met him nearly inch for inch. He smiled against her hair. "Well, maybe just a little basketball."

* * * * *

You're not going to believe this offer!

In October and November 2000, buy any two Harlequin or Silhouette books and save $10.00 off future purchases, or buy any three and save $20.00 off future purchases!

Just fill out this form and attach 2 proofs of purchase (cash register receipts) from October and November 2000 books and Harlequin will send you a coupon booklet worth a total savings of $10.00 off future purchases of Harlequin and Silhouette books in 2001. Send us 3 proofs of purchase and we will send you a coupon booklet worth a total savings of $20.00 off future purchases.

Saving money has never been this easy.

I accept your offer! Please send me a coupon booklet:

Name: _____

Address: _____ City: _____

State/Prov.: _____ Zip/Postal Code: _____

Optional Survey!

In a typical month, how many Harlequin or Silhouette books would you buy <u>new</u> at retail stores?

☐ Less than 1   ☐ 1   ☐ 2   ☐ 3 to 4   ☐ 5+

Which of the following statements best describes how you <u>buy</u> Harlequin or Silhouette books? Choose one answer only that <u>best</u> describes you.

☐ I am a regular buyer and reader
☐ I am a regular reader but buy only occasionally
☐ I only buy and read for specific times of the year, e.g. vacations
☐ I subscribe through Reader Service but also buy at retail stores
☐ I mainly borrow and buy only occasionally
☐ I am an occasional buyer and reader

Which of the following statements best describes how you <u>choose</u> the Harlequin and Silhouette series books you buy <u>new</u> at retail stores? By "series," we mean books within a particular line, such as *Harlequin PRESENTS* or *Silhouette SPECIAL EDITION*. Choose one answer only that <u>best</u> describes you.

☐ I only buy books from my favorite series
☐ I generally buy books from my favorite series but also buy books from other series on occasion
☐ I buy some books from my favorite series but also buy from many other series regularly
☐ I buy all types of books depending on my mood and what I find interesting and have no favorite series

---

Please send this form, along with your cash register receipts as proofs of purchase, to:
In the U.S.: Harlequin Books, P.O. Box 9057, Buffalo, NY 14269
In Canada: Harlequin Books, P.O. Box 622, Fort Erie, Ontario L2A 5X3
(Allow 4-6 weeks for delivery) Offer expires December 31, 2000.   PHQ4002

If you enjoyed what you just read,
then we've got an offer you can't resist!

Take 2 bestselling
love stories FREE!
Plus get a FREE surprise gift!

Clip this page and mail it to Silhouette Reader Service™

IN U.S.A.	**IN CANADA**
3010 Walden Ave.	P.O. Box 609
P.O. Box 1867	Fort Erie, Ontario
Buffalo, N.Y. 14240-1867	L2A 5X3

YES! Please send me 2 free Silhouette Intimate Moments® novels and my free surprise gift. Then send me 6 brand-new novels every month, which I will receive months before they're available in stores. In the U.S.A., bill me at the bargain price of $3.80 plus 25¢ delivery per book and applicable sales tax, if any*. In Canada, bill me at the bargain price of $4.21 plus 25¢ delivery per book and applicable taxes**. That's the complete price and a savings of at least 10% off the cover prices—what a great deal! I understand that accepting the 2 free books and gift places me under no obligation ever to buy any books. I can always return a shipment and cancel at any time. Even if I never buy another book from Silhouette, the 2 free books and gift are mine to keep forever. So why not take us up on our invitation. You'll be glad you did!

245 SEN C226
345 SEN C227

Name	(PLEASE PRINT)	
Address	Apt.#	
City	State/Prov.	Zip/Postal Code

* Terms and prices subject to change without notice. Sales tax applicable in N.Y.
** Canadian residents will be charged applicable provincial taxes and GST.
  All orders subject to approval. Offer limited to one per household.
  ® are registered trademarks of Harlequin Enterprises Limited.

INMOM00
©1998 Harlequin Enterprises Limited

COMING NEXT MONTH

#1039 THE BRANDS WHO CAME FOR CHRISTMAS—Maggie Shayne

The Oklahoma All-Girl Brands

After one incredible night spent in the arms of a stranger, Maya Brand found herself pregnant—with twins! But when her mystery man reappeared and claimed he wanted to be part of their lives, was Maya ready to trust Caleb Montgomery with her expected bundles of joy—and with her own fragile heart?

#1040 HERO AT LARGE—Robyn Amos

A Year of Loving Dangerously

SPEAR agent Keshon Gray was on a mission that could ultimately get him killed. So when his one and only love, Rennie Williams, re-entered his life, Keshon wasn't about to let her get too close. But knowing she was near forced Keshon to re-evaluate his life. If he survived his mission, would he consider starting over with the woman he couldn't resist?

#1041 MADE FOR EACH OTHER—Doreen Owens Malek

FBI bodyguard Tony Barringer knew he shouldn't mix business with pleasure when it came to protecting Jill Darcy and her father from a series of threats. After all, Tony was around for very different reasons—ones Jill *definitely* wouldn't be happy about. So until he got his answers, Tony had to hold out—no matter what his heart demanded.

#1042 HERO FOR HIRE—Marie Ferrarella

ChildFinders, Inc.

Detective Chad Andreini was more than willing to help beautiful Veronica Lancaster find her kidnapped son—*but* she insisted on helping with the investigation. So they teamed up, determined to bring the boy back home. But once the ordeal was over, could this unlikely pair put their own fears aside and allow their passions to take over?

#1043 DANGEROUS LIAISONS—Maggie Price

Nicole Taylor's business was love matches, not murder. Until her dating-service clients started turning up dead. Suddenly she found herself suspected, then safeguarded, by Sergeant Jake Ford. And falling hard for the brooding top cop who no longer believed in love.

#1044 DAD IN BLUE—Shelley Cooper

Samantha Underwood would do whatever it took to help her eight-year-old son recover from the loss of his father. And thanks to sexy police chief Carlo Garibaldi, the boy seemed to be improving. But when it came to love, Carlo was a tough man to convince—until Samantha showed him just how good it could be....